WASTED SUMMER

CATHRYN FOX

Chapter One

Speed walking along the pebbled curb leading up to Stone Cliff Resort, a popular tourist retreat in the heart of the Canadian Rockies, Melody Spencer sidestepped a deep puddle and cursed under her breath. How she'd managed to miss the last afternoon shuttle from town to the resort was beyond her. She gave a hard shake of her head, realizing that wasn't entirely true. Mr. Johnson, the elderly pharmacist at Deerfield Convenience liked to chat, and since he was one of the few people in town who was nice to her, she couldn't bring herself to cut out on him—even if it did mean missing her ride. But seriously, hadn't she learned that nice girls finished last? Or in this case, had to hoof it up Mount-Frigging-Everest because her next shift started in fifteen minutes. She couldn't be late, not again. The summer vacationers were all beginning to pile in, and if she wasn't dressed and in the dining room for the first dinner seating, her boss would have her ass—and her apron. Mel's full-time summer job might be running camps for kids, but she needed the money from this second job if she was ever going to get out of this God-forsaken town and move to a place where no one knew her, or her past.

Dark clouds knitted together overhead. Thunder rumbled with a deafening boom that shook the ground beneath Mel's feet, making her jump. Damn. Damn. Damn. Not only was she going to be late, those black clouds were seconds from opening up and soaking her to the bone. She looked at her thin tank top and frowned. The last thing she wanted was to show up in the staff lounge and have her boss think she'd participated in a wet T-shirt contest. There were enough rumors circulating as it was.

She clutched the small brown paper bag she was carrying closer to her chest. Her purpose was twofold: Shield herself from the imminent downpour, and keep the contents inside the bag dry. Mel wasn't one for luxury or brand names—every penny counted toward getting out of Deerfield—but when it came to her feminine needs, she had no problem forking over the extra money. She'd be damned if she'd borrow another Maxi pad from her friend Jaelyn. How anyone could wear those God-awful things was beyond her. Cripes, she might as well slap on a diaper, right?

She sucked in a breath as lightning zigzagged across the dark sky, and she glanced up in time to see the tall, metal spire on the resort's main registration building puncture the low hanging clouds. She exhaled a breath of relief at seeing the familiar landmark, now confident that she could make it back without getting drenched. Just then, a very expensive, very posh sports car sped by. The flashy vehicle swerved toward the rocky curb, aiming for the deep puddle ahead of her.

The wide tires split the puddle, sending water into the air. Mel gave a little yelp, but before she could dodge the deluge, cold rainwater splashed up and fell over her in a wave, soaking her from the top of her head right down to the soles of her rubber flip-flops. Sputtering and gasping for breath, Mel's feet slipped around in her shoes and it took all her balance to keep herself from landing on her ass. Her arms flailed and when she finally managed to stand straight, she worked to blink the fat droplets from her eyes. She pushed her long, wet hair from her face and looked at the boys hanging out the windows, laughing and pointing as they sped by.

Fury raced through her. She wanted to scream, she wanted to hit something, hell, she wanted to throw her bag of tampons at them. Instead, she took a breath and reminded herself that soon enough she'd be away from this place, away from all the snotty rich boys who vacationed at the resort every summer and looked down their noses at her—until they wanted to get into her pants. And eventually they all wanted to get into her pants. She hadn't met a guy yet who didn't want to go a round with the town slut.

She cursed under her breath and gathered a handful of hair. She squeezed out the excess water, breaking a fingernail in the process. Taking deep, concentrated breaths as a cold shiver wracked her body, she closed her eyes and wiped her face with her palm. When she heard another car approaching, she cringed, wishing she had a place to hide. The last thing she wanted was to get doused again. She inched closer to the embankment when a black Jeep slowed beside her. Keeping her focus on the ground, she tried to hurry to get ahead of it. She gripped the squishy, rubber flip-flops with her toes for traction, yet with each flop, water shot up the back of her legs and she slipped a little more.

The engine revved as he caught up to her. "Hey, are you okay?"

"I'm fine," she shot back, keeping her head down and her eyes on her toes.

"You don't look fine." The familiar eastern accent had her angling her head. She looked at the driver, but wished she hadn't. Ryeland Montgomery. Hot. Rich. Smart. Tight friends with the guys who'd just soaked her. She saw the iPhone on his dashboard. Perhaps he'd only slowed to get photographic evidence, so they could all laugh about it later.

"I'm fine," she said again.

He rolled the passenger window back up and sped ahead. For a second she thought he was going to leave her alone, but then he swerved onto the curb and parked directly in front of her, blocking her path up the hill. The next thing she knew he was climbing out of the driver's seat and walking toward her with that sexy, confident swagger of his, one that drove all the girls crazy, vacationers and locals alike.

Correction, not *all* the girls. She wasn't about to be drawn in by his charming smile and good looks. Even if she wanted a boyfriend—which she didn't—she certainly wouldn't fall for a guy like him, one who left a string of broken hearts behind each summer when he returned east, to a lifestyle that happened to be the polar opposite of hers. Not that she was judging. She wasn't. What he did and how he lived his life was none of her business.

Pewter-flecked eyes that reminded her of the silver spoon he'd been born with raked her over, going from the top of her sodden head to the toes curled into the soles of her mushy flip-flops. Those odd-colored irises slowly made their way back up again, and when his pupils dilated despite the lack of sunshine, Mel became fully aware of the way her shirt clung like a second skin, showcasing her ample cleavage and hard nipples— compliments of the cold puddle water. Oddly enough, his eyes didn't linger on her breasts, although she couldn't understand why, considering he was a guy and all.

He raked his hands through thick, dark hair, his

glance moving over her face before settling on her eyes. "You're soaked."

"Way to state the obvious," she huffed out. "I guess you really are as smart as they say."

The corner of his mouth twitched. "Uh, did I do something to piss you off?"

"Look, I was already running late for work when your friends thought they'd get their kicks by soaking me, so I don't have time for this, okay?"

Something dark moved over his face, but she wasn't about to take the time to examine it, not when the clock was ticking and her job was on the line. Instead, she pushed past him but he touched her arm to spin her back around. She flinched, and every muscle in her body tensed, ready to put her self-defense classes to work. Shifting her stance, she prepared to fight, recalling the last man who'd tried to touch her without her permission. She had been only thirteen at the time, and well... Her stomach clenched as painful memories intruded.

Forget it, Mel...just forget it.

Ryeland stepped back. "Whoa, sorry."

"What do you want?"

Looking confused, he shifted back and forth in his designer sneakers, his pale blue polo shirt rasping over his broad shoulders. Silence lingered for a moment, and his forehead creased, probably because he was trying to figure out why she wasn't falling all over him like every other girl he'd gifted with his presence. He opened his mouth, then closed it again, and when she was about to turn back around and hike up the hill, he finally spoke.

"I'm sorry my friends are such assholes, but all I'm trying to do here is give you a ride to make up for it. You don't have to go all Karate Kid on me." He dipped his head and his voice was soft when he said, "I'm trying to help."

Surprised, Mel narrowed her eyes to really look at him. Was he for real? *He* wanted to help *her*? Surely there had to be something in it for him. Maybe he was tired of the rich, Barbie doll blondes falling all over him and thought he'd go slumming this summer.

"Why would you want to help me?" she asked bluntly, her back straight, shoulders squared, still on the defense.

He stared at her for a moment, an equal mixture of confusion and intrigue backlighting those fascinating pewter eyes of his. "Why wouldn't I?"

While she could stand there and list a dozen reasons, mainly how those from his social circle didn't associate with girls from the wrong side of the tracks—except to sleep with them—she knew she had to get a move on it.

She backed up an inch. "You know what, I don't know you and you don't know me, so let's just both be on our way. Besides, I'm sure your friends are wondering where you are."

"You're wrong, you know."

"Wrong? What am I wrong about?"

His thick bicep muscles flexed as he drove his hands into his pockets, pushing his jeans a little lower on his hips. While she tried not to glance down—some unknown force pulled her gaze to the flash of tanned skin between his shirt and pants —he took a small step forward, moving into her personal space. He was close, too close, and while she knew she should turn and hightail it out of there, her stupid legs took that moment to betray her. Unable to drag herself away, she exhaled slowly and wondered what the heck was going on with her.

"I know you," he said, his voice so low, so incredibly soft, it momentarily caught her off guard.

She held his gaze, and when warmth moved over his handsome face, softening the hard angles, a strange, unfamiliar sensation mushroomed inside her belly. What the hell?

Despite the fact that she wanted to end this conversation, she blurted out, "How do you know me?"

He gave a lazy roll of one shoulder. "Everyone does."

"Right." She shook her head and berated herself for momentarily letting down her guard. Good God, she never let down her guard. Ever. Otherwise the things people said behind her back might get to her. Things like "slut", "town whore", "no good drunken mother", and "deadbeat dad".

Oh yeah, everyone knew Mel Spencer. Or at least they *thought* they did. Although she had to admit, some of the rumors *were* true. She mentally kicked herself for thinking he might actually be different, that he might actually know something other than the stories people spread behind her back. But how could he? She never let anyone get too close. Not anymore anyway. And truthfully, why did she even care what Ryeland Montgomery thought? He meant nothing to her, and his opinion mattered about as much as her broken nail.

"I'm Ryeland."

"I know," she answered and turned to go.

"So you know me, then?"

She caught a pebble in her flip-flop, stopped to shake it out, and moved on. "No," she lied, tossing the words over her shoulder. "I don't know you."

He jogged ahead and stepped in front of her, once again blocking her path.

Mel planted one hand on her hip and tilted her head to meet his gaze straight on. "Do you mind?"

His white teeth flashed in a smile and instead of answering he said, "You know my name and you said I was as smart as everyone says."

"And…?"

He stepped closer, closing the gap between them.

Holy hell, did this guy know nothing about personal space? He dipped his head, and as she became the sole object of his focus, an unexpected curl of heat wound through her, chasing the chill from her body.

"And…that kind of tells me you do know me," he explained.

"You're kind of legendary around here. But I don't *know* you."

She folded her arms but when he slanted his head, the boyish, totally sexy way he looked at her weakened her knees. God, no wonder everyone was crazy about him.

Her gave her a lopsided grin that set off a chain of events inside her body, none of which she welcomed. "You think I'm legendary?"

She was about to put an end to this conversation when the skies opened up and did it for her. Cold hard rain pelted them, but Ryeland didn't race to his Jeep like the pretty boy son of a rich lawyer who couldn't look less than one hundred percent put together. Instead he stood there, like he had all the time in the world to annoy the hell out of her.

Rain plastered his thick hair to his head, pushing his bangs into his eyes. She nodded toward his vehicle. "You'd better get in your car before your gel runs."

His grin widened and, despite herself, she couldn't help but smile back. Score one for the townie.

"I'm not going without you." Undeterred, he rooted his feet and folded his arms.

She tightened her grip on her paper bag, ready to tell him for the last time she wasn't going anywhere with him. But before she could voice those words her box of tampons pushed through the wet brown paper and fell into a puddle with an undignified splash.

Ryeland's gaze dropped to the ground and he scrubbed his hand over his jaw like he was trying not to laugh. She groaned low in her throat as embarrassment raced through her. Dear God, could this day get any worse?

Another rumble serrated the heavy air and Mel looked skyward, willing the next electrical bolt to hit her. Right between the eyes.

"Here, let me." Ryeland bent to grab the wet box before the lightning had a chance to put her out of her misery. He picked the carton up and it dripped with muddy puddle water as he held it out to her. "I think they're ruined. I can run you back to town if you'd like."

She snatched the box and stuck it under her arm. "No, it's fine." Thank goodness she'd bought the individually wrapped ones, otherwise they'd have soaked up the puddle water and exploded in the box.

He jerked his thumb toward his vehicle. "Come on, jump in. At least let me give you a lift back to Stone Cliff. I owe it to you after what my friends did." Water clung to his long lashes as he blinked them over those fascinating eyes while he waited for a response. She continued to glare at him, wondering what his game was. "Look, I'm not an axe murder or anything. Although I'm pretty sure you could handle yourself even if I was."

She stole a glance at her watch. Dammit. She did a quick mental calculation. There was no way she could get to work on time now if she walked. "Okay, fine. But only because I'm late." She walked past him and pulled open the passenger door. "One ride. Then we're even."

Mel slid in, pulled on her seat belt and stared straight ahead as Ryeland climbed in beside her. He started the engine, shoved the stick into first, and gave a shoulder check before he pulled back on to the road.

Loud music blared from his radio and she was thankful for the distraction. Hopefully the tunes would discourage him from trying to make conversation. The vehicle crested the hill and even though Mel kept her focus on the rain-soaked windshield, from her peripheral vision she caught the way Ryeland kept throwing glances her way.

"What?" she finally asked over the music and shifted to face him.

"It's Mel, right?"

"Yeah."

"What's Mel short for?"

"It's short for Mel."

"Come on, Mel's a guy's name. I don't want to call you by a guy's name."

"Then don't call me at all." She shifted uncomfortably, not about to tell him any more. She'd dropped her full name a long time ago. Melody was the young girl who had no control. Mel was the mature version, the one in full control of her life and her future.

"Is it Melanie?"

"No."

He tapped the steering wheel thoughtfully. "How about Melva? Is it short for Melva?"

She couldn't help but grin. "Melva? Do I look like a Melva?"

"No? Hmmm, okay maybe it's Melba."

"Like the toast?" She rolled her eyes and leaned her head back on the seat. "Yes, Ryeland, Mel is short for Melba."

He laughed. "Wait, I got it. It's short for Melody." Before she could stop herself, her head jerked his way—a clear giveaway. She noted the way his glance moved over her face in a careful assessment. He nodded and grinned. "Yeah, that's it isn't it?" He pumped his hand in triumph. "Nailed it."

"Yeah, you're a regular Rumpelstiltskin, but I don't go by that anymore." She curled her fingers in her lap and wished she wasn't so reactive, but lessons learned long ago taught her to act first, think later. "It's just Mel now."

Ryeland frowned. "Don't you think someone should get to know a person before they pass judgment?"

Was he serious? People judged others all the time for no good reason. She was a prime example. And the truth was, she might not know him, but at least her assessments were based on facts, not rumor.

"You can't hate someone if you don't know them, right?" he pressed.

She stared at him and wondered what color the sky was in his fairytale world. Then again, who was she to judge what he believed? She spent most of her nights living in her own make-believe world. The stacks of unfinished stories piled high on her desk were proof of that.

When she didn't answer, he turned the radio down and asked again, "You can't, right?"

"Yeah, you can," she shot back.

He gave a hard turn of the wheel and took the corner. "Okay, but you shouldn't." He cast her a quick glance. "I'm sure you'd agree with me there?"

"Yeah, I would." She eyed him carefully, wondering where he was going with this. Perhaps it was best not to know.

"So it's settled then. You'll get to know me. Then you'll see I'm not like my friends and there's no reason to hate me."

Mel squeezed the tampon box between her elbow and side little harder, the wet cardboard crushing under the strain. "I never said I hated you," she corrected. "I said I didn't know you."

"Which brings me back to the fact that we need to get to know each other."

"Look—" she began but then shook her head. "Wait, what? That doesn't even make..." Her words fell off when he started to drive past the main lodge and toward the staff housing. "Stop, drop me off here," she said quickly. "I don't have time to go to my room. I have to work in…" She stole a quick glance at the dashboard clock. "Damn, I'm going to be late."

Ryeland hit the brakes. "What about your clothes? You can't go to work like that."

She reached for the door handle. "I have a spare uniform in my locker."

"Hold on." Ryeland reached for her, but seconds before he touched her arm he caught himself. He pulled back, gripped the shoulders of his polo shirt and peeled it over his head. "Put this on. You're liable to draw some unwanted attention if you don't."

She was about to protest but her gaze followed his and when she saw her nipples poking through her soaked tank top she groaned. "Thanks," she murmured and quickly pulled the shirt on, but not before she noticed his hard, striated muscle and tanned skin. Ryeland had certainly grown up since the first time she saw him at the Cave all those years ago. He was hot. Hard. Cut.

In fact, his body was like a Plinko game, all those hard ridges and muscles guiding her gaze down to the thin line of hair that disappeared into his jeans.

"I'll wash it and return it right away," she managed to get out around a tongue gone thick.

"Then you'll need my address."

"No. I already know where your chalet is."

That sexy, lopsided grin returned. "Well, now, would you look at that."

"What?"

"It appears you do know quite a bit about me after all."

She lifted her chin and countered with, "Which means there's no reason for us to get to know each other better."

His smile fell, and he suddenly looked like a puppy that had just been kicked. "But you still hate me."

"No, I…" When she caught the glint in his eyes, the heated way he looked at her, she briefly shut her eyes and looked skyward. "You're a little infuriating, you know that?" Jesus, could he pour it on any thicker? The guy was all sex and charm even when he wasn't trying.

"Only a little?" His sexy laugh fell over her, and Mel noticed the way her body warmed in all the wrong places. "Wait until you get to know me better," he teased with a wink. "I'm sure there'll be lots of other things you'll want to call me."

"I can already think of a few."

"Hey, be nice. I'm one of the good guys. You'll see."

Mel had no intentions of getting to know the infamous Ryeland Montgomery, a boy who'd recently graduated Canada's Ivy League university in the top of his class and was on his way to law school to follow in his daddy's footsteps, but she had no time to argue. She jumped from the Jeep and rushed along the stone walkway leading to the main entrance. As she hurried her steps, a strange tingle raced down her spine and the sensation that she was being watched prompted her to glance over her shoulder. Her gaze collided with Ryeland's and they exchanged a long look. His eyes drilled into hers, tracking her every movement carefully.

Fighting off the strange way he made her feel, she pushed through the front doors, putting Ryeland Montgomery, his sexy body, boyish grin, and demands that she get to know him better out of her mind.

With her head low, she walked through the front foyer and dashed toward the dining room, all the while hoping to avoid a run-in with her boss. Water dripped from her bangs and she wiped her cheek on her shoulder. That's when she caught Ryeland's scent in the fabric. Dear God, he smelled good. Like the fresh outdoors, clean soap, and hard man all mixed together. If someone decided to bottle his scent, they'd surely make millions.

Jaelyn came in to the back staff lounge behind her. "Holy shit, Mel, was that Ryeland Montgomery dropping you off?" Her green eyes moved over the polo Mel was wearing and she pointed a manicured nail at the little alligator logo. "Is that his?"

"Yes and yes," Mel said, tossing the wet tampon box into her locker before pulling his shirt over her shoulders. She was about to stuff it onto the top shelf of her cubbyhole when she caught his smell a second time. Unable to help herself she buried her face in the shirt and pulled in a breath. She drew it deep, savoring the aroma as it filled her lungs.

"Mel?"

Oh, God, what am I doing?

"Yeah?" she asked, throwing the polo to the back of her locker. She grabbed her clothes and slammed the metal door shut.

"What the hell is going on?"

"He gave me a lift because his friends soaked me. That's it. And what's really going on is I need to get dressed." Dishes clanged in the dish pit outside the staff lounge as Mel paused and pointed to the dining room. "And I need to get out there before Judith realizes I'm late and cans my sorry ass."

Jaelyn gave her an odd look but didn't press for details about Ryeland, and for that Mel was thankful. Changing the subject, Jaelyn whacked Mel on the ass. "Hey, you don't have a sorry ass. You have a nice ass. Not as nice as mine of course."

Mel laughed. "Of course." Jaelyn was a good friend, and even they were opposite in almost every way, she was the one person who could pull a smile from her, the one person she could count on when push came to shove. No doubt it was because her closest and only friend was also a lost soul. Except Jaelyn was a transplant who hadn't grown up in Deerfield, which meant she was quite content to stay and work here, whereas Mel just wanted out of Dodge and to start a new life somewhere else.

After stripping, Mel pulled on her green work shirt, with the Stone Cliff logo over her left breast, tugged on her black dress pants, and wrapped her apron around her waist. She tied her wet hair back and stuffed her notepad into her pocket. She looked at Jaelyn, who was frowning at the reservation screen on the restaurant's computer.

"What?" Mel asked.

"You're working the first dinner shift on the back patio tonight right?" Jaelyn asked.

Mel stepped up to her and looked over her shoulder. "Yeah, why?"

"Because this just came in." Jaelyn pointed to a name on the screen and arched her eyebrow.

"Shit," Mel cursed under her breath.

Jaelyn puckered her painted lips, and cast a curious glance Mel's way. "You sure you don't want to tell me what's really going on between you two?"

CHAPTER TWO

Ryeland sat in his car and couldn't wipe the stupid-ass grin off his face as he watched Melody rush up the walkway, her sweet ass dragging his focus until she disappeared from his line of sight.

Melody...

The name was pretty, and suited her well, which made him wonder why she'd shortened it. From the way her face fell and body tightened when he'd guessed correctly, he suspected the reason must have been a pretty damn important one.

There was no denying that everything about her intrigued him. It had for years now, actually. Ever since he'd first spotted her at the Cave when they were teens, he knew there was something special about her, and soon enough he found himself watching her every move, searching for her in the crowd. Every year he counted on her being here at Stone Cliff, and knew she could always be found somewhere or another in the small mountain town neighboring the resort. Melody Spencer was as much a part of the landscape as the towering Rocky Mountains.

For years she worked at Johnson's Convenience, and Ryeland had made lots of excuses to stop in, even though she'd never paid him a lick of attention. After graduating high school, she started living in Wolf Creek Lodge and working at the daycare camps as well as the resort's dining room, mainly the outdoor patio section—yeah, he'd been paying attention.

He grabbed his phone and called his buddy Jared, the resort's concierge. If anyone could make things happen around this place it was Jared. The guy had his pulse on the action and knew everything about everyone.

"Stone Cliff Resort, Jared speaking. How can I help you?"

"Jared, buddy, it's Ryeland."

"Hey. Ryeland, welcome back. How's it going?"

"Things are good. Listen, I need you to do me a favor. I need you to deliver a package to Mel Spencer for me."

"You bet."

After giving him the details, he dropped his phone onto his lap, put his vehicle back in gear, and followed the road leading to his folk's chalet.

Tall trees overhead shaded the road and provided a canopy from the heavy rain. Ryeland cracked his window, and while he usually loved the drive along the mountain, and loved spending his summers with his younger siblings, today he had a peach-sized lump in his throat.

After a hard four years studying at McGill, this summer hiatus was supposed to be about regrouping before he started law school in the fall and eventually joining his father in his practice, Montgomery and Associates. But deep down, he wanted to be a physician, a specialist, more than anything, not a cutthroat shark that gave all attorneys bad names. Except his father was a driven man and not someone anyone wanted to disappoint, which left Ryeland in a tough spot.

Ryeland wanted to do something more purposeful with his life, more meaningful—at least to him anyway. If he had it his way, if he felt his future was actually in his hands, he'd become an oncologist, helping sick kids here in Canada as well as volunteering his time overseas. But how could he turn his back on his father when the man had been grooming him to take over his firm for as long as he could remember? It was important to Arthur Montgomery to have his son join him, important to keep up appearances and present a united front in his social circles. While things might not always be perfect at home, every single Montgomery had to pretend their life was flawless. No way could the hard-hitting lawyer risk the opposition digging up dirt and using it to their advantage in the courtroom.

His father might be hard on him, harder than he was on his younger siblings. But he guessed it was because some eighteen years ago, when Ryeland was five years old, he'd nearly died from childhood leukemia. His father had changed drastically after Ryeland's diagnosis, became a little colder with Ryeland, a little tougher. Perhaps it was because he felt Ryeland needed his strength and not his coddling. Regardless, his old man's hard-headedness, his unemotional, clinical approach to Ryeland's illness pushed Ryeland to be stronger, to be tougher. Although he had to admit a hug every now and then might have been nice. But his father wasn't the hugging type, at least not after the sickness—or with him. And the truth was, he hated when Ryeland showed empathy. Ryeland was pretty sure it pissed the man off when he volunteered at the resort's stables. Maybe the hard-assed lawyer in him thought compassion and empathy for others was some kind of weakness.

Birds chirped in the distance and pulled his thoughts back as he drove along the windy stretch of road that followed along beside the lake. Kids hovered near a wharf, waiting for the storm to pass before they jumped back in. Their laugher could be heard as he crested the hill leading to their summer chalet. From his distance he caught sight of Justin Beechcroft and his two buddies, Cameron and Nikko sitting on the porch railing under the awning, waiting for him.

He pulled his car up beside Justin's flashy Mustang, slammed the stick into first, and yanked on his emergency brake.

"What took you so long?" Justin asked as Ryeland climbed from the driver's seat. "And where the hell is your shirt?"

Ryeland grabbed his duffle bag from the backseat, slamming the door with more force than necessary. "You fucking asshole."

"What?" Justin asked, laughing as he feigned innocence.

"You know what. You splashed that girl on purpose."

"Like hell I did. I swerved to avoid a squirrel." Justin held his hand over his heart. "Scout's honor. Could I help it that she was walking next to a puddle?"

"Yeah, sure, Justin. Go sell your crap to someone else." Ryeland pushed his wet hair from his forehead and took the steps leading to the front door two at a time. "That was a shit thing to do and you know it."

"What, you'd prefer it if I killed an innocent squirrel? I mean, come on, don't you remember the time I shot a squirrel with a BB gun and you went all Statham on my ass? Shit, I thought you'd be happy that I avoided it."

"We were nine," Ryeland countered.

"So you're saying I should have killed a poor, helpless squirrel?"

He took in Justin's cocky smirk and suddenly wondered why they were still friends. Sure he'd known the guy since they were kids, meeting up with him and the other guys at Stone Cliff every summer. Their parents were all friends from back east which, by default, meant their kids were friends too. While Ryeland chose to go to school in another province, the other three stayed back home and went to Kingsdale and had all grown a lot tighter over the years.

"Why are you worried about her?" Justin asked. "She's nothing but the local whore anyway."

Ryeland glared at his friend, shards of anger prowling dangerously through his veins. "Don't talk about her like that."

Nikko jumped from the railing. "Shit, what the hell's gotten into you?"

Ryeland pulled his key from his pocket and opened the front door. "Nothing," he said as his friends piled in behind him. "Just don't talk about her like that. You don't know her."

"Well, when you put it like that, maybe I should get to know her a little better this summer." Justin grinned and bumped fists with Nikko. "If you know what I mean."

Ryeland reached into his duffle bag and pulled out a clean shirt. "Leave her alone."

"You got a thing for her or something?" Nikko asked as he went to the fridge to grab a cold one. "I guess she is kind of cute."

Cute? She wasn't cute. She was straight up gorgeous, with long dark hair that fell to the middle of her back and a sassy attitude that challenged him in ways he'd never been challenged before. She was so different from the girls he normally associated with, and he had to admit, everything about the tough girl who didn't like to be touched and wanted nothing from him—hell, everyone wanted something from him—made him want to get to know her that much more.

Even though she had a great body, she was a little on

the thin side, making those dark, haunted eyes of hers look ten times bigger. He'd heard the stories over the years and had been warned by his folks to stay away from the local girls, who were nothing but trouble. Ryeland, obedient son that he was, had always kept his distance. But today, oh Jesus, today after seeing her standing on the side of the road, soaking wet, looking like she was about to kill someone, he found her impossible to resist.

He grinned, thinking about the way she'd taken a combative stance with him. Christ, he had no doubt she could kick his ass, and he kind of liked that she held her own against him. He could tell from the way she talked to him, to the disdain in her eyes, that she hated him and his friends—not that he could blame her after Justin's childish stunt. But it did give him all the more reason to prove he was different. All the more reason to prove he wasn't some stereotype, because somewhere deep inside, he suspected she wasn't either, and the rumors were just that. Rumors. And truthfully, he really wanted to get to know her better. He had for a long time now.

"What's so funny?" Cameron, who'd remained quiet until now, asked.

Ryeland wiped the smile from his face and looked out the window to see his parents' car pull in behind his Wrangler. As his father walked to the trunk, the knot in his stomach tightened. Soon enough his dad would want to strategize and plot the rest of his career with him, and Ryeland knew he'd have to make one of two choices. Tell his old man he didn't want to join his practice and risk getting blacklisted from the family—yeah his father was that much of a hard ass with him—or follow in Dad's footsteps and spend the rest of his life miserable?

Shit.

Nikko dropped down onto the sofa and planted his feet on the glass coffee table. "So what's on for tonight?

Are we heading to the Cave? I hear it's supposed to clear up later." He took a long pull from his bottle and dropped it onto the table beside his feet.

"And it's initiation night." Justin rubbed his hands together. "I like my girls nice and wet."

"Right, nothing like wet, local poo-say," Nikko added.

Ryeland looked at Nikko, who'd also been accepted into law school this fall. With his apathy toward others, maybe he should be the one joining Montgomery and Associates.

"Poo-say? What are you? Fourteen?" Ryeland asked.

Nikko laughed. "What the fuck happened to you this last year anyway? You used to be fun."

"Oh, I don't know. Maybe I grew up."

Justin snorted. "You can become a stiff-ass lawyer like your old man when you graduate law school. Right now you need to loosen the fuck up, pal."

"Says the guy who takes nothing seriously," Ryeland countered. He started at Justin. The guy was smart. Scary smart. But he was also an asshole who smoked way too much weed and didn't bother trying because his daddy had a nice cushy job for him in his software development firm.

"I hate to agree with anything that Justin says, considering he's a dick and all, but this time he's right," Cameron said.

"Asshole," Justin shot back.

"Pussy," Cameron countered.

Justin grinned. "Well you know what they say. You are what you eat."

Ignoring him, Ryeland pulled on his shirt and Cameron folded his arms as they stood eye to eye. "You really do look like you need to get laid."

Ryeland exhaled and could feel the tension in his shoulders. Jesus, he'd worked so hard this last year, burying himself in his work, he couldn't even remember the last time he'd been with a girl. "You're probably right."

"Now there's the Ryeland I know." Cameron slapped him on the back. "I hear Suzette will be at the Cave tonight.

Suzette. Sweet Suzette Preston, the girl his parents wanted him to marry. Smart, educated, pretty—the perfect socialite with the right pedigree to fit into the Montgomery family. While she was a nice girl, Ryeland wasn't interested in someone whose biggest worry was whether her bag matched her shoes. He'd about nodded off last summer at a family dinner when she talked about accessories for over an hour.

"I can't. My parents just arrived and you know they like to have a family dinner on our first night back."

At the mention of Ryeland's parents, Nikko grabbed a coaster and put it under his bottle. "How about afterward?"

Before he could answer, the front door swung open and his siblings came rushing in. Ashley raced toward him, her little dog Corky tight on her heels.

"Ryeland," she said, giving him a big hug. He lifted her off her feet and spun her around as Corky went up on his hind legs and barked, wanting some of the attention. Ryeland groaned as he set her back down to look her over.

He ruffled her hair. "You must have grown a foot since Christmas."

"Well I am almost thirteen." In a fashion that mimicked their mother, she planted her hands on her hips and bobbed her head, her long blonde ponytail swishing over her shoulders.

Ryeland turned his attention to his brother Evan, who was two years older than Ashley, as he came sauntering in like he owned the place. Ryeland opened his arms, but

Evan just stood there, looking like some punk ass thug.

"What? Are you too big to hug your brother now?"

"Bro," Evan said, twisting his ball cap around until the bill was facing backward. "I'm fourteen. I don't hug."

"Like hell you don't." Ryeland grabbed the cap and tossed it to Justin.

"What the—"

Evan made a move to get it but Ryeland gathered him in a bear hug and ran his knuckles over his brother's blonde head. "I think you've grown two feet since I saw you last."

"And I'm still growing, which means by this time next year, it'll be payback time and I'll be giving you all the noogies," Evan shot back, fighting to get free.

"Ryeland." At the sound of his father's voice Ryeland let his brother go and straightened. Arthur Montgomery dropped the suitcases inside the front door and squared his shoulders. "I take it you had a safe trip here?"

Nikko removed his feet from the coffee table and stood as Ryeland shook hands with Arthur. "I did. And you?"

His father nodded, then looked over his friends. "Boys," he said. "It's nice to see you all. Nikko, your father tells me you were accepted into law school as well."

As Nikko and Arthur talked, Ryeland's mother, Eliza, came rushing in, her purse over her head in some feeble attempt to keep her hair dry.

"Ryeland," she said, squealing in delight as she gave him a big hug. She stood back and looked him over. "You're looking too thin. I'm going to have to fatten you up over the summer. And your hair is too long. I'll make an appointment to get it cut tomorrow."

"Mom, I'm fine, and I don't need a hair cut."

Ignoring him she wagged her finger and said, "You've been working too hard and need a nice meal." She pulled her phone from her bag. "I'll make a reservations at the golf course country club."

He pushed his hands into his pockets and rocked back and forth on the balls of his feet. "I thought we'd have dinner on the patio at the main lodge tonight."

Blue eyes blinked up at him. "Oh?"

"Yeah, it's supposed to clear up and it will be nice to eat outside." He gave a casual shrug, like he hadn't made the reservation so he could see Melody again, or to introduce her to his parents so they could see that she wasn't some troubled townie like everyone thought. She might come across as tough, but deep down she was sweet and funny. As he thought about her witty comebacks, he tried not to grin.

"Why do you want to go there?" Eliza's eyes narrowed curiously as her glance moved over his face. "Everyone who's anyone will be at the country club."

"All the more reason for us not to go. It's quiet on the patio and will give us all a chance to catch up." He nodded toward his sibling. "I haven't seen those two monkeys in months."

"I'm not a monkey," Ashley yelled back as she raced up the stairs to her bedroom. "You're the monkey."

His father put his hand on Ryeland's shoulder. "That sounds like a fine plan, Ryeland. I'd like to go somewhere private to talk. We have your future to discuss. I want to tell you all about the office I'm redecorating for you."

The peach-sized lump in Ryeland's throat blossomed into a full-sized cantaloupe.

Shit.

CHAPTER THREE

Tucked behind the cash register, Mel whacked her notepad on her hand and tossed Jaelyn a pleading look. "Come on, I'll do anything if you take their table for me."

Tim, the bartender-in-training, walked by and Jaelyn lowered her voice. "You know I would if I could, but then Judith will know something is up. Do you want people talking about how you wouldn't serve the Montgomerys? They're pretty important people around here, Mel."

Mel peeked over Jaelyn's shoulder, glimpsing Ryeland and his family seated outside under the canopy as the rain slowed and the late-day sun broke through the clouds.

"Why did they have to come here?" she groaned.

"Yeah, good question." Jaelyn crinkled her nose. "Why do you think they came here? Don't they usually hang out at the golf course country club?"

"Apparently he's not finished annoying me," Mel said under her breath, barely able to pull her focus from Ryeland and the sexy grin he kept aiming her way. With his hair dried, all combed back in place, and a clean new shirt that accentuated those broad shoulders he looked good. Too good.

"Annoying you? I'm not exactly sure that's what he's doing, Mel." Jaelyn gave a mock shiver and held her hands out like she was testing the air. "I can feel the tension between you both from here. There's enough sparks in the air to trigger another lightning storm."

"That's crazy." Mel worked to rub the goose bumps away before Jaelyn noticed them.

"I'm not so sure about that." Jaelyn arched a brow. "What exactly happened during that drive, anyway?" She tapped her painted nail on her chin. "I mean, you did have his shirt on."

"Nothing happened." Mel frowned, the details of her conversation with Ryeland racing through her mind. "Not really. I mean…well…he said we should get to know each other better."

Jaelyn's green eyes widened. "Oh, and you decided to leave out that bit of vital information." She gave Mel an annoyed look. "That's not *nothing*. That's something. Something big."

"It's nothing, because I have no intentions of getting to know him."

Jaelyn's face softened. "Are you really going to let one guy ruin the rest of your life?"

One guy?

Oh, how she wished it were only one guy who'd ruined her trust in men. But it wasn't. It was more— many more—her father included. But there were some things she just couldn't tell anyone, not even her closest friend.

"Jaelyn—" Mel began.

"I mean, I know after you slept with Trevor he spread rumors about you, but maybe Ryeland is smart enough to know they aren't true."

Some are true…

Mel exhaled slowly. "Why are you on his side?"

"All I'm saying is this: maybe he's a nice guy and maybe you're judging him wrong." She went quiet, thoughtful for a moment—a rarity for her—then added, "You know how much you hate to be judged, especially by people who don't know you."

She nodded. "I'm not judging. I'm stating facts."

"Which are?"

"He uses girls."

"You don't really know that, do you? Not for sure."

"I've seen him with a different girl almost every summer. That's a fact."

"Did you ever stop to think that maybe they're using him? That they want something from him?"

Mel lowered her eyes as Jaelyn's words sank in. "Well, no, but—"

"But nothing. Maybe he *is* a nice guy and is truly interested in getting to know you."

She shook her head, refusing to believe that. "I'm sure the only thing he's interested in—"

"Mel, you're beautiful and smart, with a good head on your shoulders." She grabbed Mel's hand and gave a squeeze. "You're the whole package. Someday when you're signing your bestselling novel I'll get to say, 'I knew her when she worked at Stone Cliff.' Maybe he sees what I see."

"So what about you? You going to see Cole tonight after catching him with Jessica?"

Jaelyn gave an exaggerated exhale, her shoulders slouching. "You can't help who you like." Then she blinked and said, "Hey, this isn't about me, it's about you and Ryeland."

"I don't want a boyfriend, Jaelyn. No matter how hot he is."

Jaelyn smirked. "So you agree he's hot."

Mel threw her hands up in the air. "Of course he's hot. But I have a plan and I'm not about to get sidetracked, not now when I'm so close."

"I know you do, but it can't hurt to have a bit of fun once in a while, can it? Jesus, you spend so much time in that room of yours I'm afraid you're going to start collecting cobwebs." Jaelyn pretended to pick cobwebs from Mel's hair then glanced at Ryeland. "All I know is there is a hot guy over there who wants to give you another ride, except this time I'm pretty certain he wants to use a different stick shift. If it were me, girlfriend, I'd be all over that."

But Mel wasn't like Jaelyn, and never wanted to open herself up to another guy again. Her thoughts raced to Trevor, a local boy a few years older than her who'd never paid her any attention until last summer when he returned from university. God, he seemed so nice and sincere, sweet-talking his way into her bed. In a moment of weakness, she put her past hurts behind her, forgot about her distrust in men, and gave herself to him, only for him to brag about his conquest behind her back. She cringed, recalling the nasty things he'd said—a hard lesson learned that taught her to keep the protective shield around her heart.

Jaelyn nudged her. "Well?"

"I don't…"

"Just talk to him. Give him a chance and get to know him better like he wants. I mean, he's clearly going out of his way to be around you, and he did help you after that stunt his friends pulled. If you don't like who he is, then you walk away. Simple as that. Come to the Cave tonight. It's initiation night and I bet he'll be there."

Before she could answer and tell her friend that she'd rather not go the Cave, and had no intentions of riding anything of Ryeland's—ever again—Judith came from the kitchen.

"Is there a problem here?" she asked, and both Mel and Jaelyn straightened.

"No," they answered in unison.

Judith's piercing brown eyes drilled into them. "Then why are you both standing here when there are tables waiting?"

Stepping away quickly, Mel smoothed her hand over her apron and made her way through the dining room out to the patio. She could feel Ryeland's eyes on her as she walked toward his table. She tried to act casual, like him giving her a lift earlier, not to mention his shirt, and then finding him here in her section didn't affect her. But the truth was, it did, and that bothered her more than anything. She was so close to having enough money to leave, and he was a distraction she didn't want or need.

"How is everyone tonight?" she asked, plastering on a smile even though everything in the way Ryeland was looking at her made her feel all jittery. Ryeland's kid brother sat up straighter in his chair and she turned her focus to him. She looked at him and noticed the interest backlighting his blue eyes as they dropped to her chest. Typical guy.

"Stop staring." Ryeland jabbed his brother playfully with his elbow.

"Cut it out," his brother responded, color creeping into his cheeks.

"Mom, Dad, this is Mel." Ryeland looked at her, and she didn't miss the way her pulse jumped in her throat. "I gave her a lift earlier."

"That's right," she said playing along without missing a beat. "He was a knight in shining armor who came to my rescue when it started raining." Lord knew she wasn't about to rip on his friends in front of his family and tell them why he really stopped, which, when she thought about it, was rather nice of him. Maybe she had been too hard on him. Maybe Jaelyn was right and he was a nice guy.

And maybe she should just stop thinking about him.

"It was my pleasure," Ryeland said. His smile was so charming, so sexy and inviting, a jolt of heat raced through her. What was it about this guy that had her reacting like a silly cheerleader crushing on the quarterback?

She sucked in a quick breath to pull herself together and asked, "Have you all decided what you'd like to order?"

She looked around the table, and as she took in the beautiful, happy family of five, loneliness reared its ugly head and nipped at her soul. God, what she would have done to be a part of something special like this. She quickly pushed down those feelings, refusing to give in to them. Even though her mom went from man to man and was strung out on booze half the time, and her father was a deadbeat in prison, she reminded herself that she had Jaelyn and her stories—which gave her the make-believe family she'd always wanted. She didn't need anything more than that.

Her gaze settled on Mrs. Montgomery and the warm flush coloring her cheeks as she glared at her oldest son. Mel stiffened slightly. She wasn't sure what was going on between the two, nor did she want to get involved, so she tried to redirect the woman's focus by asking, "Do you all need another minute? I can come back—"

"Actually I'm not feeling so well," Mrs. Montgomery announced, dropping her cloth napkin onto the table.

"I'm so sorry to hear that. Let me get you some more water." Mel twisted to go.

"That won't be necessary," Mr. Montgomery piped in, the firmness in his voice stopping Mel in her tracks. His chair scraped across the decking as he stood to help his wife up. "Kids, come along."

"But I'm hungry," Ryeland's little sister grumbled.

Mrs. Montgomery cast her daughter a stern glance. "Ashley, you heard your father."

"I can take care of them," Ryeland said and something in Mel's stomach tightened when he ruffled Ashley hair in such a loving way. "I'll run them back once they're finished."

"Ryeland, I'm going to need your help with your mother."

Ryeland's confused glance bounced back and forth between his mother and father before landing on Mel. He stood and mouthed the words, "Sorry."

"Nothing to be sorry about." Mel worked to keep her composure as the other guests in the restaurant watched the actions of the family. The last thing she wanted was for Judith to think she'd run the Montgomerys out of the restaurant. Jaelyn was right. They were important people and this incident could be the end of her job. "I hope you're feeling better soon, Mrs. Montgomery. If there is anything I can do please let me know."

Ryeland grabbed his wallet and pulled out a few bills. Mel closed her hand over his. "That's not necessary."

"But—"

"Ryeland," his father called out as he guided his wife toward the steps leading to the back courtyard.

"What are you doing later?" he asked quickly. "Can I see you?"

Mel looked at his folks, then turned back to him. "I'm not sure that's a good idea."

He stared at her for a moment, then his silver eyes lit as understanding slowly dawned. "Wait. What? No, Mel." He shook his head and she caught the now-familiar scent of his cologne as it fell over her, a reminder that she still had to return his shirt. After the way his folks had acted, she certainly wouldn't be walking up to his door and delivering it herself. "This has nothing to do with you. I'm sure she's not well because of the long drive here. It's probably just exhaustion."

"Ryeland," his father bellowed.

He tossed the bills on the table, despite her protest. "Meet me at the Cave when you get off," he said quickly, then turned to hurry to his family before she could either accept or decline the invitation.

Mel glared at the money. It reminded her of her father's gambling. Perhaps because she felt as insignificant and worthless now as she did all those years ago when her father had used her as collateral in the illegal, high-roller poker game that took place at the resort once a year. Her heart pounded faster, her breath a little harder to catch as those cutting memories bombarded her.

With a bevy of unwanted emotions welling up inside her, she left the money where Ryeland had tossed it and grabbed the discarded menus. Even though she'd long ago hardened herself and tried not to care what others thought of her, there was nothing she could do to swallow down the sick feeling welling up into her throat.

"What the hell was that all about?" Jaelyn asked as Mel dropped the menus back at the hostess counter.

"Mrs. Montgomery said she was sick," Mel said, shoving her hands into her apron so Jaelyn couldn't see them shaking. "But I get the feeling it has more to do with me."

Jaelyn gave her shoulder a reassuring squeeze. "Mel, I'm sure you're wrong." She blinked up at her friend, and Jaelyn's eyes softened. "Maybe this will cheer you up. Jared just dropped a package off to you."

Mel's head jerked back with a start, surprised. "What? What's going on?" Why would the resort's concierge be bringing her a package?

"Beats me."

Mel opened the brown paper bag and peered inside.

"Oh. My. God." She shook her head in disbelief. "You've got to me kidding me." Her heart gave a little leap when she pulled the sticky note off the box of tampons and read the one word written on it: *Truce*. She smiled despite herself, and something inside her stomach took flight.

Truthfully, even if she did call a truce, after the way his parents had acted there was no way the two could ever be friends, which meant she wasn't going to waste another second thinking about him, or about the sweet—yet oddly disturbing—package he'd sent her.

Chapter Four

An uneasy feeling moved through Ryeland as his mother dropped down onto the sofa, placing a shaky hand over her head. Ryeland's father folded his arms and stood over her from behind.

"What's going on?" Ryeland asked.

"Maybe we should be asking you the same question." The coolness in his father's tone chilled the room.

"I don't know what you're talking about."

"Kids," Arthur said, handing Ashley and Evan some cash. "Head to the canteen and get yourselves something to eat."

Ryeland's siblings bounded out the door and once gone, his mother turned to him. "Did you know that girl worked there?" she asked, a combination of worry and repulsion in her tone. "Is that why you made the reservation?"

Ryeland shook his head, hardly able to believe what was going on. Jesus Christ, was Melody right? "Tell me that's not why we had to leave. Please…please tell me I'm wrong."

His mother pursed her lips. "I told you to stay away

from the local girls, Ryeland."

"All I did was give a girl a ride and make a reservation at the restaurant where she works. Don't you think your reaction is kind of extreme?"

"No, I don't. And locals are nothing but trouble."

"Weren't you a local girl once?" he asked his mom. "Before you met Dad at the resort?"

His mother stiffened. "Which is why I know what most of them are like, but this isn't about me."

"What do you have against her anyway? What did she ever do to you?"

"Her mother is the town drunk and her father is in jail. And then there was that incident…" She let her words trail off.

His jaw dropped. "Come on, you don't seriously believe she had anything to do with that guy's death. That's just crazy."

His father stiffened. "Crazy or not, you need to stay away from her."

"I'm not going to let her ruin my family," Eliza said, her voice hovering on panic.

Yeah, because it was such a great goddamn family. Jesus, he didn't even think his parents liked each other anymore. They probably were just keeping up appearances because, God forbid, they come across as anything but perfect. Ryeland linked his fingers behind his head and paced.

"How the hell is she going to ruin our family?" he asked.

Arthur's jaw clenched. "Watch your language, young man."

"By trapping you," Eliza blurted out, and he didn't miss the tightening of his father's jaw. "I know her type. She'll use you to get out of this place. She'll do whatever it takes."

Ryeland stopped abruptly and stared at his parents.

"Are you serious?" he bit out, unable to believe what he was hearing. "How can you say that? You don't even know her."

"You're the one who doesn't know her," his father said, something dark and menacing in his tone.

His mother angled her head and exchanged a tense look with his father.

"What?" Ryeland asked. "Tell me what this is really all about. What do you know that I don't?"

"Stay away from her. She's trouble."

"You're wrong." He shook his head. "You're so fucking wrong."

"Ryeland," his father warned.

"I'm twenty-three years old." He ran shaky fingers through his hair, his stomach clenching. Melody was sweet and funny and didn't deserve to be treated like a lower class citizen by anyone, especially his family. "I make good decisions and I think I'm quite capable of picking my own friends." He drove his hands back into his pockets and fisted his Jeep keys hard enough to cut skin. "I've allowed you to run my life long enough." Before he could think better of it, he added, "You're not going to tell me who I can and cannot hang out with too."

"What's that's supposed to mean?" his father asked.

With his anger spiking, and not thinking with his head on straight, he blurted out, "It means that maybe I don't want to be a lawyer. Maybe I don't want to work for you."

Anger flashed in his father's eyes, but beneath it Ryeland caught something else, some deeper concern.

"You're just upset," Arthur said firmly, his even tone belying his fury. "You don't mean that."

"What if I do?" He sucked in a quick breath. With everyone's emotions running high, some small, coherent part of his brain warned that now might not be prime time to lay it all on the line, but since he was on a roll, and things had been kept bottled up for far too long, he couldn't help but toss out, "What if I do mean that?"

"What's wrong with being a lawyer? Hasn't it provided well for us all?"

Well hell! He'd already opened the door and took a tentative step out, he might as well barrel right on through. "Maybe I want to do something more…meaningful."

"Meaningful? Jesus, Ryeland, get your head out of the clouds and grow a set. If you want to be a part of this family, then you're going to be a lawyer, and that's that. No son of mine is going to hang out in the gutter and do charity work for those who can't be bothered to help themselves. It's a dog-eat-dog world, and you'd be wise to remember that."

"Ryeland, trust that we know what's best for you," Eliza said, her voice a bit shaky.

"You don't know anything about me," he shot back. Desperate to get out of there, to get himself under control before he made things worse, he walked to the front door and pulled it open. "I need to go."

"Don't you walk out on me when I'm talking to you, young man."

He turned back and looked at his dad, wanting to talk it out. But when he saw his father's resigned expression he knew it was never going to happen. "You're not talking to me, Dad. You're lecturing me." Knowing there was no point in even trying to rationalize with him, Ryeland closed the door. His footsteps were heavy as he descended the stairs and slid into his Jeep.

He peeled out of the driveway, and darkness was beginning to fall over the town as he sped down the windy road and pulled his car onto the sandy shore at the Cave.

"Ryeland," Justin called, tipping his beer his way as

he waved him over.

A warm breeze blew over Ryeland as he walked toward the crowd gathered around the bonfire. Squeals could be heard as the guys tossed the new girls into the water, everyone having fun during their annual summer initiation to Stone Cliff. While he usually enjoyed the game, tonight he was in a shit ass mood and in need of a drink.

"What's the matter with you?" Nikko asked as he handed him a cold one.

Ryeland cracked the cap and looked around, hoping to find Melody but knowing he wouldn't. No way would she show up here after the way his folks and so-called buddies had treated her. Not that he could blame her. Off in the distance, surrounded by her friends, he caught sight of Suzette and noted the way she was glancing his way as Nikko continued to stare at him, waiting for an answer.

"Nothing's the matter," he said to Nikko.

"Whatever you say, man." Nikko turned and began chatting it up with the pretty brunette beside him.

Cameron came up to him and put his hand on Ryeland's shoulder. "You okay?"

Ryeland rubbed his temples with his thumb and forefinger. Shit, even though he didn't want to talk about it, he found himself saying, "Got in a fight with the folks."

"Shit. What about?"

He looked at his friend. Cameron was a good guy, the most level-headed of the group, and the truth was Ryeland needed someone to talk to. "What do you know about Mel Spencer?"

Cameron grinned. "Ah, so you do have a thing for her."

He shrugged. "I gave her a lift after Justin soaked her."

Cameron shook his head and swallowed a mouthful of beer. "He's such an asshole."

Ryeland scoffed. "Yeah, tell me about it."

Cameron glanced around. "Is she here?"

"No."

"I don't know much about her." Cameron tossed another stick onto the fire. The wood splintered under the heat and sparks took to the sky as Cameron poked at it. "Just things I've heard. Probably the same things you've heard."

Ryeland took a long pull from his bottle, then asked, "You don't think she was involved in that incident, do you?"

"You talking about when that poker player died?"

"Yeah, I mean that's crazy right? To think she had something to do with it."

He rolled one shoulder. "I barely remember it. It was forever ago. But I'm sure that's just some of the local crazies talking." He swallowed a mouthful of beer and bobbed his head. "Small town," he added, like that summed everything up.

"You think she sleeps around like everyone says?"

"Who doesn't? Jesus, come on. We're in our early twenties. That's what we're supposed to do. It's like it's in our DNA or something."

Ryeland smiled at his friend who was going into pharmacy studies next year. "You learn that in biology?"

"No, I learned that last night with Maggie Bryce."

Ryeland laughed, and put his hand on his friend's shoulder. "Okay then."

Cameron laughed along with him. "Which brings me back to what I said earlier today, you need to get laid."

"Yeah, I do." Maybe that would help him let off some steam and work out his anger.

"Looks like you've got your pick tonight, although Suzette might have something to say about that. She's been asking about you."

Ryeland stole a glance around, giving a heavy sigh at the number of eyes that were on him, all sending out silent invitations. "Yeah, I guess I do."

"Gee, your enthusiasm is wearing me out," Cameron teased with a grin. "Come on, it's not that big of a deal. You look at your choices, pick one out and go for it."

While he'd normally go for it, tonight he wasn't in the mood for mindless sex with some random girl, which was bat-shit crazy, because he was twenty-three and always in the mood for sex.

Before he could respond, a fight broke out behind him, and his friends all took off to get a glimpse of the action. Ryeland stood there for a moment longer, then poured out the rest of his beer. Without saying anything to his friends, he walked back to his Wrangler. He drove along the winding roads, unable to get the conversation with his folks out of his head. Cracking the window, he breathed in the night air and slowed when he caught sight of a deer on the side of the road.

He pulled over and watched it for a while. Ignoring him, the animal grazed on the grass along the road, its coat wet from walking through the woods and going about its business like Ryeland didn't exist. It sort of reminded him of Mel. Standing on the side of the road alone, soaking wet and trying to ignore him. After a long while he spun his vehicle back around and headed toward the resort, passing some suicidal maniac on a motorcycle. That had to be Noah Sullivan, the crazy son of a bitch who gave white water rafting tours for the resort. He continued down the mountain and drove toward the lodge, slowing when he caught the silhouette of a girl walking along the edge of the road. His heart picked up tempo and he tapped his brakes.

She glanced his way and continued to walk, ignoring him. Not that he could blame her. Hell, she'd been insulted by his friends and his folks all in the span of a few short hours. He rolled his window down, needing to make this right with her. "Hey."

Melody glanced his way, the look in her eyes wary. She'd freed her hair from the elastic and it flowed around her shoulders as she turned, but in the dark he couldn't make out her face, her expression.

"Hey," she said in a guarded voice without slowing. She continued forward, and he crept along beside in his Jeep, his elbow propped on the window.

"It's Melba, right?"

Her feet came to a resounding halt beneath the street lamp, and when she turned to him, he thought he caught a flicker of a smile before she wiped it away.

"Ryeland—"

"Funny how fate keeps bringing us together," he said, trying to keep the mood light. "Three times in one day."

"It's late and I'm tired."

"Then let me drive you."

He caught the conflicting emotions in her eyes before she looked down. "You shouldn't be doing this."

"Doing what, trying to be your friend?"

She looked him square in the eyes and said matter-of-factly, "I'm a slut. You must know that."

A lump lodged in his throat. Jesus, he hated to hear her talk about herself like that. "Come on, Mel, don't say that."

"You've heard the rumors, saw the way your parents reacted when you introduced us. You shouldn't be here. I'll ruin your reputation."

"Are you worried about me, Mel?" he asked quietly. He tipped his head, feeling an unfamiliar tightening in his chest at her concern for him. It wasn't something he got a lot of, and coming from her, especially considering the way his friends and family had been treating her, really touched him.

Her face tightened. "Why are you doing this?"

Ryeland stopped in the middle of the road, parked, and climbed out.

She looked up at him, her eyes cautious. "You can't leave your vehicle like that. Someone is going to come along and hit it."

"Then you'd better hurry up and get in."

He stepped closer and she sucked in air. Electricity arced between them as she pointed a shaky finger at the six buildings that housed the staff. "My…my place is right there. I can walk."

"And I can drive. Besides, you sound a little breathless." He stepped closer, close enough to catch the warm, sweet scent of her skin. He dipped his head, his eyes meeting hers. "Plus, I want to apologize."

She nodded, and her lashes fluttered as she looked down. "It's okay," she said quietly. "It's not your fault." As soon as the words left her mouth, her shoulders fell, like all the energy it took to hold them up had suddenly abandoned her, and she actually trembled before him.

Fearing she was about to collapse, he grabbed her. Not giving her a chance to step back, he wrapped his arms around her tiny waist and pulled her closer. With her arms trapped by her sides she stiffened, and her mouth fell open. His gaze dropped and he fought the compulsion to press his lips to hers. Jesus she had such a sweet mouth. There was no doubt he wanted a taste of her, and even though his body had turned mutinous—his cock thickening in his pants—he knew now was definitely not the right time, or the right place, to act on his urges. Partly because she was liable to give him a good swift kick between the legs, and partly because he didn't want her to think he believed the rumors and was only after one thing from her.

He tried to keep his voice normal, a most difficult task as her softness meshed with his hardness, and damn near drove him mad with want. "Are you okay?"

She pushed against him, and he let her go. "Yeah, I'm fine."

"You don't seem fine."

"I'm tired. I've been working a lot."

"That's what working two jobs will do to you." He looked over her face. Jesus, she looked like she was about to collapse again. "You're exhausted. You need to take better care of yourself."

"I'm fine." Her gaze flew to his face and she briefly stilled. "Wait, how do you know I work two jobs?"

"I just do. Now come on. You're not fine and I'm going to take you back to your place."

She stepped back. "Ryeland, I can't do this," she said, a desperate edge to her voice. "Not with you. Not with anyone."

He brushed her hair from her shoulders and felt her tremble beneath his touch. Heat zinged between them and she sucked in another quick breath. No way did she not want this as much as he did.

"I'm not asking you for anything."

She blinked up at him and his heart squeezed. From the first second he met her he knew she was a fighter, but looking at her now, he got the sense that she'd been strong for too long. Clearly she wasn't one to ask for help, to ask for anything, which made him want to help her all the more. He wasn't sure what it was about her, he only knew he'd been drawn to her for a long time now, and if he didn't finally do something about it he knew he'd regret for the rest of his life.

Her phone buzzed as vehicle lights flashed in the opposite direction. Beneath the lamplight, Ryeland caught sight of the resort's shuttle coming down the hill and knew he should move his Wrangler. "Come on, let's go," he said quickly as she checked her message.

She blinked up at him and her voice came out

strained, anxious when she said, "I can't."

"Mel—"

She gave a quick shake and cut him off. "No, you don't understand, it's not that…I…I have to go. There are some things I have to take care of." Before he could protest, she cut across the street, flagged down the shuttle, and disappeared into the night.

He stood there dumbfounded as he watched the shuttle drive away and couldn't help but wonder what was so important that she'd flag down a shuttle and head back to town when she was drop dead tired.

Chapter Five

Mel jumped from the shuttle and moved away from the tourists as they made their way down Main Street to browse the shops or head into one of the many restaurants that catered to the summer vacationers. She cut the corner and slipped into the shadows, hurrying toward her mother's place on the other end of town. Despite the exhaustion pulling at her like a weighted serving tray, she picked up her pace. As she approached her mother's rundown apartment building, her chest grew so tight it took effort to fill her lungs.

Even though she knew what to expect—hell, she'd found her mother like this as far back as she could remember—it still didn't make it hurt any less. The warm evening breeze washed over her face, but she was so very cold inside she shivered. She wrapped her arms around her body, covering her work shirt as she peered into the night. She moved closer, catching sight of her mother slouched against the apartment's front door. A huge man stood over her, and her pulse raced a little faster. Officer Sattler, the man who was there that night so long ago, one of the few who knew the truth about what happened in that hotel room, straightened to his full height when she approached.

"Mom," Mel said breathlessly as she quickly climbed the set of stairs. "Mom, come on. Get up."

Officer Sattler turned to Mel and she tried to ignore the pity in his eyes. "Mel," he began as she averted her gaze, her stomach clenching around the lump forming in the pit of her gut. "I can't keep doing this. Someone is going to press charges one of these days and I'll have no choice but to take her in. You know that, right?"

"I know and I'm sorry. It won't happen again," Mel said, even though they both knew it was a straight up lie. Honestly, if her mother continued to drink and trash things, mainly whatever guys she was with, she was going to end up in the drunk tank and there wasn't a damn thing Mel could do about it. She bent and grabbed her mom's arm. "Come on, Mom. Get up." Sattler reached for her mother's other arm and helped Mel lift her. Once they had her standing, Mel wrapped her mother's arm around her shoulder. Mel might be petite herself, but her mom was still smaller. Thank God, because Mel had to do this far too often. She shot Sattler a quick look. "I got her. Thanks for the help, and for letting me know."

"Melody," her mom slurred. "You're such a good girl. Isn't she a good girl?" she said to the officer.

"Yeah, she's a good girl, Rita," he agreed, and once Mel fished the keys from her mom's purse, the officer turned to leave.

"You take care of yourself, Mel." Sattler's voice was so steeped with concern, Mel had to bite the inside of her cheek to keep her emotions in check.

She worked to harden herself. "I will, thank you."

Mel dragged her mother into the building, and once inside Mom's apartment she lowered her onto the sofa. "I'll make you some coffee and get you something to eat."

"Mel, come here."

"Mom, come on," she said barely able to keep the annoyance from her voice. "Let me make the coffee."

"Come here, baby."

Exhaling slowly, Mel dropped down onto the coffee table beside her mother. "What is it?"

With her head bobbing, her mother tried to focus her glassy eyes as she reached out to run her fingers through Mel's hair. "Men are no good, baby. No good. You know that, right? They take what they want and this is how they leave you."

"Okay, Mom," Mel said, cutting her off. "We can talk about this in the morning." She stood and grabbed the blanket at the end of the sofa.

"Your father, he was no good too. I never should have married him. If it wasn't for…" Her words fell off, and she pinched her lips together.

"Why don't you try to get some sleep? You'll feel better in the morning."

Her lids blinked open, and her eyes looked lost and vacant as she stared at some spot behind Mel's shoulders, but Mel heard the wistfulness in her tone when she asked, "Is everyone back, Mel?"

"Yeah, everyone is back," she said softly, knowing exactly what her mother was asking. That's when it occurred to Mel that she should have expected to find her mother in this condition tonight. Every year when the tourists started filing in, her mom would get pie-eyed drunk. Maybe it was a reminder of what they had and she didn't, but heck, if a person wasn't happy with their lot in life, they either needed to do something about it or accept it. Mel would be damned if she was going to fall into the trap of alcohol and self-pity.

"You don't come around much anymore," her mom said.

"I'm busy. I'm working two jobs now."

Her mother briefly closed her eyes, then opened them again. Instead of commenting on Mel's jobs or how she was trying to make something of herself, she turned the conversation back to her, like she always did.

"They're no better than me, you know. No better than any of us. They come here every summer and walk around turning their noses up at the locals."

"I know," Mel agreed, having no idea if her mom was talking about the tourists in general or someone specific.

"You know you have to stay away from those rich boys, baby. They'll only break your heart."

"I will." Her thoughts raced to Ryeland.

Her mother laughed, a disturbed, maniacal titter that chilled Mel to the bone. "They make promises they can't keep."

"Doesn't everyone," she said under her breath, thinking back to the last time she rescued her mom from a night in the drunk tank, only for her to promise never to drink again.

Finally her mom's eyes slipped shut, and when she started snoring, Mel tucked her in and made her way to the kitchen. She opened the fridge and scanned the contents to make sure her Mom still had food, noting that she'd barely touched any of the groceries Mel had dropped off last week. Mel pulled out the package of deli meats and mustard. She slapped together a sandwich, wrapped it in foil and put it back in the fridge. Then she cleaned the coffee pot and prepared a fresh brew for morning.

Tipping her head from side to side, she stretched out her achy neck muscles and made her way back into the living room. A quick glance at the clock told her she could still catch the last shuttle back to the resort if she hurried. There was no point in staying overnight. Like so many times before, her mother would only be sleeping it off anyway, and come morning likely wouldn't even remember that Mel had been there. Mel grabbed a sheet of paper from the broken printer propped up in the corner of the room and scribbled a note. Fighting the pang of sadness nipping at her soul as she took one last look at her passed-out mother, she left the apartment and secured the lock behind her.

She retraced her steps and ran when she caught sight of the shuttle getting ready to pull out from its stop. She flagged it down and let loose a grateful sigh when the doors opened for her.

"Thanks, Jack," she said to the elderly driver who'd been doing the night runs every summer for as long as she could remember.

"You're out late tonight." Jack smiled at her. "I don't usually see you in town at this time."

She took the seat directly behind him. "Just had some last-minute things to take care of."

His smile fell and he gave her a sympathetic look in the rearview mirror like he knew what she was talking about, so she changed the subject. "Things must be picking up now that the tourists are all back in town."

"Yeah, I did a few extra runs to the Cave. Seems to be the hot spot tonight. Is that where you're headed?"

"I…" Mel thought about it for a moment, and her first instinct was to say no, but tonight the thought of going back to her room to write until she fell asleep didn't sound quite as appealing as it had earlier. She exhaled slowly and sank farther into her seat and stared out the window, finding it a little harder to fight down the emptiness inside her. Being with her mother always left her feeling out of sorts.

Jack drove through the lamp-lit streets and glanced at her in the rearview mirror. The lines around his cloudy eyes deepened as he looked at her. "Come on, a young girl like you should be out having some fun. From what I hear it's initiation night. I dropped Jaelyn off earlier. So what do you say, you want me to drop you there too?" He winked. "Someone's got to keep that girl out of trouble."

"Yeah, okay. I guess I'll go see what she's up to." She rested her head against her seat and stared at the roof of the bus. She rarely went to the Cave, and after last year, when Trevor set out to "bag" her as he called it, she'd decided to avoid the place all together. She would never be someone's summer conquest again. Which made her wonder why the hell she said yes to Jake. She shook her head, hoping to knock some sense back into her brain. What the hell had come over her? Perhaps she was just so damn worn out she couldn't make good decisions.

Or perhaps it was because Ryeland might be there, some inner voice whispered.

Her stomach did a weird little flip-flop as she thought about him. Like it or not, he had a way about him that made her forget her resolve to stay clear of men. Maybe it had something to do with the way his eyes went nearly black when he looked at her, or how the groove around his mouth made that sexy dimple when he tossed a smile her way.

She closed her eyes. Despite her best interests she let herself think about him a moment longer. Around her, tourists talked amongst themselves and from the back of the bus she could hear a bunch of rowdy boys razzing each other. She caught a whiff of weed and figured they were gearing up for a good time tonight.

When the bus finally stopped, she exited and walked the pebbled path leading to the sandy shoreline. She searched the crowd for Jaelyn, knowing her friend would be in the midst of the fun. Heck, her friend wouldn't miss initiation night if her life depended on it. She looked at a group of guys and girls hanging off one of the vehicles as music blared from the car's radio. One of the pretty blondes climbed to the rooftop and started dancing, and the boys all began cheering her on. At least it wasn't Jaelyn this time, she mused.

Mel walked toward the bonfire, weaving her way through the throng of partiers, and scanned the crowd a second time. She approached the fire and when she looked through the flames, she caught sight of Ryeland. He stood with his back to her and she took advantage of the moment to look her fill, admiring his wide shoulders and long, hard body. He really was hot, and everything in the way those jeans hugged his ass almost made her forget why letting him get too close was a bad idea. Clearly she wasn't the only one who thought he was the catch of the night, considering all the girls hovering around him. Suzette stepped up to him. Suzette Preston: perfectly made-up face, perfectly styled blonde hair, long, lithe body that made Mel feel like a hobbit. Basically, she was the antithesis of Mel. Suzette blinked long thick lashes and looked at Ryeland with adoring eyes.

Ryeland fisted his hair, a habit Mel was becoming familiar with, and unfortunately, when he turned her way, she was far too slow to react. Her gaze flew to his and when his lips quirked into a smile, she knew he'd caught her staring. Damn.

A squeal came from the lake and Mel was thankful for the distraction. She removed her shoes and dug her toes into the sand, enjoying the warmth on her feet as she followed the sound. Water splashed in the distance, and a second later, Jaelyn burst through the surface, two guys standing over her and laughing.

Mel grinned and shook her head. In typical Jaelyn fashion, she wrapped an arm around each of the boys who, from the grins they exchanged, clearly felt she was a sure thing tonight. They laughed as they carried her to the shore. At least she'd found a way—or two—to get over Cole. When she saw Mel standing there she squealed, freed herself from the boys, and rushed forward.

"Mel, you came!" Jaelyn reached out to give her a big, wet hug.

"Don't." Mel laughed as she tried to push her away. "I spent half the day wet already and would like to spend the rest of my night dry."

"That's too bad, because I like my girls wet." Mel's heart fell into her stomach at the familiar voice behind her. She turned and came face to face with Trevor. Christ, if she'd known he was going to be here tonight she never would have come. Then again, why wouldn't he be here? No way would he miss out on the biggest party of the season, not when it was his chance to mark his next conquest.

"Go away, Trevor," Jaelyn sputtered as water dripped down her face.

Ignoring Jaelyn, he stepped closer to Mel, a predatory look on his face. "I'm pretty sure Mel can speak for herself. Isn't that right, Mel?"

"Absolutely. Now go away," Mel said, but she may as well have been talking to a piece of driftwood for all the attention he paid her. He continued to come closer, ignoring her, and Mel knew she had two choices. Give him a good swift kick between the legs like he deserved, or just get the hell out of there. Since she really didn't want to cause a scene or any more rumors, she turned to leave. But he had other ideas.

He grabbed her arm and spun her back around to face him. "Ah, come on, Mel. What are you mad about?"

She flinched as anger raced through her. While she could stand there and list a dozen reasons, she didn't want to be doing this with him—not here with everyone watching. God, what had she been thinking? Coming here tonight was such a stupid, stupid mistake.

"Drop it, Trevor," she whispered between clenched teeth, then turned her back on him again. Head down, she trudged across the beach.

"But we had some good times, baby." He followed close behind, bending to be heard over the blaring music, and she could smell the alcohol on his breath. "Why don't you stop pretending you didn't like it, 'cause I know you did."

"Go away, Trevor," she bit out again.

She heard his hand hit his chest. "You're breaking my heart, baby."

"And I'm going to be breaking your face if you don't fuck off."

Mel looked up and came face to face, or rather face to chest with Ryeland. She lifted her eyes higher and when she caught the intensity backlighting those beautiful silver orbs as he stood there glaring at Trevor, her heart pounded a little harder in her chest.

"Ryeland, don't," she pleaded, putting one hand on his chest to push him away. "It's not worth it." No, getting his ass kicked because of her past mistakes definitely wasn't worth it. And Mel had no doubt Trevor would give him a good beating. Ryeland was lean and cut, but Trevor was an all-star football player who played dirty, and a nice guy like Ryeland didn't stand a chance against him.

Nice guy?

Ryeland closed his hands over hers and held it against his packed muscles. She could feel the strong, rhythmic beating of his heart as his warm palm engulfed hers. It made her feel strange…safe.

"Cut it out, Trevor," Jaelyn said, catching up to them from behind. She grabbed his arm to pull him away, but he shook her off and she fell to the ground.

Mel pulled away from Ryeland and rushed to her, leaving Trevor and Ryeland standing there, testosterone coming off them in waves as they sized one another up.

"You got something to say?" Trevor asked, smirking as he squared off against Ryeland. While they were both the same height, Trevor had a good fifty pounds on Ryeland, which didn't bode well for anyone.

Ryeland widened his stance. "Yeah, why don't you try picking on someone your own size?"

Trevor looked Ryeland up and down and scoffed. "You know anyone?" When Trevor's friends came up to stand beside him, they laughed and bumped fists. Except Ryeland wasn't without his own friends, and when Justin, Cameron, and Nikko flanked Ryeland, Mel knew this was going to get ugly really fast.

"Fight, fight, fight," the crowd chanted, gathering around them. Everything inside Mel clenched. She shouldn't have come here tonight. Ryeland didn't deserve this.

"Well," Trevor asked again over the deafening chant. "You know anyone?"

"Yeah. Me," Ryeland said as he continued to hold his own against Trevor.

Trevor laughed and jerked his thumb toward Mel. "Why would she want anything to do with a pretty boy like you? It's not like you'd be able to make her moan the way I can." His mouth twisted. "Isn't that right, baby?

"Don't fucking talk to her like that." In the blink of an eye, Ryeland had Trevor on the ground, pounding Trevor's face into the sand. Trevor cursed and fought to gain purchase. One of Trevor's friends kicked Ryeland in the ribs to knock him off and Cameron jumped in to help out. Before Mel knew it, fists were flying everywhere. In a mass of arms and legs and sand flying into the air, Jaelyn grabbed Mel to haul her backward before anyone landed on them.

The crowd grew thicker, the chants louder, and even though Mel kept screaming, "Stop!" her pleas went unheard. Worry for Ryeland ripped through her as her heart slammed harder against her chest. Why couldn't he have just minded his own damn business?

"I need to stop this, Jaelyn," she said, her voice bordering on hysteria as she searched for her shoes to tug them back on.

Her stomach turned inside out as she listened to the chorus of violent sounds as fists hit and bones crunched. Jaelyn pulled her closer and jerked her head forward. "Don't worry. I think your lover boy can hold his own."

"He's not my…" She let her words fall off. Now was not the time to be getting into a debate on who Ryeland was or wasn't.

The sound of sirens reached them from the distance and relief washed through her.

"Thank God." Mel hugged Jaelyn tighter. At least someone had kept a level head and alerted the police.

"Shit. Cops!" some guy yelled, and the crowd took off, leaving Ryeland, Trevor, and their friends to fend for themselves.

Mel stood and brushed the sand from her knees. She looked up to see Sattler coming their way. His gaze combed the beach before bobbing back and forth between Trevor and Ryeland.

It settled on Trevor. "What's going on here?" he asked, in a hard voice that Mel had only heard him use once before, right before he took her father away in handcuffs after the incident at the hotel.

"Nothing," Trevor said, spitting out a mouthful of blood. "Just cutting loose after a hard year in school, Uncle Ronnie." He smirked at Ryeland—a look that said he planned to finish what he started. "Isn't that right, buddy?" Trevor put his arm on Ryeland's shoulder and grinned.

"Yeah, that's right." Ryeland nodded in agreement. "We were blowing off steam."

Sattler turned toward Mel and frowned. She shrunk into herself, the way she always did when she wanted to disappear. "I'm surprised to find you here."

"I was here to see..." She stopped and looked at Jaelyn, who was smoothing her hair back and looking at Sattler like she wanted to eat him alive. "Actually, I was just leaving."

Sattler hooked his thumbs into his belt loop and looked over his shoulder. "I'm headed to the resort. You want me to give you a lift?"

"I've got her," Ryeland said, shaking Trevor off and moving in beside her. He put his arm around her shoulder and pulled her close to lay claim. Mel didn't miss the way Trevor's nostrils flared in response. What the hell? Did he think she would ever have anything to do with him after the things he'd done and said?

"Mel?" Sattler asked, glaring at Ryeland with suspicious eyes.

"It's okay." Mel tried not to flinch as Ryeland held her. She really was going to have to teach him a thing or two about personal space. When Sattler gave her a dubious look, she rushed out with, "I'm okay."

He watched her carefully and she tried not to fidget under that all-knowing gaze, then he finally conceded. "All right." He turned his glare to his nephew. "Trevor, come with me."

Like a petulant child, Trevor curled his shoulders forward and walked away with his uncle, his friends following.

"Yeah that's right, you better get the fuck out of here," Nikko said, slamming his right fist into his open palm.

Cameron wiped his mouth with the back of his hand

and stepped up to Ryeland. "Well that was fun."

Justin came up from behind and put his hand on Ryeland's shoulder. "Christ, Ryeland, did you have to pick on the biggest bastard here?"

Ryeland shook his head. "Justin, this is Mel. Mel, this is the asshole that splashed you today. I think he has something to say."

"Yeah, sorry about that." Justin took a step closer to her. "Was just trying to avoid a squirrel. It won't happen again."

"It better not." Ryeland pulled her in tighter, his warmth curling around her like a wool blanket and pushing back the cold.

"You okay?" Jaelyn asked as the two boys she was playing with earlier came up to her, clearly wanting to pick up where they left off.

"Yeah, I'm fine," she said, even though she couldn't seem to stop shivering.

"If you're not, I can—"

"I am. Now go. I'm going to head back and get some sleep." She looked at the boys waiting for Jaelyn and recognized them as vacationers who came here every summer. Mel might not live the same lifestyle as her friend, but who was she to judge. She leaned in and whispered, "Have fun, but be careful, okay?"

Jaelyn hesitated for a moment. She looked at Ryeland, then back at Mel. "You sure?"

"Yes, I'm sure. Now go."

"Okay." She gave Mel a hug and disappeared down the beach with her two boy toys. Now that Sattler was gone, people were emerging from the shadows and filling the beach once again.

Ryeland jutted his chin toward his friends. "I'll catch up with you guys later. I'm going to make sure Mel gets home safely." He scrubbed his hand over his jaw and said, "And, thanks for jumping in to help."

"You know we've got your back," Cameron said before he drove his hands into his pockets and sauntered off with Justin and Nikko.

When his friends left, Ryeland turned her toward the road and started walking, his arm still around her. Mel caught sight of his Jeep, then shot a sidelong glance his way. She took in his handsome profile and the dark contemplative look on his face.

As if feeling her eyes on him, he angled his head. "Who was that guy anyway?"

"Just someone I once knew, or at least thought I knew."

His features softened when his gaze zeroed in on her, and the strength of the impact hit like a physical blow. O-kay…

"What did he want?"

Trying not to think about the way he affected her, she blurted out, "What every guy wants."

Ryeland dragged her in closer, the heat of his body wrapping around her and making her feel a little bit woozy. As her body turned mutinous, taking too much pleasure in his warmth, she stepped away in an attempt to get her control back. "Just so you know, I can fight my own battles, Ryeland. You don't need to keep coming to my rescue."

"I know you can. But I was itching for a fight anyway."

"Why…?" Her words fell off and she winced as her eyes narrowed in on his forehead.

"What?" he said.

She went up on her tiptoes and pushed his hair off his face. "You're bleeding."

He wiped his hand over his forehead and winced.

She whacked his hand away. "Don't touch it."

"Why?"

"You'll get it all infected."

His face softened again, and his voice was low when he said, "There you go worrying about me again."

"I just didn't want you to bleed all over my shirt." She continued to walk, trying to shake off the strange way he made her feel. "You'd better get home and get that cleaned up." When she realized he'd stopped walking, she turned back. "What?"

He frowned, and the muscles in his jaw flexed as he fisted his hair. "I can't go home. I got in a huge fight with my parents and I'm not ready to go back yet. I think we all need some time to cool down."

"Is that why you were itching for a fight?"

"Maybe."

Mel's thoughts raced back to the dining room incident and her throat tightened. "Please tell me this fight had nothing to do with me."

He gave a quick shake of his head and his hair fell forward, making him look incredibly sexy. "It didn't."

Her fingers itched and she linked them together to stop herself from pushing his hair back again. "Good. I don't want you fighting about me. I'm not worth it."

He took two measured steps, until their bodies were touching once again. "What if I think you are?"

"Then I'd ask how hard Trevor really hit you."

He looked at her for a moment then burst out laughing. A deep belly laugh so loud and contagious she couldn't help but laugh along with him.

When he stopped he ran his thumb along her cheek. "You've got a wicked sense of humor, Melody."

"It's Mel." Needing to break this hold he had over her she said, "Come on." She grabbed him by the shirt to drag him to his vehicle.

He followed along. "Where are we going?"

"I'm going to let you drive me home, and then I'm going to bandage you."

His teeth flashed in a triumphant smile. "You are?

Why?"

"Because I feel responsible for all this and I also get the sense that you're not going to let up until I finally give in and let you give me a lift."

"You're right."

"Then will you leave me alone?"

He threw his arms up in the air, his lips quirking. "I just got my ass kicked for you, and I probably have a concussion. I wouldn't be surprised if I wandered into oncoming traffic and got run over and this…this is how you treat me?"

"Are you always this dramatic? Maybe you should take a Midol."

"A Midol? I let Trevor use my face as a punching bag and all you're offering me is a Midol. That hardly seems fair."

Her stomach fluttered like crazy as he stood there, his expression filled with mock exasperation. "Okay, what would be fair?" she asked.

"Oh, I don't know. Maybe a little TLC."

When she caught his half-cocked grin, she rolled her eyes. "I never asked you to get your ass kicked." Although she had to admit, he was a lot tougher than she'd first thought. In fact, while he might be a nice guy, he was kind of a bad ass too, and it secretly thrilled her that he got a few hard hits in of his own. She hated violence, but Trevor had it coming.

"I know," he said, his hand brushing against her as his expression changed, became serious. "But I'd get my ass kicked a thousand times a day if it meant seeing you smile like that."

A shivered tingled all the way to her toes and her knees weakened as the rough pads of his fingers caressed her palms. There wasn't a damn thing she could do to harden herself against his charm. The guy was irresistible and if she knew what was good for her, she'd hightail it the other way and never look back.

Walk away, Mel. Just walk away.

"Come on," she said.

Dammit.

Ryeland Montgomery was starting to mess with her head.

Chapter Six

Feeling fiercely protective after their run-in with Trevor, Ryeland kept close to Mel as they walked toward the road, and it took everything he had inside him not to grab her and pull her in tighter, to tell her everything would be okay. She was still shaking, and he could tell by her eyes that the whole situation with her ex had hurt more than she let on. He had no idea what went on between the two in the past, and it really wasn't his business, but no way in hell was he about to stand there and let that bastard talk to her like that.

"Are you okay to drive?" she asked when they reached his Jeep.

He held the keys out to her. "Can you drive a stick?"

"Actually no. I don't have my license."

"Well shit." He pulled the keys back and twirled the ring around his finger. "We'll have to do something about that."

"I've never needed it," she went on to explain. "Everything is within walking distance and there's always the shuttle."

Ryeland hit the unlock button and circled the front.

He slid in beside her. "It's not hard. I'll teach you."

She crinkled that cute little nose of hers. "I'd probably ruin your transmission."

"Such little faith in your teacher, young grasshopper."

Ryeland pulled onto the road as Mel buckled herself in. He could feel her eyes on him as he negotiated his Jeep along the windy road.

"I take it you really like *Karate Kid*," she said.

Wanting to keep things light and put her at ease he said, "Don't you?"

She rested her head against the seat and stifled a yawn. "Not really."

"So what do you like?"

She shrugged. "I don't know. Anything Nicholas Sparks I guess."

"Ah, a believer in true love."

She sat up straighter and looked at him, surprise in her eyes. "So you've seen his movies?"

"Nope."

"You're lying." She laughed as she hit him in the arm. "You have. Admit it."

He rubbed his arm and feigned hurt. "Nope. Didn't see any of his movies. And that's quite a punch you got there."

She settled back against the seat and crossed her arms. "You're not a very good liar."

"Hmm, and here I thought I was."

Ryeland took the corner and headed to Wolf Creek Lodge. A few minutes later he pulled into guest parking and killed the ignition.

Her head jerked his way. "Wait how do you know which building I live in?"

"You're kind of legendary around here too."

She frowned, and went eerily still. "Right."

"Was it something I said?" Ryeland asked as he

turned to her. Unable to help himself he reached out and curled a long strand of her hair around his finger.

"No." She pulled away from him and reached for the door handle. "Let's get you cleaned up so you can go home and work things out with your folks."

This time he frowned and went still.

She turned back to him. "Was it something I said?"

"Yeah."

"I'm sorry."

"Nah, it's fine." Now that he was with Mel, the last thing he wanted to think about was how judgmental his parents were, or how he spent a lifetime being pushed in one direction when he wanted to go in another.

He jumped from his seat and walked around to her side. A couple of girls came from the lodge as they approached the side door. One was eating French fries from a cardboard container.

"Mel," she said, dipping the fry into ketchup and licking it before tossing it into her mouth. She looked at Ryeland and for a minute he feared she was going to dump that ketchup over him then lick him clean. Jesus...

"Jess," Mel returned. Mel pushed past her and grabbed the door before it closed.

"You partying at the Cave tonight?" Jess asked her, her eyes never leaving Ryeland.

"No, just returning."

"And I can see you brought your own party with you." Jess grabbed another fry, put it between her lips and slowly pushed in. "Damn, girl, I wish I'd gotten there first." She cast her glance downward to take in his body and pouted her painted lips in a way the probably got her everything she'd ever wanted. "You wouldn't happen to have a brother, would you?"

He leaned forward. "Yeah, but he's far too young to be corrupted by you."

Jess laughed and, continuing to mimic a blowjob,

eased another fry into her mouth. "I'll see you later."

When she left, he turned to find Mel staring at him, her mouth open.

"What?"

Her glance moved over his face and she shook her head. "You have no idea, do you?"

"Afraid you lost me."

"Never mind."

He laughed. "Come on. You can't say something like that and leave me hanging."

"Fine. You're like nectar to a honeybee, Ryeland." He followed close behind as she took the stairs two at a time, stopping on the fourth floor. "Wherever you go girls seem to fall all over you."

He reached past her and pulled the door open. "Not all girls."

She rolled her eyes and ignored him. "This way." She stepped into the hall and turned left. Once the reached her room, she fished her key from her pocket and let him into her dorm-style bedroom.

"Nice," he said, giving it a quick scan.

She looked a bit uncomfortable as he followed her inside. "It's temporary."

"Oh yeah?" He was about to ask more when she cut him off.

"Yeah, now sit." She gestured toward the chair in front of a small desk and he fell into it, stretching his legs in front of him. "I'll be right back."

She dropped her phone onto the desk and disappeared into her small bathroom. He listened to her turn the water on and grabbed her phone, punching in his number and taking note of hers. Carefully putting it exactly where she'd left it, he looked at her unmade bed and the yellow flower print on her sheets. He grinned. Here he'd taken her more for a Powerpuff kind of girl, or ninjas. At least she didn't have three thousand stuffed animals lining the head of her bed. Other than a picture of her and her friend on her nightstand, her walls and dresser were bare of anything personal. In his Montreal apartment he at least had a picture of his family. After a quick scan of the small space, he looked at the laptop on her desk, a stack of papers beside it. He leaned forward, wanting to get a peek. He read the first few lines on the top sheet of paper, but sat back in his chair when the water turned off.

Mel came from the bathroom and her nervous glance left his face. She darted a fast look at the papers he'd been looking at. She came closer, set a tube of ointment and a box of bandages on her desk, and in one easy movement slipped a blank sheet of paper over the pile. Clearly she wasn't quite ready to give him a peek into her personal life.

Her glance moved over his forehead and she frowned. "Does it hurt?"

He rubbed his jaw. "Like a son of a bitch." He crooked his finger, urging her closer. "I'm ready for that TLC."

She leaned over him to examine his wound and he widened his legs to give her better access. She came closer and her sweet scent washed over him. Her body aligned perfectly with his, and there wasn't a damn thing he could to do keep his cock from hardening. Shit. He shifted to hide his erection, knowing she'd throw his sorry ass out the window if she knew he was having a party in his pants.

"This might sting." She poured peroxide onto a cotton ball, but Ryeland didn't have the heart to tell her peroxide should never be used on an open cut. She pressed it to his forehead and he winced.

"Shit."

"Sorry." She looked like she was trying not to laugh as she swiped it across his wound.

"What kind of TLC is that?" She moved a little closer, standing between his legs, and he squeezed the arm of the chair to stop himself from pulling her into his lap. "I think you're being rough on purpose."

She wiped again and held the cotton out for him to examine. "It's the only way to get the sand out."

She repeated the process and as she leaned over him her hair fell into his face. All thoughts of his cut fled as he breathed deep. Mmm, strawberry.

Her back stiffened and she eyed him. "Did you smell my hair?"

"Yeah." He gave her a sheepish look. "Sorry. You just smell so good."

"I'm pretty sure I smell like puddle water."

He scoffed. "Believe me, that won't happen again."

She squeezed ointment on her finger and dabbed it on his cut. He winced again, and when he curled his fingers around the arms of the chair harder, she cast him a chastising look. "Come on."

"What? It hurts," he said, laughing.

"You're not a very good patient."

"And you're not a very good nurse."

"It's not my calling."

"No? What is?"

Instead of answering she said, "Speaking of puddle water, I never thanked you for replacing my..." She paused like it embarrassed her to say it. "Well, you know."

"Your tampons," he said, very little embarrassing him. That's what happened to a kid with leukemia. He'd been poked and prodded by hundreds of people, and if he wanted to become a doctor, he couldn't let a girl's period ick him out.

But all thoughts of that evaporated when her hand brushed his hair back, her fingers lingering a moment longer. He shifted his legs and drew them up until they were pressed against her outer thighs, wondering if she could see the saliva pooling at the corners of his mouth. Damn, he wanted a taste. Wanted one so bad his hands started shaking.

"Yeah." Her warm breath washed over him when she added, "I'll pay you back."

He swallowed. "Okay, but I get to set the terms of payment."

She narrowed her eyes and ripped open a bandage. "Oh do you?"

"Yeah?"

"You were right, you know."

"I know," he said, working to keep his voice even.

She arched a brow, and her mouth twisted like she'd sucked a lemon. Although he wished he hadn't thought about sucking, not when she was standing so close to him and his cock was so goddamn hard.

"Don't you want to know what you were right about?"

Desire twisted inside him as she planted one hand on her waist and stuck her hip out. His throat tightened. "You mean not everything."

"No, you were right when you said there'd be a lot of other things I'd want to call you."

"Oh, and what might they be."

"You're kind of wimpy."

He laughed. "Okay, let's do a tally. You think I'm infuriating, wimpy, and…adorable."

"I never said adorable."

He shifted closer, craving the heat of her body. "I know, but you're thinking it."

"Am not."

His heart beat faster, and he wet his mouth as she carefully applied the bandage. "Want to know what I'm thinking?" he asked.

"No." She inched back, but it didn't break the tension

between them. In fact, it only amplified it. "All done," she murmured.

Jesus, he didn't want this night to end. "Melody…ah, I mean Mel."

She lowered herself onto her bed and his mind raced, envisioning her sprawled out on the mattress, his body on top of hers. Kissing her…oh Christ what he'd do to kiss her. His eyes dropped to her mouth just as she wet her lips and he stifled a groan.

"Why is it you want to call me Melody?" she asked quietly.

He inched a little closer. "Because it's pretty, like you."

Her voice thinned to a whisper. "Ryeland, I told you. I can't—"

"Sorry." He pressed his hands to either side of his head. "I meant to say it's ugly, such an ugly name, I have to say it out loud because I can't keep it in my head anymore."

She stared at him for a moment then laughed. "You're crazy, you know that."

Jesus, she was so gorgeous and exciting, completely different from the other girls he knew. No makeup, no expensive haircut, yet she was more beautiful than all those girls put together.

He raked his hand through her soft hair, expecting her to shove him off at any second. "Infuriating, wimpy, adorable, crazy…and the list continues."

"I like your name too," she said, her voice a breathless whisper. She let him touch her a moment longer, then pulled away.

"Why do you shorten yours?" He turned the conversation back to her.

"Because I'm not that girl anymore."

He glimpsed a moment of vulnerability in her eyes before she quickly blinked it away, and it made him want to know about her demons. One thing was for certain, as long as he was around, no one would ever hurt her again. "Now you're 'don't-mess-with-me-Mel' tough girl. That's one of the reasons I stepped in tonight. I didn't want you to get in trouble for giving Trevor the proper beating he deserved." That pulled a small smile from her and Ryeland's gaze moved to her mouth once again. "My folks never let anyone shorten my name for some reason. It was always Ryeland. Unless of course they were mad at me. Then it was Ryeland Arthur Montgomery." He shifted his chair closer, until their knees were touching, and a jolt of heat arched between them. Melody sucked in a tight breath and he knew she felt it every bit as much as he did. He placed his elbows on his legs and leaned forward, brushing his thumb over her knee. "But if you want to call me Rye, you can. In fact, I'd like it."

A loud noise sounded in the hall, followed by laughter and a door slamming. Melody blinked and straightened, the moment broken. "You should probably go, Ryeland. It's late and I have to work tomorrow."

Okay, so she wasn't quite ready to give him a nickname. He could live with that, but it certainly wasn't going to deter him. "I'll drive you."

"It's a two minute walk from here."

"Faster by Jeep."

"I don't—"

"It's on my way."

She exhaled slowly. "You're not going to leave me alone, are you?"

"Nope. You might be a tough girl, but this time you're fighting a losing battle."

Exasperated, she threw her hands up in the air. "Fine, you can drive me." She went quiet for a moment, then in a low voice she said, "I'm too tired to argue anyway."

They both stood at the same time, and in the small

room their bodies collided. He wrapped his arm around her waist and held her. A tremor moved through her and it took all his effort not to press his mouth to hers. Christ, she was sweet and funny and so damn gorgeous he had a hard time being near her without wanting more.

The sound of her indrawn breath filled the room and her body tightened. "Whatever you think is going to happen here, isn't," she said, her voice as shaky as the look she was giving him.

"I'm not asking for anything to happen." He tucked a strand of hair behind her ear, and when she didn't flinch right away, he let his fingers rest against her flushed cheek.

She shook him off and he dropped his hand as her hair fell back over her ear again. "Every guy wants something to happen."

"Okay, I'm not going to lie. I'm a typical guy, so yeah, I'd like for something to happen. I like you, Mel, but I'm not going to push you to do anything you're not ready for."

"And if I told you I may never be ready for anything between us?"

"I'd say okay."

"Then I'd say you're not a typical guy."

"Just like you're not a typical girl," he countered.

Silence hung for a moment as they exchanged a long look, her dark eyes moving over his face like she couldn't figure him out. She finally broke the quiet and stepped back, putting a good measure of distance between them. "Good night, Ryeland."

He grinned, and even though she was kicking him out, he felt like he'd finally won a round with her. "See you in the morning, Mel."

CHAPTER SEVEN

A flock of birds chirped outside her window and Mel blinked her eyes open to watch the early morning sun cut through the crack in her curtains and slowly climbed up her wall.

She stretched her legs, her mind going back to yesterday…to Ryeland. Okay, so why was he the first thing to pop into her thoughts upon waking? Damn him. Sure, she might be attracted to him, but she was determined to keep her resolve and stay on track. Could she do that and become his friend like he wanted and keep things platonic between them? Honestly, to even consider a relationship with him was a disaster waiting to happen.

She grabbed her pillow and pulled it under her head as she turned. Her glance landed on the stack of unfinished manuscripts on her desk and she gave a humorless laugh. When it came to romance stories, the two of them might as well be the Montagues and Capulets, and look how that love affair had ended.

The noise of the others rising on her floor sounded in the hall as the staff milled about, getting ready for their workday. She threw the covers off, turned on her clock radio and jumped in the shower as the announcer told her it was going to be a scorcher. Twenty minutes later when she was pulling on her clothes a knock sounded on her door.

Ryeland…

At first her heart leapt, but then she gave herself a good hard lecture. Not only was it far too early for him to be here, getting excited to see him again was not part of the friendship plan.

She pulled her door open to find a sleepy Jaelyn standing on the other side, still dressed in last night's clothes as she held a cup of coffee out to Mel. "Happy Monday."

"Thanks." Mel took the ceramic cup and gave her friend a once-over. "Tell me you're not just getting in."

The stairwell door banged open and Mel glanced around the doorframe to see the two boys Jaelyn was with last night sneaking out.

"Nope." Jaelyn grinned. "But I didn't get much sleep."

Mel glanced at her watch. "You can come in but I have to be to work in thirty minutes."

She pushed past Mel and plunked herself on the bed. "Go ahead and get ready, I won't bother you. I'll sit here quietly."

Mel shut the door and reached for her brush, but from the curious way Jaelyn was looking at her, she knew that was a lie. Jaelyn had never sat quietly in her life. Mel ran the bristles through her hair and shifted uncomfortably as her friend continued to study her. While she wanted to ignore Jaelyn, she couldn't take her stare-down for one more minute.

"What?" Mel finally asked.

"You know what."

She held her hands out at her sides. "He took me

home, that's all."

"Do you like him?" she asked.

She took a sip of her coffee to buy herself some time then answered with, "He's nice enough."

"And hot enough. Don't forget that."

Oh she hadn't...

Mel turned the hair dryer on to drown out her friend. Jaelyn stood and walked to the window. She stared out for a second then turned around, that all-knowing grin back on her face as she leaned against the window ledge.

"Now what?" Mel asked over the loud fan.

Jaelyn wagged her finger over the unmade bed. "Something must have happened here last night."

"I bandaged him up and sent him home. That's it."

"Then why is lover boy parked outside?"

Once again Mel's heart did that weird little flip. She worked to keep her face expressionless, despite the storm going on inside her. "He's driving me to work."

"Uh-huh."

"Uh-huh, nothing. We decided to be friends."

"Let me guess." Jaelyn pointed a finger at her. "You decided to keep things in the friend zone, but he wants more."

"What makes you say that?"

"'Cause no guy gets up this early to drive someone to work when all they're looking for is friendship."

Mel turned off the dryer and sat on the bed. "Even if I wanted more, which I don't," she added quickly, "there can't be anything between us. You saw the way his parents acted. I'm sure his mom would have a fit if she knew he was here now. We're different people from different worlds."

Jaelyn sat next to her and frowned. She studied Mel for a moment, then nodded. "You know what, you're probably right."

Mel ran her hands along the bristles on her comb. "I

am right."

"A summer fling is one thing, but a guy like that could really break a girl's heart when he leaves come fall."

"It's not going to be mine," she added quietly.

"So you know what you're getting yourself into then?"

"Yes." *Hell no!* But she couldn't seem to stop herself from thinking about him, from wanting to be around him. *Oh God...*

Jaelyn's perfectly manicured brow furrowed when she narrowed her eyes. "Be careful with him then, okay?"

Mel snapped the elastic around her wrist, then tied her hair back with it. "You know me."

"I do, that's why I'm telling you to be careful." Jaelyn yawned, then jumped up. "Okay, now it's time for bed."

Mel arched a brow, happy Jaelyn was changing the subject. "Didn't you just get out of bed?"

"Okay, let me rephrase that. It's time for sleep." She walked to the door. "I'll catch up with you tonight."

"I have class."

"Oh right, I forgot. Did you want me to ride the shuttle to town with you?"

"No, I'm good. Let's do something tomorrow night after work, though. Just us."

"Sounds like a plan."

Jaelyn disappeared into the hall and Mel hurried to finish getting ready. She pulled on her uniform, adjusted her ponytail and gave herself a once-over. Outwardly she looked like she did every other day, but inwardly, there were a whole lot of other crazy things going on—compliments of Ryeland. Ignoring the sensations in her stomach, she tossed her backpack over her shoulder and took the stairs down to the first floor. She exited her building and walked toward Ryeland, telling herself that the extra zip in her step had nothing to do with Ryeland picking her up. Her steps slowed when she caught a flash of blonde hair in the passenger seat and for a brief moment she thought it was Suzette.

"Hey," Ryeland said, climbing from the driver's seat when he saw her coming. God, he looked so good this morning, all sleepy and sexy like he'd just crawled out of bed. Her glance moved over his jeans and T-shirt, and when he stepped closer she caught the scent of his skin. The storm inside her stomach jumped to category two hurricane.

"Hey yourself." She tore her glance away from him and looked at the front seat again. No way would she get in that vehicle if Suzette was with him. Girls like Suzette didn't mesh well with townies.

As if sensing her unease, he stepped even closer, once again invading her personal space. He grabbed her backpack and threw it over his shoulder. "I'm dropping Ashley off at the camps."

"Oh," she said. "I didn't realize."

That lopsided grin that weakened her knees returned. "Told you it was on my way."

Needing to get her heart back to a regular beat before she hyperventilated, she walked toward the passenger side and Ashley jumped into the backseat. "Hey, Ashley," she said as she pulled open the door and slid in. "Ryeland tells me you're going to one of the camps."

Ashley nodded. "Yup. Mom signed me up for tennis."

"Then you'll be with Sara Eckhart. She's a lot of fun."

"Which camp do you run?" Ashley asked, dark lashes blinking over those startling blue eyes of hers as she looked at Mel's work shirt.

"Adventure Runs. We do a lot of hiking, canoeing,

horseback riding, and overnight camping trips. All outdoor stuff. In a couple of weeks we're camping out at Big Rock."

Her eyes lit. "I wanted to do that but Mom is worried about me getting bites or poison ivy."

"I can switch you out," Ryeland said as he climbed into the driver's seat.

"But Mom—"

"Don't worry. I'll talk to her."

Ashley squealed and gave him a neck hug and Mel couldn't help but smile. "You're a good big brother."

"Anything to impress my girl," he teased. "Now buckle up." He tossed the words over his shoulder to his kid sister, and when she sat back in her seat Mel looked at him, worry gnawing at her. "Are you sure you won't get in trouble for switching her?"

"They're already pissed at me." He rolled one broad shoulder. "What's one more thing?"

Mel wanted to ask what was going on with him and his folks, but it wasn't her business and even though she'd love to know more about him, the less she knew the better off she'd be when he was gone. You couldn't miss what wasn't there, right? She looked out the window as he drove her to the other side of the resort. Camp counselors and kids were already convening outside Beaver Lodge, the log building where registration was taking place. She looked at the big beaver head mounted above the door. God, could they be anymore Canadian? Then again, the resort had a lot of American visitors and they seemed to love it.

Mel pointed to the building. "You'll have to check with Beatrice inside to switch her."

Ryeland squeezed his Wrangler between two large SUVs, and pulled his seat forward for Ashley.

Noting the way the other counselors were watching her get out of Ryeland's vehicle, Mel looked at him over the roof, fully aware of the curious glares aimed her way. "Thanks for the ride."

"What time are you off?" He tapped the black roof and watched her.

Her stomach flipped. "Why?"

"I'll pick you up."

"Don't you have anything better to do than drive me around?"

"Nope."

"I'm off at four, but I'm busy tonight." She wasn't about to tell him about her creative writing class at the community center two towns over in Copperville. Some things were private, and because he was going to be a lawyer, he'd probably criticize her choices, thinking they were frivolous and impractical. And heck, maybe they were. What did she really know about being a writer—a romance writer at that? Did she really know anything about romance outside of books and movies? No. But she loved getting lost in her stories, creating worlds a million miles away from the one she lived in, where everyone lived happily ever after.

He pulled Ashley's backpack as well as Mel's from the backseat. Ashley grabbed hers and bounded toward Mel.

"Will we get to ride horses today?" she asked, her eyes wide with excitement.

"You bet," Mel said, finding it hard to keep her focus as Ryeland came close, so close it made it a little harder for her to draw in air.

"Busy doing what?" he asked, placing the backpack on her shoulder and then pushing his hands into his pocket.

"Are you always so pushy?"

He nodded. "Yeah."

"I suppose that's a good trait for a lawyer."

A muscle in his jaw ticked. "Can whatever you're

doing wait until after dinner?"

"Ryeland…" she said.

"What? Friends have dinner together all the time. I spent all last semester craving one of Grizzly's famous moose burgers."

Instead of answering, she pointed toward the registration building, needing to be away from him before she sagged against him and said yes to anything and everything he was asking. God, what was it about him that did this to her? He was trouble and he made her feel so…so out of her comfort zone. So fluttery inside. "You better get her switched before it's too late."

"Come on, Ryeland." Ashley grabbed his arm. As she dragged him away, Mel smiled. She knew there was a reason she liked the kid. "I don't want to be late."

"You have to eat, right?" he asked, clearly undeterred as his kid sister kept tugging.

"Yes, but—"

The corner of his mouth turned up. "Then you'll eat with me. I don't see what the big deal is."

Good Lord did he always have to be so pushy, argumentative…*adorable.*

"The list is getting longer, Ryeland," she said, finding it harder and harder to keep her resolve around him.

He laughed and she smiled, wondering what the hell she was getting into with him. Maybe Jaelyn was right and she needed to be a little more careful.

Mel turned and made her way to the lodge to check in with Beatrice. She picked up her assignment for the day and then found her group of ten kids waiting for her. Ten rambunctious girls between the ages of nine and thirteen. Chatty little rich girls who'd likely never spent a day in the woods. She did a roll call, checked to make sure each child had all the necessary gear, then turned to Jaelyn's ex-boyfriend, Cole, who had his own group of boys in the line next to her.

She looked at him, still pissed that he'd slept around on Jaelyn. Even though it appeared this morning that Jaelyn had gotten over his betrayal last night—in duplicate—she knew before the summer was over they'd hook up again. Like Jaelyn said, you can't help who you want, but as far as Mel was concerned, that person should treat you with respect. And if they cared anything about you in return, they'd put your well-being above their own. Yeah, she really was a true romantic at heart.

"I heard what happened at the Cave last night." He lifted his head so he could see her under the bill of the Blue Jay's ball cap pulled low on his forehead.

From her peripheral vision she caught Ryeland walking to his car, his gaze burning into her and Cole with the power of a thousand suns. The intensity in the way he stared made her feel a bit breathless.

"What did you hear?" she asked, trying for casual.

Cole nodded toward Ryeland. "What are you doing with that guy anyway?"

Mel tried not to show a reaction. "He gave me a lift, that's all. What do you have against him?"

He gave her a cocky grin. "Only one reason a pretty boy like him is sniffing 'round your backdoor, sunshine."

Her insides tightened. "Don't be crude. He gave me a lift and that's it."

"Yeah right." He tapped his head. "I thought you were smarter than that, Mel."

"There's nothing between us."

"It ain't 'cause he don't want there to be."

She didn't answer right away. Heck, what was she supposed to say? Last night Ryeland so much as admitted he wanted more but wouldn't ask for it if she wasn't ready. Cole smirked, like he'd nailed it on the head, and added, "Hey, when I'm right I'm right."

"Doesn't matter."

He adjusted his ball cap. "Oh, it matters. You'll see."

She looked at the group of boys under his charge, and when she saw two at the back of the line kicking rocks at a couple of girls a few rows over, she asked, "Shouldn't you be controlling your boys?"

"Just remember. It's the townies who don't leave a string of broken hearts at the end of the summer."

"No, they just leave them broken smack dab in the middle of it," she shot back, thinking about what Trevor did to her last June and what Cole had done to Jaelyn a few weeks ago.

"Yeah, well, you're one of us, and the local boys around these parts don't like sharing what's theirs with the vacationers."

Sensing he was threatening her—and Ryeland—an uneasy feeling moved through her. "I'm not one of *theirs*, and I'm not some object that can be shared." Despite the heat of the morning, a cold chill raced down her spine.

He shrugged but the warning was clear in his eyes as he pitched his voice low for her ears only. "Hey, look, I like you, and I say you can fuck whoever you want. But some don't see it that way."

By some she guessed he meant Trevor. Wanting to put an end to the conversation, she turned from him and shaded the sun from her eyes as she scanned the crowd, looking for Ashley.

"Mel," Ashley called out when their gazes collided. Mel waved to the girl as Ashley yelled, "I got in!"

While Mel liked the little girl, she was happy Ashley was placed in Cassandra Wilson's camp and not hers. She was pretty certain Ryeland had lied to her, and his fight with his folks had everything to do with her. The last thing she wanted was to cause any more trouble between them.

"Okay, girls, who's ready to hit the trails?"

A chorus of yesses sounded and Mel grabbed her ball cap from her bag and pulled it on. She guided the girls into the woods and for the first half of the morning they walked the trails. Mel pointed out different things to them, like which berries were edible and which weren't, as well as all the animal tracks they came across. They made their way along Stone Squaw Trail, Cole's warning rattling around inside her head. She didn't want Trevor and his buddies going after Ryeland, not because of her. Her stomach grumbled, effectively turning her attention from Cole. She stopped the girls at the peak of the mountain, so they could all have a snack.

"Miss Spencer," one of the girls asked as Mel ripped in to a granola bar. "Can I bring Fluffy on the camping trip?"

She looked at Sasha, the cute little redhead in pigtails. It reminded her of the way her mother used to do her hair, before her father went to jail and her mother turned to the bottle—and to a barrage of different men. She gave one of pigtails a little tug. "Who's Fluffy?"

"My dog." She held her hands out about eight inches apart. "She's little, and doesn't like to sleep alone."

"We're not supposed—" She stopped when she saw the girl's chin tremble slightly, a good indication that it wasn't really about Fluffy sleeping alone. Damn. Even though she could very well get into trouble—and hadn't she recently lectured herself on nice girls finishing last— how could she say no? "Okay, but it will be our little secret."

The grin that lit up her little face was so precious that Mel grinned back. "Now go finish your snacks." Sasha plopped back down onto the ground, and after everyone had finished eating, Mel asked, "Who's up for horseback riding?"

"Me. Me. Me," they all chimed in at once.

"So that's a no?" Mel teased, stealing a glance at her

watch. One by one they began jumping up, yelling "yes, yes, yes". "Okay, let's go then."

Mel led the girls along the path, coming out at the other end where the corrals were located. "Hey, Blake," she said to the head ranch hand. "Looks like I have a group of girls who want to ride the horses this afternoon."

Blake tipped his Stetson, showcasing his graying hair. "Well, what do we have here? You little fillies looking to lasso some cattle? I've got me some misbehavin' sheep over there."

The girls giggled and all started talking at once and pointing to the horses in the corral.

"All right, come this way." A sparkle danced in his blue eyes as he winked at Mel. She followed along at the end of the line and when they entered the shaded barn and passed by one of the stalls, Mel's heart jumped into her throat.

What the hell?

Even with his back to her, she'd recognize Ryeland anywhere. Hot. Hard. Cut. With a cowboy hat on his head, he stood there shirtless, his broad shoulder muscles flexing and relaxing again as he brushed down one of the horses. Her gaze fell lower, taking pleasure in the way his jeans hung low on his hips, showcasing one the finest backsides she'd ever had the pleasure of setting eyes on.

As the temperature inside the barn jumped, she suddenly realized Blake was talking to her. "Uh…what?" she asked.

"How about we get Ryeland to help out?"

At the sound of his name, Ryeland turned. The way his eyes narrowed in on her, like she was the only one in the barn—the only person in the universe—had her throat nearly closing over. Good God, he looked so hot in that hat, his bare chest all slick with moisture. She swallowed down the dryness in her throat and tried to keep things light. "Sure. I guess. I mean, if he knows what he's doing."

"I know what I'm doing," Ryeland said, tipping his hat in such a sexy way she thought her knees were going to give.

"Well okay, then," she said for lack of anything else and gave an easy shrug.

A grin tugged at the corner of his mouth. "I didn't expect to see you so soon."

"I guess I can say the same." Honestly, it surprised the hell out of her to find him here, getting his hands dirty in one of the stalls nonetheless. She had no idea Ryeland knew anything about horses. She wondered what else she didn't know about him but then pushed that thought aside. Getting too close was not in her best interest.

"Why don't you take these little fillies outside and give them each a ride," Blake suggested.

"I'm on it." Ryeland dropped the brush and looked over the girls. "Who's first?"

All hands went in the air, and he walked around them, tapping each child on the head and giving her a number from one to ten. As the girls all blinked up at him it occurred to Mel that there was just something so sweet about him, something that drew everyone in and put them at ease. He really did have a way with little girls—and big ones too.

The girls all took off to line up outside, and he turned to her. "How about you, sunshine. You want a ride?"

Before she could answer, Jamie came in with her group of ten. "Ryeland," she said, looking him over like he was a big slab of meat and she'd just come off a vegetarian diet. "I hear you're giving rides today?" she said, the suggestion behind her words more that obvious. Good God, could she be any more blatant?

He nodded his head toward the corral and reached

into the stall to grab his shirt. "You bet." He took off his hat and after tugging on his shirt, he rolled his shoulder for everyone to follow.

Keeping her distance, Mel followed him out and hung back as he took turns giving lessons. Every now and then he'd cast a glance her way, wagging his brow for her to climb on for her own lesson. Even though she kept refusing him, Jamie quickly took him up on the offer. Before she knew it the rest of the morning slipped by, and as the sun rose high in the sky, her stomach grumbled once again.

"Okay, girls. Lunch time," she called out.

After a round of grumbles the girls all lined up and Ryeland gave her a grin as he tipped his Stetson at her. Ignoring the way Jamie was looking at her, Mel left the stables and walked the kids to the canteen so they could grab lunch. She grabbed a slice of pizza and sat down at the counselors' table. Shifting her chair to keep herself shaded under the umbrella, she bit into her pizza and chased it with a soda.

"What's up with you and Ryeland?" Jamie asked, taking the seat opposite her. "Have you two hooked up?"

Mel looked into a pair of dark curious eyes. "No, we're just friends."

"Could have fooled me. He was all up in your stuff."

"Why? Because he helped me with the kids? That's hardly up in my stuff."

"Yeah, well you didn't see the way he was looking at you."

Her heart gave a little start, because yeah, she had caught the way he looked at her. And dammit, it was stupid of her to like it so much. "We're friends, that's all."

"Yeah?"

"Yeah."

She looked past Mel's shoulders, like she was

searching for him. "So it'd be cool if I checked him out."

"Sure. Go ahead." She felt an unwise pang of jealousy as she chewed on her crust and swallowed.

Jamie leaned in her voice all conspiratorial as she asked, "When did he get so hot, anyway?"

He's always been hot...

"Who's hot?"

Cassandra sat down next to her best friend Jamie, and as the two discussed Ryeland Mel's phone pinged. She grabbed it from her backpack and slid her finger across the screen. A jolt raced through her when she saw that the message from Ryeland. Wait! How the heck did he get her number? Or better yet, how did his contact information get put in her phone?

Moose burger... Mmmm.

She grinned, despite herself. As she shoved it back into her bag, it occurred to her how much she was looking forward to tonight. When she looked up, she found two sets of curious eyes looking at her. Ignoring them, Mel finished her lunch, then gathered up her girls, deciding it would be a nice afternoon to spend at the pool. They spent the rest of the day swimming and playing in the water, and as the end of the day approached, Mel marched them all back to Beaver Lodge where she found their parents waiting for them.

As she approached the log building she couldn't help but look for Ryeland, and her stomach twirled when she found him there waiting for her—and Ashley of course. He no longer had his Stetson on, and there was nothing impersonal in the way he looked at her as she lined her kids up for pickup.

Once the last kid was gone, she sauntered toward him to find him smiling down at his kid sister.

"I take it you had fun," Mel said to Ashley, careful to keep her eyes off Ryeland and her mind off how wired she felt.

"Thanks you so much for switching me, Ryeland," she rushed out. "I made two new friends and I can't wait to go camping." Ryeland took both Ashley's and Mel's backpacks, and as Ashley continued to chat endlessly about her day, they all climbed into his Jeep. Ryeland kept throwing glances Mel's way, his grin so damn cute she couldn't help smile back.

He pulled up in front of Wolf Creek Lodge, and when she reached for the handle he said, "I'll be right back. I need to get a shower."

"Me too," she said.

"Twenty minutes. That's all I need."

"I might need longer," she said.

He rolled his eyes at his sister. "High maintenance girls," he teased, then he turned to Mel, his face serious. "What if I told you I won't be able to wait a second longer?"

"Then I'd add impatient to the list."

He laughed, grabbed her backpack from the backseat, and handed it to her. He leaned in and whispered, "Take as long as you like, but I'm warning you now, I can't be held accountable for what I do after twenty minutes. I might just come up there and grab you from the shower."

She glanced at the clock and jumped from the seat. "And I'll do anything to avoid that."

Mel could still hear him laughing as she hurried inside the building. She bolted up the stairs two at a time and quickly stripped off her clothes when she entered her room, the essence of Ryeland's presence still lingering from last night.

The water was still cold when she jumped into the shower, so she washed fast, scrubbed her hair, and jumped out. After another quick glance at her clock, she stood before her closet trying to figure out what to wear. Clothes weren't a huge priority for her, and other than jeans, a few tank tops and blouses, along with a couple sweaters, her closet was pretty much bare. She grabbed a short sleeve white blouse and tugged it on. It was the least flattering of all her tops and despite her rather ample breasts, it hung awkwardly on her body made her look like a twelve-year-old boy, but since it had been discounted so heavily, she'd went ahead and bought it. Tonight it would be perfect. She didn't want to give Ryeland the impression that she was trying to look good for him.

Leaving her hair loose and face makeup-free, Mel stuffed her notepad and laptop into her backpack. After a quick glance at the clock, she darted downstairs to wait for Ryeland, only to find him already waiting for her, leaning against his Jeep, legs crossed at the ankles.

Ryeland Montgomery. The catalyst for the fierce storm brewing inside her. Honestly, he was the kind of guy every girl wanted, yet he'd passed them all up, seemingly determined to get to know her better. What she couldn't figure out was why. If she wasn't giving him sex, then what did he really want with her?

"That was fast." Ryeland removed his sunglasses, his pewter eyes raking over her clothes.

"Not high maintenance at all," she returned, her voice coming out a little higher than she would have liked.

"Not at all," he returned, and the smile that came over his face sent heat careening through her. "You look beautiful."

He leaned forward and pushed off the Jeep. She instantly became aware of his closeness when he took her backpack from her and put it in the backseat. He left the door open for her, and she watched him circle the front of the vehicle, everything about him making her feel jittery.

He climbed in and gestured with a nod toward her backpack. "You going somewhere?"

"I told you I had plans for tonight already."

He looked at her carefully as she pulled her door shut. "Overnight plans?"

"No, just plans." Because she didn't want to talk about it, she rubbed her stomach and changed the subject. "I'm starved. It's been a long time since I've had a gigantic moose burger, but maybe tonight I'll splurge." He pulled onto the road and when he looked back at her she said, "Although if you keep driving me everywhere, I might want to think about getting a salad."

"No way. No girl of mine is going to live off salads." She was about to tell him she was *not* his girl when he tossed her a wicked grin. "And ice cream for dessert. I've also been craving a chocolate swirl."

"You can't get ice cream in Montreal?"

"Not the way they make it at the Big Scoop."

"They do make the best. But I hear they have the best smoked meat sandwiches in Montreal. Are they as good as they say?"

"Oh yeah," he said. "Do you like smoked meat?"

"To be honest, I've never had it, but I watch the Food Network when I have time and I saw it on one of those road shows."

He nodded. "You should have a smoked meat sandwich," he said matter-of-factly.

"Okay. If I ever make it to Montreal, I'll have one."

She pressed back into her seat, enjoying the easy conversation as he drove them down the hill and into the town center. He parked a block away from Grizzly's and met her on the sidewalk when she jumped out.

The streets were fairly quiet for a Monday, a few tourists browsing the shops as she walked with Ryeland to Grizzly's, which, come the weekend, was the town's hottest club. Fully aware of how he kept rubbing up against her as they moved down the sidewalk and the way his hand kept brushing hers, Mel worked to keep her legs moving. When they reached Grizzly's, Ryeland pulled the heavy front door open for her and waved her in.

"Thanks," she said, and stepped past him into the dimly lit bar. Like the streets, the bar was quiet as well, so they walked past the dance floor and grabbed a booth in the corner.

The hostess, Holly, brought them menus but Ryeland didn't even open his. "We already know what we're having." He rubbed his hands together and said, "Two moose burgers and two pints of whatever's on draft."

"Soda for me," Mel piped in.

A surprised look came over Ryeland's face. "Oh, sorry. I should have asked." He looked at Holly. "Make that two sodas." After Holly left he looked around. "I missed this place."

Mel groaned. "That's because you don't live here year round."

His eyes moved over her face for a moment, like he was remembering something. "So I take it you plan to leave, then. You did mention your place being temporary."

He remembered that?

"Eventually," she said, not wanting to talk about herself too much.

"Where would you go?"

She shrugged. "Toronto. To a big city where no one knows me." Fearing she already said too much and wanting to get the conversation off her, she asked, "Do you like living in Montreal?"

"It's a great city."

"Is that where you're going to go to law school?" At the mention of law school, he rubbed the back of his neck. Mel frowned and folded her hand on the table in front of her. "Was it something I said?"

Ryeland reached out and closed one hand over hers.

"I don't know. I just…my father is pushing me to go to law school."

Okay, that took her by surprise. Holly brought their drinks, and Mel freed her hand. Once they were alone again, she asked, "Is that what the fight with your folks was about?"

"Yeah."

She poked her straw into the lemon wedge hooked to the side of the glass. "What do you want to do?"

"I want to go to medical school."

Surprised once again, she said, "Why would he be upset about that? Doesn't every parent want his or her kid to grow up to be a doctor?"

"Everyone but mine, evidently. He wants me to join his firm. He's a total hard ass about it too."

She nodded. "He's your father. He cares about you. That's actually nice, Ryeland."

"If he really cared, he'd back off and let me do what I want. But he's been guiding me down this path since I was a kid. I can see it for Ashley and Evan, they seem cut out for it, but it's not for me."

"I guess you're the black sheep of the family," she stated as he reached for her hand again. His thumb brushed over the inside of her wrist and heat traveled all the way to her toes.

"What about your folks, Melody?"

The way he said her name, so softly, so intimately, made her forget she hated her full name. In fact, she kind of liked the way he said it.

"What do they want for you?" he asked, pulling her thoughts back.

"It's just my mom and me. Dad isn't in the picture anymore. He hasn't been for a long time."

Fortunately, Holly came with their food and Mel didn't have to explain that her dad wasn't in the picture because he was in prison. Ryeland let go of her hand as she stared at the gigantic burger and plate of fries in front of her, her stomach grumbling as the delicious smells reached her nose.

"I'm never going to finish this," she said as she tried to pick it up.

Ryeland bit into his, and juice dripped down his arm. He chewed and swallowed and went for another bite. "Damn, that's good," he said as he dove back in for more.

"You really have been craving them." Mel laughed as she watched him, seeing another side to the rich boy who, from the surface looked like he had the perfect life. It actually made her feel a little less embarrassed by hers. Only a little, though.

She took a bite of her burger and her tomato slipped out the back and fell to her plate. She picked it up and tossed it into her mouth all the while watching Ryeland. Honest to God, he looked like a kid on Christmas morning.

Unable to help herself, because yeah, she wanted to know more about him, she asked, "So a doctor, huh?"

He wiped his mouth. "Yup."

"Why a doctor?"

"I don't know. Maybe because I was a sick kid."

Her head jerked back. "You were?"

"Childhood leukemia." He took a drink from his glass, then finished off his burger. He looked like he was a million miles away as he chewed. Then he said, "I remember the doctors and volunteers. They were all so amazing. I guess I just want to make a difference in a kid's life."

"Then it makes sense."

"What does?"

"Why your father wants you to work in his firm. You were sick and he probably wants to keep you close because it scared him. He's scared of losing you."

Ryeland went quiet for a moment and she could see the sadness on his face. "Maybe you're right." He picked up his soda and leaned back in his seat. "I don't want to hurt him or let him down."

"I know." Jeez, what she'd do to have a parent who cared so much. "I think he has your best interests at heart. But you have to do what's best for you, Ryeland. You know that, right?"

The door to Grizzly's opened and a warm breeze brushed over them. She turned to see Trevor sauntering in. She shifted in her seat as he plunked himself at the bar and gestured to Trent for a beer.

Mel took one last bite of her burger, leaving over half of it on her plate and said, "We should go."

Ryeland went deathly still, those pewter eyes staring at her with such intensity Mel was sure he could see into the depths of her soul. "I'm not going to let him hurt you, Mel." His voice was hard, raw, and so dangerously calm, she actually believed him, but even still, she didn't want to be there any longer.

"I'd like to go."

"Okay." He pulled out his wallet, and she reached for her money. "I got this," he said. She was about to protest when he said, "You can get the ice cream."

"You can't expect me to eat ice cream after that."

"Different compartment, sunshine."

They slipped from the booth, and Mel could feel Trevor's eyes on them as they walked out the front door. She worked to fight down her unease as Ryeland bumped against her and gave her a nudge with his elbow.

"Mel?"

"Yeah?"

"Where are you going tonight?"

"I have this thing to do."

"Can I drive you?"

"No." When she caught the dejected look on his face, her stomach turned over. "You don't have to drive me everywhere."

He nudged her again, his touch sending sparks rocketing though her. "But I want to."

"I'm only going into Copperville. I can take the bus."

"What's in Copperville?"

She planted on hand on her hip. "Do you really need to know?"

He grinned. "I kinda do."

"Fine. I'm taking a course at the community center. It's no big deal."

"What kind of course?"

Intrigue danced in his eyes as she angled her head to see him. She looked at him long and hard and guessed he wasn't about to give up. "You won't laugh?"

"Why would I laugh? I told you what I wanted to do and you didn't laugh."

"Becoming a doctor isn't anything to laugh at."

He stopped, turned to her and put his hands on her shoulders. Dark eyes latched onto hers and he said, "Neither is becoming a writer."

She looked down, feeling slightly self-conscious. She wasn't embarrassed about wanting to become a writer, but Ryeland obviously read from the stack on her desk, and she just wasn't ready to share her stories with anyone.

"Hey, don't." He lifted her chin. "You don't ever have to be embarrassed with me, okay? I think it's great that you want to be a writer."

"You do?" she croaked out.

"Yeah. And let me guess. You write romance."

"What makes you say that?" she asked, not about to give it away so easily.

"You love Nicholas Sparks, so I assumed."

She shook her head, shocked at how he was able to

take in and process everything he'd learned about her. "Yeah, that's me, the hopeless romantic." As she looked at him, really looked at him, it made her wonder what it was about him that had her sharing so much.

"I don't know why I'm telling you this. I don't even know you."

"It's because I'm adorable."

"I'm not sure that's the word I'd use."

He smiled. "Come on. Let's get ice cream and go do something fun before I drive you to Copperville."

"I actually don't have time. Class starts soon and I need to get going." She nodded toward the bus stop. "And I really should take the bus."

He nodded, but she could tell from the look on his face he had every intention of driving her. Good God, the guy was trouble, of that she had no doubt. He threw her off balance and made her feel so out of control. She swore a long time ago that she'd never let anyone have that kind of power over her again. Which made her wonder why she was letting him into her life. But she already knew the answer to that. Ryeland Montgomery was nice, easy to be with, and so damn adorable.

CHAPTER EIGHT

Darkness had fallen over the town as Ryeland leaned against the front of his Wrangler and watched a handful of students exit the community college. When he caught sight of Melody walking with some guy down the sidewalk, his territorial instincts kicked in. "Oh *hell* no," he muttered as he pushed off the hood and came up behind her.

"Hey," he said, taking her backpack from her and tossing it over his shoulder.

Mel spun around, eyes wide, hand pressed to her chest. "Ryeland," she gasped. "You scared the life out of me."

He shifted the pack on his back and dipped his head, his hair falling into his eyes. "Sorry about that."

She frowned and looked around. "What are you doing here?"

Instead of answering, Ryeland glared at the guy walking a little too close to her, with way too much interest in his eyes as he smiled down at her. He had a briefcase in his hand and because he looked like he had a good five years or so on Ryeland, he didn't get the sense that he was a student. Ryeland straightened to his full height, standing eye to eye with the man.

"Oh, this is Professor Steele. He teaches my class," Melody said.

"It's Marcus," he said offering his hand to Ryeland.

"Right." Mel shook her head. "I can't seem to get used to that. Marcus, this is my friend Ryeland."

Ryeland stepped closer to her and nodded to Marcus, accepting his hand and giving it a good firm shake before letting it go. Then he turned his attention to Melody. "You ready?"

"I was just about to grab…" her words fell off as the bus sped past them, driving straight by the empty stop, "…the bus."

"I can give you a lift home," Marcus offered.

Ryeland took a step closer to Mel. "I'm driving her."

Marcus looked from Melody to Ryeland, then back to Melody. "Okay, I'll catch up with you later, Mel," he said, then turned and drove off.

"What was that all about, Ryeland? He's my teacher, and you looked like you wanted to kill him."

"I didn't like the way he was looking at you."

"I'm his student. I need an A before he'll submit my chapters to a publisher, and he said with a little private tutoring he could help me accomplish that?"

"Private tutoring, huh? Well, let me tell you what *he's* trying to accomplish."

"What's that supposed to mean?"

"He likes you, Melody."

"Well, I am his student," she repeated, looking at him like he was dense or something. For a girl who claimed to have such a bad reputation, she was damned innocent about some things.

"Yes, and he doesn't just want to tutor you on…" he paused and leaned in for emphasis. "…your writing."

Her chin came up. "What are you trying to say? That

he only offered to tutor me to…to…" Her words trailed off as realization set in.

Ryeland almost wished he'd kept his mouth shut when her shoulders fell, but hell, he'd rather she be pissed at him for pointing out the obvious than the alternative.

He looked at her and cocked his head. "You don't read people well, do you?"

Her body suddenly tightened. "I…" She stopped talking, like she was remembering something from her past—probably that asshole Trevor. Or maybe she was thinking he was no better than him, and that if she was such a bad judge of character then she shouldn't be hanging with him either.

"I'm sorry, Melody. I just…I get protective at times." Especially when it came to her. "It's in my nature."

"You know I can take care of myself, right?"

He made a fist and nudged her chin playfully. "I know. My little fighter. Come on." He leaned into her, giving her a little push. "Truce?"

"I shouldn't let you off so easily."

"But you will because I'm adorable."

"I will because I missed my bus and you're my only way home," she countered.

He laughed. "Good, then let's go, because we never did get that ice cream."

He stepped close, his body brushing hers in an intimate way. She felt her body come alive and her breath sounded shallow when she said, "I'm not sure I'm up for ice cream."

He scuffed his toe on the pavement. "But I haven't been able to stop thinking about that chocolate swirl all night."

She shook her head and looked at him like he was a petulant child. "Fine, we'll get ice cream but then I need to get to bed." She cast him a glance as they walked across the street.

"What?" he asked.

"Why did you wait for me?"

All teasing gone from his voice, he said, "I didn't want you taking the bus back in the dark."

"I've been taking care of myself for a long time now, Ryeland."

"I know, and that's why I'm here."

She went quiet and he stepped closer to her as they crossed the street. She opened her mouth like she wanted to say something, then closed it again. The trip back to Deerfield was made in silence, with Mel staring out the window, now and then biting her lip, lost in thought. Ryeland let her have the time to consider her teacher's motives, grateful he'd been there for her. When they reached the ice cream shop, Melody glanced around as though surprised they were already there.

Melody unhooked her belt. "I must say, that was a lot quicker than the bus. I could get used to this."

"Good."

"Good? Why Good?"

He turned in his seat and leaned into her. "Because a girl like you should always have someone there for her."

She looked down, like he'd hit a sore spot. "You make it sound like I'm someone special. I'm not."

"Yeah you are," he said, and needing to see her smile, he opened his door. "Let's go get the biggest ice cream they have."

"You really like food, don't you," she said, a small smile tugging at her mouth. God that mouth. He wanted to do right by her, but damn, he was just about ready to forget chivalry and kiss the living hell right out of her. "How do you stay so…"

She stopped talking, like she'd said too much, so he thought he'd help her out. "You mean ripped?" He sucked in a breath and rubbed his stomach. "Like a badass cage fighter."

"You have no filter, do you?"

"So you think I'm ripped?"

She laughed. "I think you're something."

He leaned closer and dipped his head, his mouth so close to hers. "Want to know what I'm thinking?"

"No." She inched back and reached for her door. "Now, about that ice cream I owe you."

"Right."

They made their way to the ice cream shop and he pulled the heavy glass door open for her. He entered behind her and blinked against the bright lights as he took in all the teenagers hanging out. Melody crossed her arms, her shoulders tightening as she hurried to the counter, but Ryeland caught all the glares aimed her way—not to mention the whispers. She pulled a ten-dollar bill from her pocket, and while he wanted to pay, he knew he had to choose his battles carefully.

After they each ordered a chocolate swirl in a sugar cone, he turned to her. "Want to walk?"

"Yeah," she said and moved toward the door.

They stepped outside and strolled aimlessly along the sidewalk, the night air dropping in temperature as they ate their cones. She wrapped one arm around herself.

"You cold?" he asked, looking at her thin blouse. "I have a jacket in the car."

"I'm okay. Besides, I still have one of your shirts that I have to return."

"So tell me more about this A you need," he said.

She looked confused for a moment, then said, "Oh, if anyone gets an A on the story they're working on during the course, the prof will submit it for them."

Ryeland thought about that for a moment. "You know, my dad is a lawyer and I'm sure he has friends who are literary attorneys. Those guys know people who know people."

"No," she said quickly. "I'd never ask you to do that. Never."

He shook his head and smiled as his glance moved over her face.

"What?" she asked.

"Nothing. You're different." When she gave him a strange look, he said, "In a good way."

They soon found themselves on Union Street, off the beaten path where the street lamps didn't quite reach. "Come on, there's something I want to show you."

He grinned. "Oh yeah, there's something I want to show you too."

"Ryeland," she warned, but her grin told him she wasn't upset by his comment. "We're just friends remember?"

"What?" he asked, pretending to take offense. "I just meant that I wanted to show you this freckle here." He held his arm up and pointed to a spot on the back. "See."

She laughed and punched him in the bicep. "You're ridiculous."

"And you're frigging strong." He rubbed his arm. "That's going to bruise."

"Look." She pulled her phone from her pocket and hitting her flashlight app. She pointed it at the wall, and he stared at all the graffiti splashed over the bricks. "Trent, the guy who works at Grizzly's and his friends did this."

"I don't know much about graffiti, but this is pretty cool." He ran his hand over the patterns. "I like it." He bit into his cone as she aimed the light his way.

"You do?"

"Sure."

"I never took you for the artsy type."

He angled his chin in triumph. "There are a lot of things you don't know about me, which takes me back to why I told you we needed to hang out."

She turned the light back to the wall, and stood there for a moment admiring it. While she examined the art, Ryeland crushed the bottom of his cone in his palm and let the pieces fall to the ground.

"Why did you do that?" she asked, hitting him with the light.

Blinking against the glare, he brushed the crumbs from his hands and took the phone from her. "I don't eat the bottom."

She laughed as he powered her phone down and handed it back. "That's weird. Why not?"

"Because—" he began giving her a little nudge to set them back in to motion, "—when I was a kid, I found a big ass house fly in the bottom of the cone." He cringed. "I almost ate the damn thing too."

"Eww, no way!" Melody said. "That's gross."

"Oh believe me, I know. Now I can't bring myself to eat all the way to the bottom."

She eyed him skeptically. "Did that really happen?"

"Yes." He pointed to her cone and made a face. "And if I were you I'd check that before I bit into it."

When they reached Main Street and found themselves back outside the Big Scoop, Melody stepped under a streetlamp and looked into her cone. "No fly," she said, turning back to him and tossing it into her mouth. That's when Ryeland noticed the smudge of chocolate on her upper lip. He moved close, and felt a shiver race through her, the smile falling from her face as he leaned into her, caging her between his body and the streetlamp. Her sweet scent wrapped around him and it took all his effort not to groan.

He brushed her cheek, her skin so goddamn soft beneath the rough pad of his thumb his body tightened, wanting to touch more of her, all of her. "You have chocolate on your mouth."

"Oh," she said, standing perfectly still as he wet his

thumb and swiped her upper lip clean. Damn, what he'd do to lick it off with his tongue.

He looked over her face, taking in the heat in her eyes. One taste, one small taste was all he'd take. "Mel?"

"Yeah?"

"Want to know what I'm thinking now?"

She went quiet for a moment, like she was actually considering it, then she answered with, "No," and bumped into him to try to push him back. "It's late and I need to go. I have to get up early for work."

"Okay," he said, but neither one moved as sparks arced between them. Ryeland's heart crashed against his chest, as he pressed against her and lowered his head, his lips inches from hers. "Mel," he whispered, then swiped his tongue over his bottom lip.

When a chorus of loud voices sounded from the dark, Ryeland stiffened and turned. Shit. He squared his shoulders as Trevor and one of his asshole friends came out from the ice cream shop.

"Well, well. What do we have here?" Trevor asked, stepping up in front of Ryeland and looking so much braver when he was with his friends. He looked over Ryeland's shoulder. "Mel," he said, smirking. "You took off too fast the other night. We never got a chance to talk."

"There's nothing for us to talk about," she said, moving to stand beside Ryeland.

"Sure there is."

"No, there isn't," Ryeland said and positioned Mel behind him, blocking her from Trevor. She might be a fighter, but as long as he was around she didn't need to be so strong. Besides, he could tell how much Trevor rattled her, even though she tried to hide it.

Trevor laughed and widened his stance. Ryeland prepared himself, ready to kick the shit out of the guy once and for all. Trevor looked around. "What? You don't have your buddies to jump in and fight with you."

"I don't need them."

"That's not the way I saw it."

"Then you saw wrong."

The smile fell from Trevor's face as he squared off against Ryeland. "It's time you learned a lesson, pal."

"Trevor, stop it!" Melody yelled from behind Ryeland's back.

Trevor poked his finger in the air. "This rich fucker needs to learn that he can't come riding in to town every summer and think he can take what's mine."

"I'm not yours," Melody shot back, her voice rising.

He smirked. "That's not what you said last summer when you were moaning for me, baby."

"Back the fuck off," Ryeland said.

A group of kids came pouring out of the ice cream shop when they saw Trevor all up in Ryeland's face. They came closer, circling them to get a better glimpse of the action. The door over Mr. Johnson's pharmacy jingled, and when Ryeland and Trevor turned to see the elderly owner of the store reaching for his cell phone as he glared at them, Trevor took a small step back.

Melody's hand curled in the back of his shirt and gave a little tug. "Ryeland, please don't. I don't want to cause a scene."

Her shaky voice had him turning to see her and when he caught the panic in her eyes he cursed under his breath. He handed her the keys and nodded toward his vehicle. "Go get in the Jeep. I'll be right there."

She tugged on his shirt. "No. Come with me now," she pleaded. "This isn't worth it."

Like hell it wasn't. While he'd like nothing better than to finish this with Trevor, he knew it would have to wait. Melody was tough enough, but Trevor rattled her, and he needed to get her out of there.

"Okay," he said.

He pulled her against him and Trevor made a move to block their way, until a police car rounded the corner. He smirked and waved his hand to clear a path. Ryeland led Melody away. As the car pulled up to the curb and he could hear Trevor talking to his uncle and cracking jokes.

Melody climbed into the Jeep and he slid in beside her. "You okay?"

"Yeah." Something dark moved over her face, something that reminded him she had demons. "I just hate violence."

His heart squeezed. "I'm sorry."

"It's not your fault. He started it."

"You know I'm going to have to finish it, right?"

"No, you don't."

"He's not going to leave you alone until I do."

She turned to him. "Maybe you should stop hanging around with me. Then he'll stop bothering you."

"You think I'm going to let an asshole like Trevor scare me off?" He put his hand on her headrest and leaned into her. She went quiet. "Mel?"

"Yeah?"

"What's his problem anyway?"

"I don't know."

"He seems hell bent on winning you back. Were you two close?"

"No, yes. I guess. I thought we were anyway."

Her body sagged slightly and he touched a strand of her hair, curling it around his finger. "You want to tell me what happened?"

"Not really."

"You don't have to," he said quietly. "It's not my business." He shoved his key into the ignition and turned it. "Let's go."

"I was nothing but a joke to him, some stupid conquest," she blurted out. Ryeland let go of the keys and slowly leaned back. "When he finally got what he wanted, he said some pretty nasty things about me." Ryeland grabbed the steering wheel and squeezed. Jesus. No wonder she found it so hard to trust him. "Trevor's uncle is a cop and he thinks he's untouchable around here." She blinked up at him, worry darkening her eyes. Ryeland knew Trevor had upset her, but he sensed there was something more, something else she was holding back. "He's trouble, Ryeland."

"I won't let him hurt you."

She folded her hands in her lap, and looked down. "What if he hurts you?"

He smiled, and ran his thumb over her cheek. "There you go again, worrying about me." She glanced back at him, and the seriousness on her face killed his smile. "Hey, there's nothing he can do to hurt me. And for the record, Melody, I'm nothing like him."

She frowned, like she was still so unsure of him. Ryeland inched back. "Let's get you home."

"Okay," she said.

"And tomorrow night, maybe we can take the horses out for a ride up the mountain."

"I can't. I'm hanging out with Jaelyn tomorrow."

"Cave?"

"No, I hate that place."

"Next night?"

"We'll see," she said.

He spun his Jeep around and headed up the hill toward the resort, reminding himself he needed to take it slow with her, no matter how much it frustrated him. Melody stayed quiet but he could tell how much Trevor had hurt her. It made him wonder more about the lies that asshole had spread.

He stopped in front of her lodge and she opened the door. "Thanks for the lift," she said. "And for dinner."

"Don't forget your backpack."

Ryeland grabbed her bag and met her by her door. She reached for her pack, but he threw it over his shoulder. "I'll walk you."

She didn't protest. Instead she fell into step beside him.

They climbed the stairs and after she opened her door, he handed her the bag. "Good night, Melody."

"Good night."

"I'll see you in the morning."

She disappeared inside and he stood there long after she closed the door. It was only when he heard her shower turn on that he made his way to the stairwell, taking the stairs to the main floor two at a time. As he drove home, he rehashed his entire night with Melody. When he pulled up to the chalet, saw all the vehicles in the driveway and heard the voices coming from the backyard, his stomach dropped. Shit. He was wound up tight as it was, and the last thing he felt like doing was playing the perfect son in front of company. His mother and father had barely spoken to him since their fight that first night. They probably figured the silent treatment would help him come to his senses. Maybe he could slip past and get to his room unnoticed.

He closed his door quietly, but before he could even take two steps, his father and Benjamin Preston came out from around back. Beyond their shoulders near the flowerbeds he saw his kid brother watching Benjamin's daughter—Suzette's younger sister—Samantha. Oh yeah, the kid had it bad for her.

"There you are, son," his father said. "I was just telling Benjamin here that you were taking the summer to recoup and would have plenty of time to practice and play doubles with Suzette to prepare for the resort's tennis match." There was a dark warning in his eye when he added, "Proceeds go to raise funds for local charities, so I'm sure it's something *you* can't say no to."

CHAPTER NINE

"So what do you want to do?" Jaelyn asked as she threw herself on Mel's unmade bed.

Mel fished a tank top from her closet and pulled it on. "Doesn't matter to me."

"Well I don't care where we go, just as long as Cole isn't there."

"You're still not talking to him?"

"Not talking and over it," she said, but from the sad look on her face, Mel knew it wasn't true. "I want to do something fun," Jaelyn said, rubbing her hands.

"Last time you said that you nearly got us both in trouble."

"Trent and his gang spray paint the buildings all the time, how did I know the cops would show up when I decided to try."

"How about we do something quiet?"

"Off resort?"

"We could catch a movie."

"Or go to the drive-in."

"A drive-in with no car, now that might be challenging."

Jaelyn wagged her eyebrows. "I can jack one."

Mel laughed. "And how is that doing something quiet?"

"Movies it is." Jaelyn pulled out her phone to check what was playing at the small cinema in town as Mel finished dressing.

Twenty minutes later they were sitting on the shuttle on their way to Main Street. Most of the passengers got off at the Cave and while Jaelyn looked on longingly, because there was no doubt Cole would be there and she really did want to see him, Mel patted her hand.

"Think about all that popcorn with extra butter," Mel said.

"Yummy."

"Although with the way I've been eating, if Ryeland keeps driving me everywhere, I'll never fit in to my clothes."

Jaelyn looked at her carefully. "I knew he was driving you to work and back, but now you're telling me he's driving you everywhere?"

"Well, I just mean he drove me to class and then home again last night." God, she needed to stop thinking about him, talking about him, otherwise Jaelyn might get the wrong idea.

"Shit, Mel."

"What?"

"You like him."

Too late...

She gave a casual shrug, and stood when the shuttle came to a stop in town. "We're friends."

"Who are you trying to convince of that? Me or you?" Jaelyn asked as she followed Mel off the bus and down the sidewalk.

"He's nice, Jaelyn."

"Yeah, but you're the one who told me there could be nothing more, and don't forget that's what you said about Trevor too."

"Trevor and Ryeland almost got into it again last night. If it wasn't for Mr. Johnson, I think they would have had it out right in the middle of the street. I have no idea why he's still bothering me, and I don't want Ryeland in the middle of it." She cringed as she thought about the things Trevor had spread about her. Telling everyone she was a great lay, probably because she had so much practice fucking all the poker players for money when they all convened at the resort once a year. Then he laughed about the man they'd taken away by ambulance, alluding to the fact that he'd died because she's fucked him so good. She thought back to that horrible night the poker player died. Part of what he said was true. A man had been taken away by ambulance, but there was no money put in her hands.

"Maybe Trevor wants what he can't have," Jaelyn said pulling her thoughts back. "Guys are like that; they always want what other guys have."

Not wanting to dredge up any more painful memories, she hooked her arm in Jaelyn's. "Let's go have some fun, okay?"

They bypassed a familiar group of girls—summer vacationers—who darted glances their way as they walked to the theater. No doubt they were wondering what Ryeland was doing hanging with her. Ignoring them, they bought their tickets and grabbed the biggest buckets of popcorn.

The theater was pretty quiet for a weeknight, so they settled into seats in the middle of the theater and chowed down. Just as the movie was about to start, she spotted Nikko and Justin combing the aisles in the dark. They took two seats a couple rows in front of Mel and Jaelyn and the weed on their clothes overpowered the smell of popcorn.

"I don't like those two," Jaelyn said, pitching her

voice low.

"I know. He apologized for splashing me, but there is something about him that rubs me the wrong way." Like Ryeland said, she might not be a great judge of character, but those guys filled her with unease. Call it woman's intuition, but she didn't trust them.

The movie came on and they settled in for the next hour and half, and once it was over, Mel grabbed Jaelyn arm, wanting to get out of there before she had to make conversation with Ryeland's friends.

They hurried outside and pretended not to hear when Justin called out to them.

"Where to now?" Jaelyn asked.

"Anywhere those two aren't."

"I know where that will be," she said as they stopped outside The Inside Story, the town's only bookstore.

Mel laughed, and her phone vibrated in her back pocket. "You're right." She grabbed her phone to check it. She couldn't help but smile when she saw the message was from Ryeland.

If you need a ride, text me. Or even if you don't...

She shoved the phone back into her pocket without answering.

"Let me guess, lover boy?" When she didn't answer Jaelyn asked, "What did he want?"

"He wanted to know if we needed a ride anywhere."

"Are you going to answer him?"

"No."

"That's probably for the best, right?"

"Right," she agreed, and opened the door to the bookstore.

Once inside Jaelyn went straight to the magazines. She bought one and sat at the small coffee shop at the back of the store, flipping through it as Mel browsed the shelves and read the back blurbs on at least a dozen novels. She normally read on her laptop, but there was something about the smell of an old-fashioned novel that she loved.

Deciding to treat herself to one, she took one to the cash register. She glanced out the window as the cashier rung her up and saw her mom out on the street, exiting the small café where she waitressed.

Mel's heart tightened at the sight of her. She looked tired, sad, smaller than usual as she hustled down the street in her too-high heels and too-tight mustard-yellow uniform that her breasts were ready to spill out of.

Mel felt a twinge of guilt that she hadn't called to check up on her after tucking her in. She shot a glance Jaelyn's way. She hated to bail on her, but after seeing her mom, she felt the need to check in on her.

Mel paid for her book then sat down next to Jaelyn, the sweet smell of her friend's cinnamon latte drifting past Mel's nostrils.

"What?" Jaelyn asked when she looked up to find Mel watching her

Mel twisted her lips and nodded her head toward the street. "I just saw my mom. She was leaving work."

Jaelyn nodded, understanding flashing in her green eyes. Jaelyn might be loud, fun, and flirty most of the times, but always came through at times like this. "You should go."

"But we were supposed to hang out."

"I can wait for you if you want?"

"No. Why don't you go to the Cave? I know you want to."

Jaelyn closed her magazine. "Are you sure? I don't mind."

Mel put her hand over Jaelyn's and squeezed. "Go. Have fun. I have no idea how long I'll be anyway."

"Okay. Text if you need me."

"I will."

Mel gave Jaelyn a hug and left the bookstore. She

hurried her steps to catch up to her mom. She came up from behind and put her arm around her mom's shoulder.

"Hey, Mom," she said.

Her mom's tired eyes lit. "Mel, you scared me."

"Sorry." She gestured toward the bookstore. "I was just in there and saw you leaving work. I thought I'd walk home with you."

Her mom's heels clicked on the sidewalk and she could tell the strain of being in them all day was taking its toll. "I can make you something to eat and run you a nice hot bath," Mel added.

"You're a good girl, Mel." She looked at the bag in Mel's hand as they cut the corner. "What are you reading these days? Still those ridiculous love stories."

Mel felt her heart fall. "Yeah," she said.

A noise sounded in her mother's throat, a half laugh, half groan. "The sooner you learn there is no such thing as happily ever after, the better off you'll be."

Unable to help herself, Mel countered with, "You must still believe in it. You date all the time."

"That's different."

Yeah, it probably was. Mel constantly had to remind herself that her father hadn't just hurt her, he'd hurt his wife too, and now her mom lost herself in booze to self medicate and numb the pain. It couldn't be easy living with the things the man she'd married and loved had done to his own daughter. And, like a lot of women, her mom couldn't stand to be alone, which accounted for all the different men—she wasn't looking for love, she was looking to forget.

They climbed the stairs to her mom's place and, wanting to change the subject, Mel said, "I was chatting with Mr. Johnson the other day. He's such a nice man."

"He's been very good to us, especially after…" Her mom unlocked the door and she let her words fall off as they made their way to her apartment. Inside, Mel went straight to the window to open it to air out the stale smell of alcohol. Her mom kicked off her shoes and fell onto the sofa.

Mel sat on the coffee table and faced her, and even though they'd been over this a million times, Mel couldn't help but ask again. "Mom, when I leave here, please come with me. We can start fresh, somewhere new. Maybe we can even get a place with a balcony, like you always wanted." God, the last thing Mel wanted to do was leave Deerfield without her mother, especially when she needed help.

"We've been over this, baby." Her mom patted Mel's knee. "I'm not going anywhere. I'm too old to pack up a life and leave."

"But you hate it here."

"You go and stop worrying about me. I'll be fine."

Mel wasn't so sure about that.

Her heart squeezed at the defeat she saw on her mother's face. She'd basically given up on life, and herself, after the incident. She'd also long given up on being a mother, choosing instead to lose herself in the bottom of a bottle.

"Why don't I run you a bath, and while you're soaking I'll make you something to eat. Then maybe we can watch a show together. You know, like old times."

"I can't, baby. I have a date tonight."

"Oh." Mel tried not to show disappointment. Honestly, she couldn't expect her mother to just drop everything and be there whenever she wanted her to.

A girl like you should always have someone there for her.

As if thinking of Ryeland had suddenly conjured him, her phone pinged and a text came in from him. Her heart did a flip.

Where are you? I just saw Jaelyn, but can't find you.

I'm not at the Cave.
Home?
No, I had some things to take care of.
She stared at the phone, and could tell he started a text and stopped. Finally he asked, *Everything okay?*
Yeah.
You need a lift?
She grinned. *No. But thanks.*
Text me later?
Since she wasn't sure that was a great idea, considering she was beginning to think about him more and more, she texted, *G'night.*

With that she powered down her phone and stuffed it back in to her pocket.

"Who you texting, baby?" Her mom reached for a cigarette.

"No one."

"If it was no one then why are you smiling?"

"I'm not."

"I hope it's not some boy." She waved her cigarette. "They only break your heart."

"It's just a friend." Mel walked to the bathroom and turned on the water, adding a few drops of scented bubble bath to the water.

After her mom slid in, Mel opened the fridge and rooted around until she found some carrots and potatoes. She grabbed a can of tomatoes from the cupboard and whipped up a bowl of soup, making a note to pick up a few more groceries for her. She stayed with her mom while she finished eating, then left when she disappeared into her room to get ready.

The sky was pitch black and overcast by the time she exited the apartment, and she hugged herself against the chill in the air. Hurrying to Main Street to catch the shuttle, Mel tried to fight the pang of sadness building in her.

She climbed onboard and nodded to Jake, then took a seat in the middle, simply because she wasn't up to making conversation. They drove by the Cave and she could see the fire still burning brightly, all the kids having fun. Would Ryeland still be there? She pulled her phone out and opened his messages. As she reread she stifled a yawn. God she was tired, and not just physically. Being with her mom always left her feeling a little raw, a little emotional.

She stared at her phone, her thumb scrolling over her exchange with Ryeland. She shouldn't text him back. She really shouldn't. If she knew what was good for her, she'd climb into bed and go straight to sleep, and if there ever was one girl who knew what was good for her, it was Mel.

The shuttle stopped in front of the resort and she walked to her room. She looked around, half expecting to see Ryeland leaning against his Jeep, looking like sex in a T-shirt as he stood there waiting for her—as always. When she didn't find him, disappointment sat heavy in her gut, and she gave herself a quick lecture.

She made her way to her room, and threw herself on her bed, her finger still scrolling over Ryeland's messages. She looked at her laptop and thought about writing, but then turned back to the phone. A war waged inside her, and while logic dictated that she end this with him—she didn't want things to get any more personal—she found herself punching in a quick text.

Maybe she was reaching out to chat, a distraction to get her mind off her mother. Or perhaps it had more to do with the fact that it was Ryeland and she just simply wanted to connect. Either way, she clearly didn't know what was good for her.

A text from him came back instantly and butterflies took flight in her stomach.

Want to do something.

She thumbed back. *It's late.*

Okay, it's late, want to do something?

Mel drew her bottom lip between her teeth. God, he was so persistent, and well…there was something about it that that she found charming.

What do you want to do? she texted.

I'll tell you when I get there.

I never said yes.

But you were thinking it.

The list Ryeland…it's getting longer.

HAHA, on my way.

Mel ran to her bathroom, combed her hair, brushed her teeth, then gave herself a once-over in the mirror. She tugged on a sweater to ward off the evening chill in the air and left her room. She probably shouldn't be so excited to see him, considering they were just friends and all, but she couldn't deny that it felt like a boa constrictor had just wrapped itself around her lungs, making it a bit more difficult to breathe.

His Jeep pulled into the parking area and she walked down the pebbled walkway toward him. He jumped from the driver's side and came toward her. She took in his confident athletic gait, his quick purposeful steps.

"Hey," he said, those pewter eyes raking over her face in a way that made her feel all warm and jittery. God, when he focused his entire attention on her like that it made her forget why getting too close to him was a bad idea. She forced herself to breathe slowly.

"So." Her voice came out unusually high. "What do you want to do?"

"Hop in and I'll show you."

She planted her hands on her hips and took in his grin. "You're not going to get me into any trouble are you?" she asked.

He laughed. "Me? Never."

"Ryeland—"

"Trust me." He opened the passenger side door and motioned for her to get in. "I'd never lie to you."

She slid in and after he settled in next to her, he headed up the mountain, going in the opposite direction from town. They drove past the empty gondolas and the grassy ski hills, which were still lit up despite it being the resort's off-season, and climbed higher and higher into the mountains.

He pulled onto a dirt road and she eyed him as they went over rough terrain. "Back way to the lake," he explained.

"You want to go swimming? I didn't bring a suit."

He stopped at the end of the long dirt road, pulling into the large parking lot that was empty at this time of night. He eyed her and she hugged herself, because she was almost sure he was going to suggest she didn't need one—a typical male response. She was not about to go skinny-dipping with him, and was about to tell him so, but what he said next took her by surprise and had her closing her mouth.

"Switch seats with me."

As he reached for his door, she stared at him, certain she'd heard wrong.

"Why would I switch seats with you?"

"So you can drive."

"Are you crazy? I can't drive."

"I know and that's why we're here. So you can learn."

"Why do I need to learn? I don't even have a car."

He lifted his hands. "Let's say we were out for a drive and my appendix burst. I mean, I wouldn't be able to drive to the hospital or anything, and if you didn't know how to drive the Jeep, I could very well die. So, basically, learning is a matter of life and death."

She sat there staring at him, a laugh bubbling up in her throat. "Maybe you're the one who should be the writer, because that's a really good scenario."

"It could happen, you know."

"Or I could wrap the Jeep around a tree and kill us both right here and now."

"Nah, come on. I can teach you."

She opened her door and walked around the Jeep. "Ryeland, I don't know about this." He passed her at the front of the vehicle, his body brushing hers, then slipped into the passenger's side.

"You're going to be a natural. I can tell."

She jumped in and said, "You'd better buckle up."

Once they both had their seat belts on, Ryeland gave her the rundown. Taking his time to explain how the clutch worked, when to press on the gas, and how to shift gears.

"Okay, so I let the clutch out until I feel it pull, then hit the gas?"

"It's that easy."

While she wasn't so certain, she followed his instructions, only to end up stalling and jerking forward.

She pursed her lips. "Still think I'm a natural?"

"Of course. Everyone does that the first couple of times. Let's try again. It took me a few tries to get it right."

"I doubt it. I'm sure you do everything right the first time."

He gave her a lopsided grin full of suggestion. "There are some things I'm quite a natural at."

Of that she had no doubt.

She turned her focus back to the road, not wanting to go there with him. Well, maybe she did, but she wasn't going to. "Okay, hold on." She tried it again, and actually managed to get the Jeep moving. "Now what?" she asked as she circled the outside of the parking lot.

"Now you have to shift to second. I'm going to help, okay?"

She nodded, even though she had no idea how he could help from the passenger seat. She gripped the stick shift and his hand closed over hers, his rough palm so warm and distracting on the back of her hand she instantly stalled out.

"What happened?" he asked without removing his hand.

"I…uh…I'm not sure," she said. She cast him a quick glance. If she didn't know better, she'd think this was his way of holding her hand. But she did know better. Right? Okay, maybe she didn't. She was about to call him on it when he gave a small, reassuring squeeze.

"Try again," he urged.

She positioned her feet and concentrated on the feel of the clutch as she pressed down on the gas. Once she got the vehicle moving, she drove around the empty parking lot, and when she picked up speed, Ryeland gave her a nod.

"Ready?"

She eased off the gas and compressed the clutch again as Ryeland helped her slide into second.

"Now let off the clutch and slowly ease down on the gas pedal."

She did exactly as he said, and soon enough she was tooling around the parking lot, paying no attention to the signs or road markings. She cast a quick glance his way, giving him a big smile. "I can't believe I'm actually driving."

His thumb brushed over her hand. "Fun, huh?"

"Yeah, kinda." She cut through the parking lot, picking up even more speed. "Should we go to third base?"

When his hand tightened over hers, the heat of his fingers burning into her flesh she shot him a look. Something moved over his face, something so hot and sexy her inside began trembling. They exchanged a long heated look and everything inside her warned that he was thinking of sex. That's when she realized what she'd said.

Oh, Jesus.

"It's not baseball, Melody." His glance dropped to her mouth again. "Or sex."

"Gear," she said quickly, wondering what Freud would have said about her mistake. "I meant third gear." Flustered, she turned her attention back to the steering wheel, but her feet fumbled and the vehicle jerked forward, almost hitting the one and only guardrail in the lot. She turned the wheel quickly, and came to an abrupt stop.

Ryeland groaned low in his throat, but she guessed it had nothing to do with her near accident.

She pulled in a breath. "Sorry."

"Nothing to be sorry about. You did great."

She eyed him skeptically. "Why is it I don't believe you?"

"You should." All humor fell from his face. "I'd never lie to you."

She looked at him carefully, taking in the honesty in his eyes. She wanted to believe him. Wanted to believe that Ryeland Montgomery really was a trustworthy guy.

"It's late," she said, suddenly out of her comfort zone. "I should head back."

"Do you want to drive?" he asked.

"I think if we want to make it back in one piece, I'd better leave that to you."

He leaned into her, his thick muscles bunching as he turned in his seat. "Don't worry, by the end of the summer you'll be a pro," he said, his mouth so close to hers for a minute she thought he was going to kiss her. And oh, God, how she secretly wanted him to.

She reached for the handle but his voice stopped her. "Mel."

"Yeah?" she asked, her blood pounding harder through her veins.

"I think maybe you should slide over me?"

"What?" she asked, her body tensing. "What are you talking about?"

He opened his door, and it hit against the guardrail. "I can't get out and you can't get in. Not unless you want to move us away from the rail."

"I should move us." Completely rattled by the way he was staring at her, she started the Jeep only to stall out. With her brain and body no longer functioning on the same wavelength, she failed miserably at putting the vehicle into motion. Three tries later, Ryeland closed his hand over hers.

"Maybe you should just slide over me."

Good God, if she wasn't the one who'd blocked him in, she'd be second guessing his suggestion, wondering if it was his way of getting her onto his lap. Wait! Maybe he thought she'd done it on purpose.

"I didn't mean to block you in," she said.

"I know."

"Okay," she murmured and swallowed against the tightness in her throat. "As long as you know."

He slid toward her. "You go over, I'll go under."

Mel threw her legs over the stick shift and proceeded to shimmy over Ryeland. He gripped her hips when she landed in his lap, and if she wasn't mistaken she was sure she'd heard him bite back a moan. He lifted her like she was feather light and then his hands fell to his thighs after she pulled away from him. When she reached her seat, she tried not to think about what if felt like to be in his lap, how his strong hands held her so carefully, so gently, or how much she liked every minute of it.

Ryeland cleared his throat and gripped the steering wheel hard. "You all set?" he asked, his voice coming out a little deeper.

"Yeah." She grabbed her buckle, snapped it in, and stared straight ahead.

They both remained quiet, lost in their own thoughts as he drove her home, and when he pulled into a parking space outside her building, all she wanted to do was escape Ryeland and the way he made her feel, but she knew he wouldn't let her off so easily. And maybe she really didn't want him to. God, she was in way over her head here.

He slid from his seat and walked her to her door. After thanking him for the lesson, she stepped into her small room and was about to close the door when his voice stopped her.

"Mel?"

She turned back to him. "Yeah?"

He braced his hands above her door and leaned in to her. "Want to hang out tomorrow night? I can give you another lesson if you like."

She nodded toward the stack of papers on her desk. "I have to work on my paper."

"How about on the weekend?"

"I work the afternoon shift at the restaurant. I clock out around six."

"After you get off, have dinner with me."

His warm breath whispered across her face and she became acutely aware of his closeness. It excited her, overwhelmed her. Stirred the storm raging inside her.

"Ryeland."

He dipped his head, his hair falling into his eyes. "Hmmm…"

"You can call me Melody, if you want."

"Yeah?"

"Yeah."

"Okay, Melody." One warm palm touched her cheek and she suddenly found herself leaning into it. "About Saturday night. Have dinner with me."

"I think—"

His pewter eyes narrowed and when they dropped to her mouth, her words dissolved.

"You want to know what I'm thinking?" he asked.

She looked at him long and hard, her thoughts racing a million miles an hour, trying to make sense of the things he made her feel, things she knew better than to feel.

"No," she said and stepped back.

He smiled, his voice a low murmur when he said, "G'night, Melody."

"Night, Ryeland," she whispered.

As she shut her door and sagged against it, she knew she was in all kinds of trouble, because she really and truly *did* want to know what he was thinking.

Chapter Ten

Ryeland spent his entire Saturday afternoon playing tennis with Suzette in preparation for the end of the summer tournament. She was a great player, trained by professionals back home, and they had a great shot at winning the junior championships. Except being on the court with her was the last place he wanted to be and had only agreed to appease his father, and of course, the money raised would be going to good cause.

It was also his father's way of putting the two of them together, but that didn't mean Ryeland was suddenly going to fall head over heels for her. No, he was completely caught up in Melody, despite the fact that his parents had come right out and told him to stay away from her. Too bad, because he had no intention of listening, and he'd be damned if he was going to sneak around with her. She deserved better than that from him.

Another couple took to the court as Ryeland put his racket down and grabbed his towel to wipe his forehead. Suzette came up to him, looking all cute and bubbly in her little white tennis outfit.

She offered him a big smile and placed her racket and

towel on the bench. "You going to the Cave tonight?" she asked as she pulled her long blonde hair from her ponytail and let it fall over her shoulders.

He tossed his towel over his shoulder. "No, I actually have plans."

"Oh," she said, disappointment on her face as she plucked at an imaginary piece of lint off her skirt. "I just thought we could hang out. You're never around anymore."

"We just did hang out."

"Not like this." She waved toward the courts. "Somewhere private."

Ryeland liked Suzette well enough and while he didn't want to hurt her feelings, he didn't want her to think there could be anything more between them either.

"I'm meeting Melody for dinner tonight."

Her eyes narrowed in on him. "Melody? As in Mel Spencer?"

"Yeah."

Disgust moved into her eyes, and Ryeland noted the quick change in her personality.

"Do your parents know about this?" she asked.

"Who I see is my business, not my parents'."

She gave him a dubious look and asked, "What are you doing with her anyway?"

"I like her."

She put a hand on his chest and blinked thick lashes over blue eyes, a move she probably had perfected in the mirror. "Ryeland, if it's sex you want…"

Ryeland removed her hand and stepped back. "I'm with Melody, Suzette," he said, and turned to walk away."

"It won't last, you know."

He swung back around. "What's that supposed to mean?"

She lifted her head high, tipping that judgmental nose

of hers in the air. "She's a whore, Ryeland. She's only hanging around you because she wants something. When she gets it, she'll toss you away like you were yesterday's garbage and move on to the next guy." She folded her arms and tapped her foot, the look on her face daring him to challenge her. "You'll see."

Ryeland clenched down on his jaw to keep his anger in check. "Don't talk about her like that."

"She's probably already sleeping with some guy behind your back."

His thoughts raced back to the night she'd hopped on the shuttle and took off into town, saying she had some things to take care of. Then he considered last night when she left Jaelyn because she had something to do. She never did say where she was or what she was up to. Then again, he'd never asked.

Ryeland shook his head and quickly pushed those dark thoughts right out of his mind. Melody was not what everyone said she was, and he refused to let anyone plant anything in his head that said otherwise.

"If you want to go slumming this summer, fine, go slumming. But don't expect me to be here forever. Just so you know, Ryeland, I'm only going to wait until the end of the vacation season. After that, don't expect me to be here when you come crawling back." She scooped up her racket and towel and darted to the women's change area, leaving Ryeland standing there staring after her, hardly able to believe what he was hearing. He fisted his hair. Jesus, did she think she could talk about Melody like that and expect him to want her if didn't work out.

Ryeland threw his towel over his shoulder and walked away, determined to put Suzette out of his head. He had a great night planned with Melody and had been looking forward to it for days now. No way would he let Suzette get in his headspace and ruin it.

He checked his watch. He had just enough time to

grab a quick shower and dress before the courier arrived with the package he'd sent for. At least his parents were out at some party tonight and he wouldn't have to field questions when they saw what he'd had shipped across the country.

He hurried back home. Inside the chalet he found Evan playing video games as he babysat Ashley and her new friend, Tabitha, as they played with Corky.

"Ryeland," Ashley said her eyes lighting when she saw him. "Want to take Corky to the lake with us?"

He felt bad that he hadn't spent much time with the two of them since they'd all arrived. But Ashley had been at camp all week, and when Evan wasn't out with his friends, he was flaked out on the sofa playing games.

"Not tonight, kiddo. I'm heading out." When she frowned he found himself promising to take her and her friend to the drive-in tomorrow, and that seemed to make her happy. He caught the spark of interest in Evan's eyes before he quickly blinked it away and turned back to the television.

"Listen, bro, you think you can come help me out with the girls?" Ryeland asked.

"No," Evan said. "And the drive-in is lame."

"Yeah, well I heard Samantha is going to be there."

Samantha Preston, aka, Suzette's kid sister. Ryeland had seen the way Evan had been looking at her the other night when Ryeland got stuck chatting with his father and Mr. Preston in the yard. No doubt his father had already put that relationship into motion too.

"How do you know that?"

"Because you're going to ask her." He pushed on Evan's ball cap, driving it over his eyes.

"I guess she can come if she wants." Evan adjusted his cap. "But the only reason I'm going to go is because Ashley probably wants me there. Right, Ash?"

"Yup," she yelled out as she threw a ball for Corky.

With that settled, Ryeland made his way to the shower. He washed quickly, splashed on his favorite cologne, then pulled on a pair of cargo shorts and white button-down shirt. The doorbell sounded and he rushed down the stair, getting there before Evan could even lift himself from the sofa.

He paid the courier and carefully packed the delivery into a cooler bag. He checked the clock again. If he hurried he could catch Melody clocking out.

"Catch up with you guys later." He scrubbed his hand over Ashley's hair, then hurried down to the lodge's main building. Melody was just exiting.

"Hey." He leaned into her and gave her a little nudge to set her in motion.

"What are you doing here so early?"

"I couldn't wait any longer."

She looked down at her work clothes. "But I want to shower and get changed."

"I can wait."

"Ryeland—"

"I don't mind."

"You're crazy, you know that."

"Yup." *About you.*

She laughed, "Okay, let's go." She slipped in beside him, and he noted the way she looked him over as he pulled onto the road. "You look nice," she said. "Where are we going?"

"It's a surprise."

He drove her the short distance to the staff quarters and parked. She looked at him, a moment of hesitation on her face.

"Did you want to wait inside?" He bolted from his seat and met her before she had a chance to change her mind. She laughed. "I take it that's a yes."

"That's a hell yes," he said.

He followed her to her room, and once inside she

pointed to her chair. "I won't be long."

Ryeland stretched his legs out, and nodded toward her manuscript. "Can I read?"

"No," she said quickly, then grabbed a magazine off her nightstand. "Read this."

He looked at the cover and then back to Melody as she rooted around inside her closet. "Uh, just so you know. This is bullshit."

"What?" she pulled a white dress off a hanger and turned back to him.

Gripping the magazine in two hands, he turned it so she was looking at the cover. "How to turn him on in three easy moves."

She gave an embarrassed laugh, a pink flush crawling up her neck. "I buy it for the pictures."

He laughed along with her, "Yeah, and guys buy *Playboy* for the articles."

"You buy *Playboy*?" She planted one hand on her hip and arched a brow.

"I never said *I* bought *Playboy*," he teased. "And for the record, Melody, you don't need any moves to turn me on."

"Ryeland," she warned, pointing toward her door. "You want to go back outside to wait?"

"Nope." He flipped open the magazine. "I'm going to sit here and take this quiz here on how to rate my mate."

Melody rolled her eyes and disappeared into the bathroom. He flipped through the pages, and listened to the shower turn on, then off. A few minutes later her hair dryer sounded, and when she finally came out, looking more beautiful than ever in the sleeveless white dress, the magazine fell from his hands and he stood.

Her sweet smell filled the room and he breathed deep. He cleared his throat to stifle a groan, but there was nothing he could do to stop his blood from growing hotter. It raced through his body at breakneck speed, building momentum like an unleashed tornado. Every muscle tightened and bunched, one in particular. He fisted his hand to stop himself from pulling her against him, and crashing his mouth down on hers. Her unmade bed taunted him, had his brain conjuring up images of the two of them on it, her body pinned beneath his, while he kissed a path downward.

"…Ryeland."

"What?"

"Are you ready?"

"Oh, yeah." He shook his head to clear it, and wondered how he'd make it through the night without touching her, tasting her. He wanted her so goddamn much, but promised her he wouldn't ask for anything. Damned if that wasn't just about killing him.

He drove them up the mountain, parking on a trail that led to the hot springs. She eyed him curiously when he grabbed a blanket from the back and the rest of the supplies.

"What are you up to?" she asked trying to peek inside the bag.

"You'll see in a minute."

She went up on her tiptoes. "Want me to carry one of those bags?"

"Nice try," he said, and handed her the blanket.

They entered the pebbled path and Melody looked around. "This trail leads to the hot springs."

"Yup. It's a great spot for a picnic, don't you think?" They trekked through the woods a little longer and when they finally reached their destination, the sun had dipped lower in the sky. He took the blanket from her and spread it out in the clearing near the water. He sat and as he patted the spot beside him, he noticed the look on her face.

"What?"

She sat next to him and crossed her legs, tugging her

dress over her knees. "I just…I didn't expect this."

"You've never been on a picnic?"

"No."

"Then you've been hanging out with the wrong guys, sunshine."

"Apparently. Like you said, I'm a bad judge of character."

"Until you met me, right?"

"The jury is still out."

He laughed, "Okay, fair enough. For now. You hungry?"

She nodded and rubbed her stomach. "Starved."

"Good." He pulled two wine glasses from his bag.

She shook her head and held one hand up, palm out. "Ryeland, I don't—"

He produced a bottle of juice. "It's alcohol-free fruit juice."

"Oh."

He tapped his head, liking the pleasantly surprised look on her face. "I remembered." He twisted off the cap and filled their glasses. "How come you don't drink, anyway?" She looked down, her lashes lowering, coving her eyes…her expression.

"Hey, I'm sorry. I didn't mean to upset you."

She blinked back up at him. "It's okay. It's just…well." She took a sip of her juice, then said, "It doesn't do nice things to people I care about."

He thought about the rumors he'd heard about her mother and guessed she was too embarrassed to talk about it. Never wanting her to feel shame with him, and wanting her to trust him enough that she could share hurtful things, he said, "Yeah, I know what you mean. There is rarely a day that I don't see a glass of wine in my mom's hands. And when she's had too much she gets all emotional and talks a lot about when I was a sick kid."

"Yeah?"

"Yeah, but I don't want to talk about her. I want to talk about this." He pulled the food from the cooler bag and handed a foil wrapped sandwich to her. "In case you never make it to Montreal," he said.

"Oh My God." Melody's mouth fell open when she unwrapped the foil to reveal a thick smoked meat sandwich, all the way from Schwartz's in Montreal. She looked at him. "How…why?" She shook her head, her lashes blinking rapidly. "I can't believe you did this."

"Special delivery, and because I wanted you to have one," he said, answering her questions in order. "I mean, you did treat me to a chocolate swirl the other night, so I wanted to treat you to something famous from my city."

"This is incredible."

"Wait until you taste it."

"I can't believe you did this," she repeated. She went quiet for a moment then in a soft voice said, "Ryeland, you really can't be this sweet."

He tossed her his best lopsided grin. "You think I'm sweet?"

That pulled a smile from her. "You're a lot of things, remember?"

"Of course I remember. You never let me forget. You can add sweet to the list later, but for now, let's eat." Ryeland unwrapped his sandwich and bit into it. Melody did the same as he let loose a loud groan. "Damn, that's good."

"So good," Melody agreed around a mouthful of meat. She chased it with her juice then took a big bite of her pickle. "Oh my God, so good."

Ryeland laughed and went to work on making another huge dent in his sandwich. They both grew quiet, a comfortable silence falling over them as they ate, and after awhile Melody looked at him, her eyes serious.

"Ryeland."

"Yeah."

"If being a doctor is important to you, what are you going to do about it?"

"I don't know. I took the LSATs and I've been accepted to law school. I guess I'd have to take the MCATs and start applying to med schools. It's too late to get accepted anywhere now. I'd have to wait a year."

"What will your father do?"

"I don't know. I understand a man wanting his son to follow in his footsteps, but it's not like I'm throwing my life away and bringing down the family name, which is the most important thing in the world to him. I wish he could just accept me for who I am and I don't get why he can't. Unless I become a lawyer in his firm I'll never be good enough." He scoffed. "None of my choices are ever good enough."

"Like me?" she asked quietly.

His eyes snapped up. "No, Melody. No, don't say that."

"You told me you'd never lie to me, but you lied about that fight didn't you?"

"I didn't want to hurt your feelings, and the fight was more than just about you. So it wasn't really a lie."

"They're never going to like me, Ryeland."

"What matters is that I do."

"Why?" she asked.

"Jesus, you have no idea, do you?"

She shook her head.

"You're so tough, a girl who fights for what she wants, but yet you're so sweet and genuine. You're real, not fake, and you have this fire inside that drives you. You're different from anyone I know." She continued to stare at her sandwich in her lap, plucking at the foil wrapping. Wanting to pull a smile from her, he said, "You're not even the kind of girl who worries about what her hair looks like."

Her eye lit and she punched him. "Hey," she said. "I combed it and blew it dry for you."

He angled his head. "You did that for me?"

"Well I couldn't go out with it wet," she said, like she was trying to backtrack. "It gets cold in the mountains at night."

"Yeah, you're right." He pointed toward her food. "Now finish your sandwich."

She nodded and took another bite, smearing mustard all over her mouth. She licked it off and said, "I'm so full. I don't think I'm going to be able to finish it." She held the other half of her sandwich out to him, a pleading look in her eye. "Help?"

"You sure?" he asked.

"Positive." As he took it from her and caught the warm smile on her face, he fought the urge to lean in for a kiss. Christ, she was so sweet, so…everything. For a brief moment he thought about asking where she was the other night, but he didn't. Except asking meant he was letting others get into his head, and he refused to do that.

He finished eating then crinkled the foil, tossing it into the bag. He leaned back on his elbows and glanced around at the clearing. Crickets chirped in the distance and a noise sounded in the underbrush. Melody stiffened and he wondered if it had more to do with the way he'd shifted closer than the animal lurking nearby.

"You okay?" he asked.

She wrapped her arms around herself and stared at the sky. Ryeland followed her gaze and took in the streaks of pink and purple bruising the horizon.

She rubbed her hands over her arms. "Yeah, it's just, the sun is going down and the temperature is dropping."

"We could always get in the hot springs."

"I don't have a suit."

"We can wear our clothes."

"I guess it wouldn't be the first time you caught me

soaking wet and fully dressed."

"Then I take that as a yes." He jumped to his feet and pulled her up.

She yelled when he scooped her into his arms and carried her to the edge. "No, I was kidding." She whacked him and wiggled to get free. Jesus, he wished she wouldn't wiggle like that. "And we just ate."

"Don't care." He jumped, and she wrapped her arms around his neck to hold on as the warm water enveloped them. She pushed away from him and they both came up sputtering.

Laughing, she swiped her hair off her face and swam away. "You're crazy."

"You think?"

"Yeah, I think."

He moved closer when she stopped swimming, watching the way the water dripped down her face, making her look so sexy, so damn tempting. His cock thickened, need propelling him forward and urging him to act on what he was feeling. Her smile fell and her mouth opened slightly as his gaze dropped to her lips.

He took a breath and let it out slowly as he closed the distance between them, standing so close he could feel the pounding of her heart. "You want to know what I think?"

She stared into his eyes and he could almost hear her brain buzzing. She opened her mouth and closed it again. When she finally spoke, her voice was so soft, so quiet he had to strain to hear it.

"Okay," she whispered.

With his heart picking up tempo, he ran his thumb over her cheek then cupped her chin. "What I think is I'd like to kiss you." When she didn't flinch, he leaned forward and pressed his mouth to hers. His lips moved over hers, reveling in the warmth, the softness.

"Ryeland," she whispered into his mouth.

"Yeah?" he asked, barely able to think straight as she melted against him. His body tightened, pleasure racing through him.

Her breath grew shallow, her chest rising and falling quickly against his. "What are we doing?"

"We're kissing."

"Friends don't kiss."

"Friends kiss," he murmured.

"No, they don't."

Breathing hard, he rested his forehead against hers, working to keep his shit together. "Do you want me to stop?" he asked, his voice so tortured he barely recognized it. "If you want me to stop, I will. Just tell me and I will."

She didn't speak for a long moment, then she finally whispered, "I don't."

Thank you, Jesus.

He pressed his lips back to hers, his hungry mouth coming down hard this time, savoring, tasting, his tongue slashing urgently against hers because he couldn't quite get enough. Fuck. She tasted like candy and sugar and honey all rolled into one. In fact, she tasted so goddamn good, so incredibly sweet, his body screamed for more. His cock thickened, aching to be inside her.

She moved against him, the warm water heating his body even more. Her nipples were hard, scraping against his chest in mind-blowing ways. He pushed her wet hair back and his brain shifted through all the things he wanted to do to her, all the places he wanted his mouth, as she shivered under his touch.

Jesus he wanted, needed, more…everything. Her hands slid around his back, her fingers surfing over his body, tentatively at first, then with more urgency. He tugged her impossibly closer. She was so soft, so warm. His blood pounded harder and he could feel his brain shutting down, his body taking over. He breathed harder, deeper, struggling to keep his head on straight and his shit together before they did something she wasn't ready for. No matter what, he wanted to be the kind of guy she needed, the guy she could trust. He inched back and sucked in a few shaky breaths to get it together.

He wasn't some selfish high school jock anymore, who wouldn't think twice about taking her right here in the hot springs. Yeah, he wanted her—goddammit he wanted her—but he didn't want to rush her and ruin things between them. Fighting an internal battle, he grabbed a fistful of his hair and tugged. He growled and that's when he caught the way she was looking at him.

"What?" he croaked out.

"Do you want to know what I'm thinking?"

CHAPTER ELEVEN

Mel had never seen Ryeland look at her like that before, everything about him so intense, so serious. For a moment she couldn't think, breathe…all she could think about was his mouth and how incredible it felt on hers. One of her hands brushed his without thinking, and she entwined her fingers through his.

"Tell me," he said, his voice rougher than she'd ever heard it. He leaned into her, his breath warm on her face. Sexual tension arced between them and with exquisite gentleness he cupped her cheek, his callused palms rough against her flesh. "Tell me, Melody."

"I think you should kiss me again."

His eyes closed like he was in complete distress, and he crushed his hands in her hair. "Jesus, I want you so much," he whispered as he leaned into her and breathed a kiss over her lips, his tongue sliding over her mouth, like he was savoring the taste of her. Her toes curled and she moaned, a soft, barely there sound but it seemed to do something to him. He wrapped his arms around her, pulling her against him as he deepened the kiss, his tongue once again slipping inside to tangle with hers.

She'd never tasted anything so incredible, so intoxicating. Ryeland was right, there were some things he was naturally good at because she'd never, ever been kissed like this before.

He broke away from her lips and his mouth moved to her neck as one knee pressed against her thighs to widen them. His lips surfed over her skin, teasing the sensitive hollow of her throat as she in turn ran her hands through his hair, loving the feel of his hot mouth on her body.

"Melody," he murmured, his breath whispering across her collarbone and pulling a quiver from her. "Jesus, Melody. You taste so good."

"Rye," she said. As soon as that one word left her mouth, Ryeland pulled back. His glance met hers, the pewter in his eyes deepening as he sucked in harsh breath. "Rye," she said again, loving how his shortened name sounded on her tongue, but more importantly, how it affected him. She put her hand on the side of his face, noting how he lacked his usual steadiness. "Kiss me."

This time his mouth came down harder, crashing against hers. A growl ripped from his lungs and he slipped his hand under her shirt, running his fingers over her back. Her nipples tightened more, aching to be touched, but there was some small working brain cell telling her it was too much, too soon to be chasing second base.

But she wanted him, wanted to feel his mouth on her body, wanted to put her lips on his in return. Wanted to feel his naked skin, his muscles, to breathe in the scent of him. Good God, she'd never felt so out of control...yet so safe. That last thought took her buy surprise. *Ryeland made her feel safe*. Honestly, she could no longer kid herself that they could just be friends. This thing between them was powerful, explosive...dangerous.

His fingers burned her body, and he inched back

slightly to touch her stomach. He shifted his stance, angling so he could better position himself. She could feel his hardness against her hip as his palms journeyed higher, sweeping the outer edges of her breast. His breathing changed, became faster, the water splashing around him as they moved against each other.

She moaned and pressed her mouth to his neck, right where it met his shoulders. The salty taste of him danced on her tongue as his thumb brushed over her nipple. She murmured his name as her body flushed hotly.

She was caught up in Ryeland, so consumed by the way he was touching her, and the things he made her feel she didn't hear the voices until they were right beside her. She pulled back, and dipped lower into the water to hide her body's reaction.

"Sorry, dude," some guy said as he stood there holding his girlfriend's hand. "Didn't mean to interrupt." He jerked his head behind him. "Want us to leave…so you can, uh…"

"It's okay," Mel said as the girl eyed her, a smirk on her face. Mel's stomach plummeted. Damn, she could only imagine the rumors that would spread tomorrow. "We were just leaving."

Ryeland caught hold of her hand and positioned her behind him. She rounded her shoulders into herself, and crossed her other arm over her stomach.

"You think you can turn around?" Ryeland glared at the guy and spun his finger in the air.

"Oh, yeah, sure dude," the guy said, his gaze lingering on Mel for just a moment longer.

The two turned and Ryeland and Mel climbed from the water. As if sensing her unease, Ryeland kept her close, shielding her body from the intruders, and she couldn't deny that it felt nice to be held by him. He grabbed the blanket off the ground, and when he wrapped it around her shoulders, it occurred to her how sweet and protective he was. No one had ever been so protective of her before and she was beginning to believe he was too good to be true.

"All yours," he said, tossing the words over his shoulder as he guided her back to the parking lot. He kept his arm around her. It was crazy how far they'd come since he'd picked her up on the side of the road, crazy how much she liked his touch and wanted to be with him.

He tossed his bag into the back of his Wrangler and opened the passenger door for her. Before she got in he leaned into her and pressed a soft kiss to her mouth. "Just so you know, now that I know what it's like to kiss you, I'm never going to stop."

Her insides fluttered, because the truth was, she didn't want him to stop. "Okay," was all she could manage to say, her throat so tight, her body so needy it was a wonder she could even think coherently.

He brushed her hair from her face, his eyes moving over hers, like he was trying to read her. "I want you, Melody. I want you so much, but I don't want to do anything you're not ready for." He pressed his lips to her forehead, and when a shiver moved through her, he mistook it for her being cold. "Get in. I'll get the heat on."

A short while later he parked and walked back to her room with her. She stepped inside and hesitated. Would he want to come in? Would she let him? What would happen if she did? What did she want to happen?

With a million questions going through her mind, she turned to look at him, and he stopped outside her door, making the decision for her. He jammed his hands deep into his pockets and leaned into her, dropping another kiss onto her mouth. He moaned, licked his lips, then fixed her with a look that said how much he wanted her…wanted more.

"Melody."

"Yeah," she said as electricity crackled between them.

"You'd better shut this door on me."

His hair fell over his eyes and she fought a shiver. "Why?" she asked, her brain only partially functioning.

"'Cause I'm real close to coming in and tossing you on that bed and fucking you all night long, and we both know you're not ready for that." She sucked in a breath and he continued. "I'm trying to do right by you, but Jesus, girl, a guy's only got so much control. So shut the damn door, already." With the non-negotiable piece of advice, she inched back and bit her bottom lip, then made a move to take the blanket off but he stopped her. "Keep it for now."

She took another small step into her room and he growled and pulled her back, planting his mouth on hers once again. "Fuck," he murmured, clearly having a hard time reining himself in. Who was she to talk? She wanted more too. "I love the taste of you," he groaned. His mouth moved over hers and a moan caught in her throat when he sucked her bottom lip. "I can't get enough."

Her body reacted to his, and as much as she liked seeing him so crazed, if they kept this up, things were going to go too far too fast. "Rye," she whispered.

He exhaled sharply, gripped her shoulder and nudged her backward. Forehead creasing like he was in total agony, he said, "I know, I know. I'm going now." He hesitated then said, "I'm taking my brother and sister to the drive-in tomorrow. Come with us."

She shook her head. "I can't. I need to do my homework for Tuesday's class."

He leaned into her again—a move she was growing accustomed to—and the softness on his face made her really believe his interest in her went deeper than sex. In fact, everything about the way he acted, treated her, told her he saw her as something more than the local whore.

"Will I see you tomorrow?" he asked.

His scent washed over her and her body tingled. Truthfully, it scared her a little how much she wanted to say yes, to forget about everything and just lose herself in him—again.

"I work and then I have homework."

"I can help you with your homework." He gave her a playful grin.

She gave him a little shove. "I won't get anything done if you're here," she said, but as she thought about it, an idea formed in the back of her mind.

"Good night, Rye."

"Good night, Melody." He hesitated for a moment and shifted uncomfortably, then a teasing look came over his face. "Just so you know, I'm a total wreck right now."

"Yeah," she whispered. "Me too."

Mel closed her door and tore her wet dress off. She threw herself on the bed, her insides completely rattled. With her lips still tingling, she touched her mouth and couldn't help but feel all ridiculously giddy inside. While it was silly, it was also the best feeling in the world. Heck, she really hadn't anticipated how much that kiss would affect her.

Ryeland.

Oh, God, Ryeland. She hadn't meant to get in so deep so fast, but she wanted him. It wasn't logical, it sure as hell wasn't smart, but like Jaelyn always said, you can't help who you like.

Her phoned pinged as she made her way to the bathroom to brush her teeth.

Want to know what I think?

She laughed and texted back. *No.*

You will. Soon enough. Get some sleep, Melody.

You too.

She held her phone close and quickly got ready for bed. She flopped onto the mattress and pulled the blankets up, hugging herself. As she drifted off to sleep, she relived every minute with Ryeland tonight, anxious to be in his arms again, no matter how bad of an idea that was.

Before she knew it Tuesday night was upon them and right after class, knowing Ryeland was outside waiting for her, she rushed to the library. When she found what she was looking for she sent him a text.

Meet me inside.

On my way.

Mel hurried to the front door just as Ryeland was coming through it, that sexy, confident swagger of his doing ridiculous things to her pulse. His mere presence drew the attention of the other female students, but he ignored them and closed the distance between them. A question formed in those gorgeous pewter eyes as he focused solely on her and a fine shiver moved through her. Goodness, she was so aware of him, the way he moved, smiled, looked at her. Heat sang though her veins, but she forced it down.

"What's up?" he asked, bending to drop a soft kiss onto her mouth.

She grabbed his hand. "Come on. I want to show you something."

He grinned. "Oh yeah, there's something I—"

"Ryeland," she warned, whacking him. When she saw her teacher, Marcus, walking from the classroom, she dropped Ryeland's hand and straightened. She didn't miss the wounded look on Ryeland's face as she put a small measure of distance between them.

When Marcus left through the front doors, Ryeland pulled her to him. "What was that all about?"

She gave an easy shrug. "Nothing."

He frowned. "Are you embarrassed to be seen with me?"

"No," she said. "It's not that."

"Then what is it? It better not be because you like him."

"No, of course not." She crinkled her nose and grabbed his hand. "He's my teacher. I don't want him to know anything about my personal life, and well, people talk."

"I don't care, Melody." He fisted his hair, a distressed look on his face. "I don't care who knows how I feel about you, or what they say."

She looked at his chest. "I don't want any more rumors."

Ryeland cupped her chin and lifted her face until they were eye to eye. "You let me deal with that, okay?"

Not wanting to think about that anymore, she said, "Come with me." She led him through the busy hall, students passing them by as they exited their classrooms, and guided him to the library.

She took him to the reference section and pulled out an MCAT book. "Now," she began, "we can study together."

He took the book from her, and his face fell as he looked at the cover.

Unease moved through her. "What? I'm sorry. I thought—"

"Melody," he said cutting her off. "You did this? You looked for this book for me?"

"Yeah." She pulled her phone from her back pocket and pulled up a website. "I also looked into the dates for taking the test. If you register now, you can take it at the end of the summer. They have a testing site in Jasper, driving distance from here. I could go with you, if you want."

"I just...I..." he said, and dropped the book on the

shelf behind her. He scrubbed his palm over his chin and a look she couldn't quiet identify moved over his face. His nostrils flared and his silver eyes went to hers.

She swallowed, wondering what was going on with him. "Don't you want to—"

Before she could finish, he put his hand around her head and drew her mouth to his. "Yeah, I want to," he whispered into her mouth. "But first I want to kiss you."

His mouth found hers and he slipped his tongue inside. He kissed her softly at first, then backed her up against the shelving unit and deepened it. He pushed against her, and she could feel his arousal.

She kissed him back, sliding her arms around his waist, loving the way his body shook beneath her touch.

Someone cleared their throat and Ryeland jerked away. They both turned to see the elderly librarian glaring at them over the rim of her glasses.

"Sorry," Mel said quickly, grabbing the book from behind her and trying not to sound as breathless as she felt. "We were about to check this out."

"That's not what it looked like to me," she said.

"It's the MCATs," Ryeland explained, trying to keep the grin from his face. "What you saw here was just us doing a little hands-on research. They encourage that in chapter five right, Melody?"

"Yeah, chapter five," she agreed, pinching herself to stop from laughing.

The librarian jerked her thumb toward the door. "Take it somewhere else," she said, and while she kept her face stern, Mel was sure she caught a hint of a smile pulling at her.

Ryeland grabbed her hand and tugged, and as she caught his grin, her insides turned over. Honest to God, the boy was trouble with a capital T.

Chapter Twelve

Ryeland turned the page of his book and stole another peek at Melody as she punched away on her laptop. Here it was Friday night, and they were once again working together at Edible's café in Copperville, like they had every other night for the past week. It was a quiet place to work—and because he wanted to be alone with her—here in Deerfield's neighboring town, they were less likely to run into people who knew them, people who would bother them.

"Are you ever going to let me read it?" he asked, eyeing her over his book.

She looked up at him. "No."

"Come on." He dropped his book onto the table. "You let Marcus read it."

"He's my teacher."

"I'm your boyfriend." A strange look came over her face. "What?" he asked.

"I just…I guess I never…"

"Thought of me as your boyfriend?" She opened her mouth to say something, then shut it again. He reached out to touch her hand and slid his thumb over her wrist.

He lowered his voice and asked, "Are you ever going to open up to me, Melody?"

"It's a romance novel," she said. "You don't read romance."

He pointed to his medical book. "Well, I'm reading a lot of things I never thought I'd be reading."

She pursed her lips. "You won't laugh?"

"No."

She went quiet for a moment, like she was having second thoughts, then said, "Maybe another time."

"I'm going to hold you to that." She returned to her work and he listened to her click away. Curious, he asked, "How many books have you written anyway?"

"Four," she said.

"Have you ever submitted any?"

"No."

"Why?"

She gave him a look that showed her annoyance with him, but then said, "If you must know, I've never really finished any."

"How come?"

"I don't know." She curled a strand of hair around her finger and shrugged. "I guess I just don't know how to end them. I mean, I've read a lot of books, and books on the craft. I've studied how it's done, but when it comes to mine, I can't seem to nail the happily-ever-after."

"Maybe it's because you haven't experienced it yet." He winked.

"That's kind of deep for a Friday night, Ryeland," she said, a teasing look on her face. She pointed to his book, clearly wanting to drop the subject. "We still have another hour, so get to work."

He gave her his best mischievous grin, finding it hard to concentrate when all he wanted to do was kiss her again. "And if I don't? Will you get out the whip?" He pretended to look over the top of her laptop. "Didn't I see you writing about that?"

"I don't write those kind of stories," she said, then under her breath she added, "I only read them."

They both laughed and that's when the door opened and in sauntered Justin and Nikko. Before Ryeland could close his book and put it away, Justin came bounding over. One look at his eyes told Ryeland he was high.

"What the fuck?" Justin said his gaze bobbing back and forth between the two of them. "So this is where you two have been hiding." He put his hand on Ryeland's shoulder and sank into the chair next to him. "You're missed at the Cave, pal. Everyone thinks you're hiding from Trevor."

"I'm not," he said coolly.

He watched the way Melody stiffened, and beneath the table he pressed his knees to hers. Her gaze darted to his and he hated the worry he spotted there. He reached under the table and gave her leg a comforting squeeze.

He turned to Justin, "What are you two doing here, anyway?"

"Justin's got the munchies," Nikko said as he settled in the seat next to Melody, sitting entirely too close. Possession raged inside Ryeland as he glared at Nikko. Ignoring him, Nikko pointed to the pastry shelf. "We're here to get a dozen." Nikko turned the question back on them as Melody closed her laptop and placed it over his MCAT book. "What are you two doing here?"

"Better yet…" Justin gawked at Melody and jerked his thumb toward Ryeland. "What are you doing here with this douche when I'm available and he's not?"

Ryeland stiffened. "Back off, Justin."

"Hey, I'm only kidding." He gave Ryeland a playful punch. "Sort of."

"What do you mean?" Melody asked, her voice low, her eyes cautious as they zeroed in on Justin.

"He doesn't mean anything," Ryeland said, gripping her knee. "Melody, look at me." She turned wary eyes his way and he said, "He doesn't mean anything."

"So she doesn't know, then," Justin said, so freaking high on weed he probably didn't even know the trouble he was stirring up. Then again, maybe he did, and maybe before the night was over he'd end up with Ryeland's fist in his face.

Melody's face paled, and it reminded him that she'd been hurt before and didn't trust easily. "What don't I know?"

"Our boy here is practically married. His old man has a pretty little thing all lined up for him. The right girl for Daddy's little protégé." He winked. "And you can bet your ass what his daddy wants his daddy gets."

"You're high, Justin, and have no idea what you're talking about, so fuck off and get out of here."

Justin laughed and stood up. "Yeah, maybe you're right. Let's go," he said to Nikko. "But Suzette's been looking for you. If we run into her again should we tell her you're here?"

Without taking his eyes off Melody, he said. "I don't care what you tell her."

"I guess you can tell her yourself where you've been, since you'll be seeing her on the court tomorrow," Justin said, and Ryeland shot him a quick glance, catching the wry smirk on his face.

"Oh yeah," Nikko added. "You two are playing doubles this year, right?"

"Only because my father arranged for us to be in the end of the summer tournament together," Ryeland explained through gritted teeth.

Justin bumped fists with Nikko. "Like I said, what Daddy wants Daddy gets."

"I only agreed because it was for charity." He looked at Melody, desperate to explain. "And to get him off my back for a bit."

Justin backed up. "Hey, whatever, pal. Not my business."

When the two walked away, Ryeland fisted his hands under the table and resisted the urge to go punch his former friend in the throat.

"Ryeland," Melody said, stuffing her laptop into her bag, the tension in her shoulders like a hard slap to the face. "We should go."

"Melody," he began, grabbing her hand to stop her. "I'm with you. Only you. You have to believe that. Justin is an asshole and a troublemaker. You of all people know that."

She went quiet for a moment, then nodded. "I know he is, but…" She exhaled slowly, sounding unconvinced about everything else. "Maybe we shouldn't be doing this, Ryeland." She waved her hand back and forth between them. "Maybe this is all…wrong."

Ryeland stood and pulled her up. Her body crashed against his and he dropped his mouth to hers. Despite the audience, and lacking any sort of discretion, he kissed her long, hard, and deep, holding her so tightly, so fiercely, there was no way she could even think he cared about anyone else.

When he finally pulled back, he said, "Did that feel wrong?"

She sucked in a breath. "No," she whispered.

"Because it's not," he said, and caught the smirk Justin aimed his way before he exited the café. "Let's forget about what Justin said, and if you want me to quit the tournament, I will."

"No," she said quickly. "It's a great charity."

"I would have told you about it, but I just didn't want to talk about Suzette when I was with you." Those expressive eyes blinked up at him. "You're the one I want, Melody," he said, kicking himself for not mentioning it. Hearing it from Justin wasn't going to help him prove he was trustworthy. "The only one."

Melody looked around, and shrugged into herself when she noticed all eyes on them. "Let's get out of here," she said.

He grabbed her backpack and tossed it over his shoulder, and during the drive back to her place she remained relatively quiet. Music and laugher spilled onto the road as they passed the Cave and when he finally pulled into a parking space outside her lodge, she turned to him, a frown on her forehead.

"Ryeland," she began, and everything inside him tightened.

"Yeah?"

She looked at her hands folded in her lap, then her lashes fluttered as she glanced back at him. "Want to come in for a minute?"

Worried about what it was she had on her mind, and hoping like hell what Justin had said wasn't getting to her and giving her second thoughts about the two of them, he followed her inside. She remained quiet as she opened the door to her room. As he stepped in behind her, she turned back to him and the worry in her eyes had him wrapping his arms around her waist and pulling her to him. Christ, her body felt so good next to his, so right, all he wanted to do was kiss away her reserve and put an end to her fears. He was not going to hurt her. He'd never hurt her.

"What's up?" he asked.

"I want to show you something."

Relief moved through him. He exhaled slowly and wanting to lighten the mood he said, "Oh yeah, well I want to—"

She broke from the circle of his arms, and his words died an abrupt death as she inched away. She held her hand out and he gave her a confused look.

"My backpack," she said.

He slipped it off his shoulder and handed it to her. She reached inside, grabbed her laptop, and powered it up. A second later she put it on her desk and gestured toward her chair. He sat, and when he realized what she was doing, his heart squeezed.

She sat on the bed behind him, her glance flickering to the screen. "I think the opening is good," she said. "If you want to read it, you can."

"Are you serious?" he asked, so goddamn ecstatic that she was trusting him enough to give him a glimpse into her private life. It meant so much to him, especially after the stunt Justin had pulled tonight. That asshole could have ruined everything.

"Yeah," she answered quietly as he sat here a moment longer, marveling at the curious shift in her.

He turned to the computer and started reading, all the while listening to her clothes rustle as she fidgeted restlessly on the mattress behind him. He scrolled through the manuscript and couldn't help but smile. Melody's quick humor was all over the page. She stepped up to him, and her hand went to his shoulder.

"I'm surprised you didn't try to skip to the good parts." Her warm breath fell over his neck, and when she leaned over him and the sweet smell of her hair reached his nostrils, desire slammed into his gut, carrying the impact of a sucker punch.

"Good parts?" he asked, his heart racing, his body urging him to turn and take her right there. Jesus, he wanted to touch her, taste her, to show her how good they could be together.

She whacked his arm playfully. "You know what I mean."

He looked over his shoulder and when he saw a pink flush on her cheek he realized what she was talking about. "I do now." He hit *page down* about five times looking for the sex scenes before Melody stopped him.

"Don't," she said, laughing. "That will embarrass me."

He spun his chair around and put one arm around her waist, resting his hand on the small of her back. "You don't ever have to be embarrassed with me." He sucked in a breath when her eyes dropped to his mouth. Her sweet pink tongue darted out to swipe her bottom lip and he rubbed his temples with his thumb and forefinger, fighting for a measure of control.

"Do you have any idea what you're doing to me?" he bit out, his voice rougher than it was only seconds ago.

"I think so," she said, her tone so soft, so seductive, he considered the possibility that the glimpse into her life just might be her invitation for more.

Excitement surged through him. "I want you, Melody."

She lowered her lashes and when she opened them again he saw the raw hunger. "I want you too," she whispered.

He pushed to his feet and grabbed her, moving her back until her legs hit the bed. "I don't want to go too fast, but Christ I need to taste you. It's all I can think about." When she didn't answer, he tugged on his hair, his heart hammering. "I promise to go slow and will stop anytime you tell me to."

She eased away and that's when he thought he had his answer. He rolled his tongue around a suddenly dry mouth and was just about to kick his own ass for pushing too soon, but then she dropped onto her mattress, pulling him with her. He growled and followed her down, bracing his hands on either side of her head.

"Are you sure?"

"Yes," she whispered, but barely managed to get that one word out before his mouth crashed down on hers.

He kissed her hard, deep, and she shuddered beneath

him as he sank into her warm, wet heat. She kissed him back, her tongue tangling, stroking, driving him wild with need. He slipped an arm under her and then shifted her to the middle of the mattress. Once he had her where he wanted her, he crawled over her body. His mouth found hers again and she immediately opened for him, welcoming him back. He settled on top of her and pushed one knee between her legs to widen them. His blood pulsed hot as she writhed beneath him, her hands racing over his back and tugging at his shirt.

His cock thickened and pressed against her leg as he slid down her body, his lips trailing over her neck and lower, until his mouth hovered over her breasts. "You smell so good," he murmured, brushing his lips over her nipples as they poked against her cotton shirt.

"Rye," she murmured, her voice reverberating through his blood as his cock ached to be inside her.

Desperate to touch her, kiss every inch of her, he slipped a hand under her shirt and met her glance as he slid it upward, trailing his fingers over her warm stomach as he sought her breasts.

Melody raced her hands through his hair, and when he lifted her shirt enough to expose her bra, she made a whimpering sound.

"Sit up," he growled, and when she did he tore her shirt off and removed her bra. Her breasts spilled free, her nipples so pink and hard he damn near lost his shit then and there. She swallowed, and the sound filled the room as she dropped down onto her pillow. Ryeland went back on his heels, eager to just look at her.

"You are so beautiful," he murmured. Jesus her breasts were so full, so perfect. But it wasn't just her body he liked. It was her.

"Rye..." She reached for him and he fell over her again, his mouth wrapping around one pert nipple as his hand closed over the other breast, stroking, massaging, kneading her flesh. Her nipple swelled even more inside his mouth, and he clamped down gently, grazing her with his teeth.

"Oh, my God," she cried out, her hands clutching his shoulders and urging him on.

He sucked deep and swirled his tongue around her hard peak to ease the sting of his bite. She moaned louder and cupped her breasts, offering him more. He sucked in a sharp breath and tried not to tumble over the edge.

Fire burned through his blood as he indulged in the sweet taste of her, sliding his hands and mouth over her skin. Christ he wanted her, wanted to tear his pants off and fuck her long and hard, but he wasn't that greedy adolescent who took without thinking. Not anymore, and definitely not with her. Tonight was about Melody and he wasn't going to forget that, no matter how much blood had left his brain to settle deep between his legs.

He licked her other nipple, making a slow, leisurely pass, then blew on the wetness his tongue left behind. Goose bumps formed on her skin, and she visually quivered, which made him the happiest goddamn guy alive.

"Oh, God, Rye," she cried out.

He shifted his body and reached for the button on her shorts, dying to bury his face in the heat between her legs. "I need you naked, baby," he said, sweat collecting on his brow. "I need to taste you so bad."

With her chest rising and falling rapidly, she lifted her hips, letting him unzip her shorts and pull them off. Her lace panties quickly followed, and he tossed them away, taking a long moment to gaze at her nakedness.

As he teetered on the edge of sanity, he shook his head, his hair falling into his eyes. "Melody…Jesus, Melody." He brushed his hair back and tried to remember how to breathe.

"What?" she asked, her voice a hesitant whisper as she tried to cover herself with her hand, like she was suddenly uncomfortable under his hungry gaze.

"Don't." He pulled her hands away and pressed them into the mattress at her sides. "Don't ever cover yourself. Not with me."

"But…you're staring," she said quietly.

"That's because you're so beautiful and I can't believe I'm here with you."

"Rye, you don't—"

"Yes, I do," he said. "I'm not lying, Melody. I told you I'd never lie to you."

Honest to God, she made him feel the way no other girl ever had, and he couldn't believe that she was his, spread naked beneath him, opening herself up to him like this. His glance met hers again and his body burned hotter, loving the way she was gazing back with need, desire…trust. He cleared his throat, rattled by the things she made him feel. His gaze shifted to the apex between her legs, his brain so rattled it took effort to think.

He lightly stroked her thighs. "Open for me."

She widened her legs, and when he saw how wet she was for him, the way her pussy glistened so invitingly, he groaned, his cock throbbing so hard against his jeans he was about to rip them open and finish himself off in two quick strokes. Yeah, he was that hot for her.

Clenching down hard on his jaw, he reached out and swirled his finger through her slick heat, circling the pad of his thumb around her clit, coming closer and closer, but never quite touching.

"Please, Rye," she begged, her fingers biting into his shoulders as she shifted her hips, trying to force his hand to the spot that needed it most.

He grinned, wanting to tease her longer, to make her as crazy as she made him. Her hips came off the bed, but he pressed on her gently, forcing her back down. She was practically trembling from head to toe when he pulled his hand away.

She whimpered, but it turned in to a moan when he gripped her legs and spread them. The sweet tang of her arousal filled the air and as he drew it into his lungs, it fueled his need.

He settled between her legs and ran his tongue over her thighs, taking pleasure in the taste of her skin. He moved higher and when he reached her pussy, he widened her lips with his fingers and shot her a glance. She was up on her elbows, desire swimming in her eyes as she watched him.

"You want this, baby? You want my mouth on you?"

"Yes, please…" She cried out and fisted the sheets.

"Good."

With single-minded determination, he lowered his head and gave a long swipe with his tongue before his mouth pressed hungrily against her clit. Her breathing hitched and a moan sounded as she fell back onto the bed. He slowly slipped one finger inside her. She was tight. So damn tight.

He stroked deeper, and as her pleasure resonated through him, he took full possession of her body. He greedily drew her clit into his mouth, and her body spasmed as he found the bundle of nerves inside. She rocked against him and moaned as he lapped at her clit and pumped a little quicker.

He could feel the tension building insider her, her pussy growing slicker with each stroke.

"Rye," she cried out, her voice sounding tight. "Please…" she begged, but he wasn't quite ready to take her over. He wanted to spend the rest of the night playing with her, tasting her, pleasuring her. Her hips rocked and as he indulged himself, he took her higher and higher, wanting this to be so good for her.

"I feel…" she said, and a moan replaced her words.

"So good."

He sucked harder, the soft blade of his tongue lashing against her clit as he inserted another finger.

"Oh, my God, that feels so good." He pumped deeper, harder, and knew she was so damn close. "Don't stop," she cried out.

As tension escalated and her breathing grew more erratic, he applied more pressure to her clit. He stroked and rubbed, then shot her a glance, ready to take her where she needed to go.

"Ride my face, baby."

She made a whimpering sound and lifted her hips, grinding her sweet pussy against his mouth. She rode his face furiously as he pumped into her, and in no time at all her body responded to the dual pressure.

"That's it, Melody. Come for me."

Her muscles tightened and contracted around his finger as he continued to lap at her clit. She cried out his name, her body shuddering and surrendering to the onslaught of pleasure. She released in his mouth and he changed tactics, licking gently to draw out every delicious pulse of pleasure, all the while ignoring the way his body was screaming at him to impale her, to drive into her hard and deep and take what he needed.

He drew a breath to center himself, and when she finally stopped spasming, he dusted a soft kiss over her pussy, soothing her sex until her breathing returned to normal. With her passion receding, he slid up her body and settled on top of her. He pushed her damp hair from her face, and the warm, satisfied way she looked at him nearly stopped his heart.

"Rye, that…that…"

"Should we add amazing to the list?" he asked, teasing as he came to her rescue.

She laughed. "Yeah." Her gaze moved over his face. "What about you?" she asked, her lips going to his neck, her lashes fluttering against his skin.

He inched back, desperate to get his head on straight. "Not tonight, baby."

She placed her palms on his cheeks, her hands still trembling from her orgasm. "Rye?" she asked, confusion written all over her face. "You don't want me to touch you?"

"Yeah, baby, I do. You have no idea how much I want you to touch me, but tonight was for you, Melody. Just for you."

She looked at him long and hard, then gave a slow shake of her head. "Who are you?" she asked.

"I'm the guy who wants to do right by you." Even if it meant sporting a pair of blue balls.

<h1 style="text-align:center">CHAPTER THIRTEEN</h1>

"What the hell is the matter with you?" Jaelyn asked as she plopped herself down on the bed.

"Nothing," Mel said and tugged her unflattering green work shirt on over her head. "And shouldn't you be getting dressed?" She pointed to her alarm clock. "We work in twenty minutes."

Ignoring the time, Jaelyn continued to glare at her, then shrieked, "Oh, my God! You had sex. You had sex with Ryeland."

"Shhh…" Mel said, unable to stifle the giggle rising up from her throat. "And, no, I didn't."

Jaelyn did that head-bobbing thing. "Like hell you didn't."

Mel bit her bottom lip and pretended like she was in deep thought. "Well, then again, maybe I did. I guess it depends on how you define sex."

"Tell me everything," Jaelyn said, her eyes going wide. "Everything!"

Mel dropped onto the bed beside her friend and stared up at the ceiling. She told Jaelyn exactly what happened, and how Ryeland, after giving her the best sex of her life, had left to take a cold shower.

Jaelyn rolled onto her side and propped herself up on her elbow. "What the hell? You've got to be kidding me."

"No, I'm serious. He said it was about me, not him." Mel gave a contented stretch of her body, muscles that she hadn't used in a long time aching pleasantly.

"And you didn't touch him?"

"No."

"Did you want to?"

"Oh yeah."

Jaelyn's hair flared as she gave a bewildered shake of her head. "Jesus, who is he anyway?"

"Funny, that's what I asked."

"Why the hell can't I meet a guy like him?" She threw herself back down. "The guys I sleep with care only about getting their rocks off. It's never about me."

"Yeah." Mel nodded, her thoughts going back to Trevor, but then she quickly put him out of her mind, refusing to let him drag her down when she was flying so high—perhaps even dangerously high—with Ryeland.

"Uh, oh," Jaelyn said quietly.

She turned her head to see Jaelyn staring at her. "Uh, oh. What?"

"You're crazy about him."

Mel put her hands over her face. "I know," she said, her words muffled as a quiver moved through her. "I really do like him. He's so nice and thoughtful, and he's so…I don't know, Jaelyn. He's just…unbelievable," she said, reaching for the pillow. She hugged it to her chest and rocked on her bed. "He's insanely funny too."

Jaelyn pushed herself up to a sitting position and crossed her legs. Mel followed suit.

"So you two are an item, then?" Jaelyn asked, her voice serious.

"I don't know. I guess. Yeah. He did say he was my boyfriend."

"What happens at the end of the summer?"

"I haven't thought too far ahead," Mel said.

"But you always think ahead. It's what you do."

"Maybe I don't want to this time." She shrugged. "Maybe I just want to enjoy this right now, and how he makes me feel."

Jaelyn went quiet for a moment, then made a face. "You still know what you're doing, though, right?"

"Yes," Mel lied. Truthfully, she was so caught up in Rye, she had no idea what she was doing. Yes, they were different people who came from different places. Not only that, she had secrets about her father, that night in the hotel so long ago, and he had a family who hated her and wanted to control his future. But for the first time in her life, she felt important, cherished, like someone really cared about her as a person and not what they could get from her.

"I mean, you were the one who said it could never work out, right?" Jaelyn said quietly.

"But it is working, Jaelyn." She buried her face in the pillow. "It's actually working."

"I just don't want to see you hurt, you know, when vacation season…" She let her words trail off, like she couldn't bring herself to remind Mel what happened every year at Stone Cliff.

Mel jumped up, not wanting to think about where this relationship could go, or more importantly, where it couldn't go at the end of the summer. "Come on. I don't want to be late."

She followed Jaelyn to her room and waited while she dressed. They walked outside and Mel couldn't help but look around. Honestly, she'd gotten so used to Ryeland always being there for her it felt odd not to find him perched on the bonnet of his car waiting for her, legs crossed at the ankle and looking so damn sexy. But he had tennis practice with Suzette, and Mel had insisted he go.

Fifteen minutes later they walked into the dining room, ready for another shift, but tonight Mel didn't mind the hard work because she'd be meeting Ryeland afterward and that gave her something to look forward to. As soon as they entered the busy dining room, Judith barked out her instructions, and Mel was soon lost in her work.

The dinner rush eventually died down but Mel's sigh of relief was short lived, because as the crowd cleared, she caught sight of Justin Beechcroft at the bar. Great. Just what she needed tonight. He ordered a beer from Tim and watched Mel walk across the room as he tipped it to his lips.

Working to ignore him, she pushed into the kitchen, and found Jaelyn collecting her order. "Justin's here," Mel said.

"Yeah, I saw him. What's up?" she asked when she saw how agitated Mel was.

"I don't know. I just don't like him."

"Ignore him." She waved a dismissive hand. "You're off in an hour."

She helped Jaelyn with her trays and went back to check on her tables. An odd, nervous sensation settled in her bones, and every time she turned around she found Justin staring at her. On her next trip to the kitchen, he called out to her.

"When are you off?" he asked.

"Soon."

He dropped his empty bottle onto the bar top and dug his heels into the metal bar circling the foot of the stool. "You want to do something?"

That stopped her in her tracks. What the hell? "I'm meeting Ryeland."

He made a noise, something that sounded like a laugh and a cough. "He's not the guy for you, Mel."

Her stomach tightened, but she didn't want to show a reaction in front of him. She breathed past the anger. "That's where you're wrong."

"I'm not wrong." He pushed off his stool and when he came closer she noticed the red lines in his eyes. "If you were mine, I wouldn't be off fucking around with Suzette." He tugged on a strand of her hair that had fallen from her ponytail and she jerked away from him. "I'd be off fucking around with you."

She took a shaky breath, hating how much he could rattle her and dredge up old, painful memories. "You should go," she said.

"Come with me."

She swallowed hard and strived to keep her composure. "I'm not going anywhere with you."

Tim caught her eye from behind the bar and telegraphed her a message. Justin looked at her, then Tim, then back at her. "I'll catch up with you later, Melody," he said, his sly grin making her feel nauseous.

"It's Mel," she responded.

"That's not what Ryeland calls you."

Before she could respond, he left the restaurant and she grabbed the edge of the bar to support herself.

Tim came over. He'd only started working at the bar a few weeks ago and she didn't know him all that well, but he was nice, and very protective of all the servers. She heard he used to be a bouncer, and from the way he was built, she guessed he was probably very efficient at his job, seeing as one look from him was enough to scare Justin off.

"What was that all about?" he asked

"Nothing," she said quickly. "Just a friend."

"That didn't seem like a friendly conversation." He tossed his dishrag over his shoulder. "You want me to talk to him?”

“No,” she said quickly, not wanting to draw any more attention to herself. Like the Montgomerys, Justin Beechcroft and his family were also very important people around here. “Everything is fine.” She stole a glance at her watch and plastered on a smile. “And it’s my quitting time.”

She took off her apron and tossed it into her locker, debating on whether to tell Ryeland about what had happened with Justin. After giving it a considerable amount of thought she decided against it. There was enough tension between the two guys as it was, and she didn’t want to add to it, or bring him any more trouble.

She slammed her locker, said a quick goodbye to Jaelyn, and hurried outside to see Ryeland. She just somehow knew that being in his arms again would make everything all right again.

Her heart fell when she raced through the front doors and didn’t find him standing there. Following the lit path, she made her way to the parking lot and looked around.

When her glance came up empty, she tried to shake off the uneasy feeling. Old, hurtful memories were quick to surface, but she reminded herself Ryeland was not Trevor. He wasn’t the kind of guy to ditch her after getting what he wanted from her. She pulled her phone from her back pocket but found no messages from Ryeland. She turned toward the road and began the short trek to her place.

A few minutes later a vehicle slowed beside her, and she turned to see Ryeland’s Jeep. He slowed, and rolled down the window.

“Need a lift?” he asked, that lopsided grin of his doing the most delicious things to her.

“I live right there.”

He gave her a playful wink. “But I’ve got candy.”

She laughed and her heart lightened as she slid in next to him, and the next thing she knew he had his hand around her head and was drawing her mouth to his. He kissed her deeply, and she melted like a summertime Popsicle. She touched him in return, her hands sliding over his arms as they steamed up the windows. Her body grew hot, achy as he deepened the kiss, his hand sliding around her back. There was no awkwardness between them after last night's intimacies. In fact, there was a new closeness. She honestly had no idea what she was doing with Ryeland or where things could go from here, all she knew was that he could leave her heart broken at the end of summer if he left without looking back. Unnerved by that thought and wanting to only think about the incredible way he made her feel, she pushed it from her mind. She moaned into his mouth as his warm, familiar scent curled around her. Their tongues tangled, and she touched his face. God, he tasted so deliciously sweet, like cinnamon and sugar. Candy.

When he pulled back, they were both breathless. "That's all I could think about all day," he murmured. She caught his mischievous grin when he added, "Among a few other things." His eyes moved over her face. His smile instantly fell and he stiffened, his muscles tightening beneath her hands. "What's wrong?"

"Nothing," she said, realizing how well he could read her and how impossible it was to keep anything from him.

"Is it because I'm late?" he asked.

"Of course not," she said, Justin's words still pinging around inside her brain. *I wouldn't be off fucking around with Suzette.* God, why was she letting him inside her head? Ryeland had offered to quit the tournament and she was the one who insisted he stay.

"We were late getting a court, so we ended up going over to make up for it," he went on to explain anyway.

"It's fine, Rye."

He pushed her hair back and cupped her cheek, his hands so strong and protective as he held her. "Something's wrong, Melody. Tell me what it is."

"Nothing, really." She didn't want to get into this, but she knew Ryeland wasn't going to let up. "It's just that Justin came in tonight and told me you weren't the guy for me, and then asked me to do something with him."

"Fuck," Ryeland said, as he briefly closed his eyes. "What the hell does he think he's doing?"

"He was high."

"He's always high. I'll talk to him."

"No, don't. Just forget it, okay? He's not worth it."

"But you are." He brushed his thumb over her cheek and she closed her hand over his. "Don't worry, he won't bother you again. I'll make sure of it."

"I don't want to talk about Justin anymore."

When lights flashed behind them, Ryeland stepped on the gas and drove past the staff buildings. He shot her a glance. "Know what I want to talk about?"

"What?" she asked, wanting to forget about everything and anything but Ryeland and the way he made her feel.

"Last night," he said.

She felt heat move into her face. "What about it?"

"Oh, I don't know. Maybe just how much I liked it, and how much I want to make out with you again."

He spun around and headed down the hill toward town. "Where are we going?"

"I thought we'd go to the drive-in."

"You want to make out with me at the drive-in?"

He flashed a big smile her way. "Yeah."

"I thought you were supposed to be studying tonight and I was supposed to be working on my assignment."

"Technically this is work."

"Really? And technically how?" she asked, her heart

racing a bit faster as she thought about feeling his mouth on her body again.

"Chapter five." He grinned. "And well, really this is about me helping you with those sex scenes." He shot her a look, his expression full of mock exasperation. "The sacrifices I'm willing to make for you."

She laughed. "Oh, is that what you'd call it?"

"Doesn't matter, because in ten minutes the only thing you're going to be calling is my name…"

Chapter Fourteen

After the movie, and a hot and heavy make-out session, Ryeland dropped Melody back at her place, and now here he was combing the streets looking for Justin. Figuring he'd be at the Cave, he headed to the beach area and shot him a text. Except Justin didn't answer. Ryeland found Cameron, who had his arm wrapped around Maggie, a cute brunette who vacationed here yearly.

"Where you been hiding?" Cameron asked.

"Not hiding. Just hanging out with Mel." He looked past Cameron's shoulders. "Is Justin here?"

"Yeah why? What's up?" Cameron asked.

"I want to talk to him."

"You actually look like you want to kill him." Cameron dropped a kiss onto Maggie's mouth, then whispered something in her ear. A second later she disappeared.

"What's going on?" he asked when she was out of earshot.

"Justin hit on Mel."

"What is it with him anyway? The guy needs some

serious counseling. Last I saw him he was doing a line of coke."

"Christ."

"You might want to wait until he's sober to talk to him."

Just then he caught Justin out of the corner of his eyes. Then he spotted a drunken Suzette coming his way. Shit. Jamie, the camp counselor he'd given horse rides to, caught his eye and started his way but stopped when Suzette pushed past her, giving Jamie a look that could kill.

"Ryeland," she squealed, a wide smile on her face. "About time you showed up." Before he knew what was happening, she threw her arms around his neck and planted a kiss on his mouth.

"Suzette," he said, peeling her arms from his body. She whimpered in protest and flung herself at him again. "You know I'm with Melody." That's when he spotted Jaelyn watching him, her face stone cold.

"Come on, Ryeland," she half purred, half slurred. "We all know what you're doing with her. Just taking your turn like everyone else."

With his anger raging, he cast Cameron a pleading look. Cameron grabbed Suzette's arm. "Come on. Let's go get Ryeland a drink."

"Oh, good idea. I'll be right back," she murmured and left with Cameron. Ryeland went to find Jaelyn, wanting to explain what she saw, but instead stumbled upon Justin.

"Ryeland," Justin said. "What the fuck are you doing here, man?"

"Looking for you."

Justin reached into the cooler and pulled out a beer. He held it out to Ryeland. "You finally ready to loosen up and have some fun, or what?"

Ryeland didn't take the beer, instead he said, "Stay

away from Mel."

Justin shrugged, then uncapped the bottle in his hand and took a huge swig. "What the fuck you talking about?"

"She told me what happened tonight."

Just then a giggling little blonde came up to Justin, and he tossed his arm her shoulder. "Nothing happened."

Ryeland stepped closer and lowered his voice. "And nothing ever will happen, so stay the fuck away from her."

Justin laughed. "Hey, man, whatever happened to bros before hoes?"

Ryeland clenched down hard and through gritted teeth he warned, "Don't ever call her that." His nostrils flared and he worked to pull himself together before he did something he would only regret. Justin was wasted and the last thing Ryeland wanted was to get in a physical fight with him. That would only give his parents the fuel they needed. He had no doubt they'd use it to their advantage and remind him that there'd be no tension between friends if it wasn't for Melody. He scrubbed his chin and glanced around, noticing Trevor in the crowd. The douche has his lips smashed with some girl's and Ryeland was glad. He didn't want to deal with him tonight too.

Ryeland fisted his hands. "All I'm saying is if you bother her again, next time we won't be talking."

"Hey, come on, what do I need with your girl when I've got my own." He pressed his mouth to the blonde's and she giggled and kissed him back.

"That's what I'm wondering too."

Cameron came up to them and Ryeland turned from Justin. "Want to get out of here?" Cameron asked. "We could head in to Grizzly's for a beer. You look like you need to cool down a bit."

"Yeah, sure," he said, needing to get away from

Justin and that smirk on his face. "But what about Maggie?"

"I told her I'd catch up with her later."

They drove to town, and a short while later, they both took a seat at the bar and gestured Trent for a beer. Still unable to shake his anger, he turned to Cameron.

"What the hell did Justin think he was doing anyway?"

"He's an asshole, and like any asshole, he wants what someone else has."

"He doesn't know her, you know. She's not what everyone thinks." He looked at Cameron pointedly. "She's not a whore."

Cameron took a sip of his beer and planted the bottle on the tabletop. "I don't know her, but if you say she isn't then she isn't."

"She's incredible, Cameron."

"Then it doesn't matter what anyone else thinks right?"

Ryeland blew out a breath. "It matters to my folks."

"Yeah, I kind of thought it would. Your father is a bit of a hard ass."

Ryeland exhaled slowly. "He wants to see me with Suzette and warned me away from Mel."

"What do they have against her?"

"She's a local, and my mother automatically hates her because of it. Jesus, my mother grew up here, so I don't know what her problem is." He took a small pull from his bottle. "Apparently she thinks Mel is using me and is only hanging around because she wants something." Christ, Ryeland was used to people wanting things from him. His father and mother expected the perfect son, a child who would follow the path they set out for him without question. Suzette wanted to become a Montgomery, to marry into the right kind of family. Then there were the girls he'd been with in the past.

They all wanted something from him, whether it was a roll in the sack, or for him to open his wallet and buy them pretty things. Only Melody seemed to like him for him, and asked for nothing.

"I'm crazy about her, Cameron."

"Then you should be with her."

"Shit," Ryeland said. "I'm sure Jaelyn's planning on telling her she saw me at the Cave with Suzette."

"You'll explain. If she's as great as you say, she'll understand."

Cameron finished off his beer and Ryeland pushed his to the side. "I should go talk to Mel, to explain what happened. I just hope Jaelyn hasn't texted her yet."

Cameron checked his phone and grinned. "Yeah, Maggie sent a few texts already. She's going to pick me up here. Her folks are out for the night, so we're heading to her chalet."

"I'll catch up with you later." Ryeland slipped from his stool and walked outside. The cool night air washed over him, and he breathed it in as he linked his hands behind his head and stretched. He crossed the road and he reached for his car handle, but when a movement on the sidewalk caught his attention, he looked up, catching a flash of dark hair swishing beneath the light of the lamppost before disappearing around the corner. Melody?

What the hell?

He hopped in his Wrangler and followed, and when he caught her rushing up the steps to an apartment building and disappearing inside, he killed the ignition and opened his door. The street was quiet, only a few cars passing as he sat on the bonnet, and he stole a glance at his watch. Soon minutes turned into hours, and as he sat waiting for her, small doubts crept into his brain. While he didn't believe his mother and the things everyone said about Melody, there was nothing he could do to keep the words of warning from rattling around inside his brain like dice in a Yahtzee cup. When she finally came out and caught him sitting there, panic moved over her face.

"Hi," he said as she slowly came down the steps.

"Hi," she returned and shot a glance around. Her voice cracked when she asked, "What…what are you doing here?"

"I thought you might need a lift." She stood there staring at him, so he pushed off the engine bonnet and opened the passenger door. "Hop in."

With her arms crossed, she hugged herself and moved toward him. "Thanks," she said quietly. "How did you know where I was?"

He braced his hand on the top of the Jeep and leaned toward her. "I caught a drink with Cameron at Grizzly's and saw you when I was coming out."

"Oh."

He shut the door after she got in, and took note of the way she was shivering. Ryeland circled the Jeep, jumped in and turned the heat on high. Melody remained quiet, too quiet, and while he wanted to ask what she was doing he kept his mouth shut.

"It's not what you think," she finally said, breaking the quiet.

He turned slowly, his eyes meeting hers, then looked back at the road. "I never said what I thought."

"I wasn't with another guy."

"I never thought you were."

"You didn't?" she asked, sounding surprised.

His hand slid across the seat and captured hers. He gave a little squeeze. "No, I didn't," and while that was true, he couldn't help but wonder what it was she was hiding from him. When he dropped her off earlier, she told him she was going to do some writing and then go to sleep, because she needed to be well rested for the overnight camping trip with the ten little girls she was in charge of tomorrow night. Then again, he told her he was going to study and hit the sack too, but instead had gone and looked for Justin, despite her not wanting him to.

He listened to her breathing change, and when he looked at her again, he could see her swiping at her eyes. Everything inside him tightened. "Melody," he whispered. "What is it?" he finally asked, hating to see her hurting. "What's going on?"

"I don't want you to think less of me," she choked out.

"Could never happen," he said.

She went quiet for a long time, her hand still in his. They drove past the Cave and up the hill, and it was only when he was nearing her lodge that she broke the silence.

"Remember when you asked me why I didn't drink?"

"Yeah, you said it didn't do nice things to the people you care about."

"I was talking about my mom. She drinks too much. She gets angry, really angry, and often ends up in fights with whatever guy she's with. Most times Officer Sattler calls me to get her, but one of these days he's going to have to lock her up. Tonight I was able to save her from that."

He swallowed. Hard. "I'm sorry."

"It's okay, it's not your fault. I'm lucky Sattler was able to get ahold of me tonight."

"Officer Sattler, as in Trevor's uncle?"

She nodded.

"He calls you?"

"Texts."

"That's good of him. He must really like you."

"More like pities me," she said quietly.

She looked down, hiding her eyes, and he sensed

there was more to the story with Sattler. He squeezed her hand tighter, hating that for a moment there he'd let others plant doubt in his head. Melody didn't deserve that from him.

She cast a quick glance his way. "He also told me he talked to Trevor. He won't be bothering us anymore."

"I can handle Trevor, but he better damn well stay away from you." She leaned her head back on the backrest and stared at the roof. "What's your mom so angry about?" he asked.

"For one, she hates the vacationers. She feels like they all look down their noses at the locals. I guess she's just not happy with her lot in life but doesn't want to do anything to change it."

"And what else?" She angled her head his way and gave him a confused look. "You said for one, so I thought there must be a two."

"Oh." She turned and continued to stare at the roof. "I don't know. I didn't mean to say that." There was a deep sadness on her face, and Ryeland knew she was holding something back. Sweet Melody Spencer had secrets and plenty of them, and damned if he didn't want to help her slay the demons that haunted her.

He pulled into his usual parking spot and walked around to her side. He pulled her to him, holding her shaking body. It occurred to him that Melody had an incredible sense of responsibility for her mother, yet no one was taking care of her.

"You never have to go through this by yourself, Melody. Not again."

He walked her up the stairs and to her room, and when she opened her door, the loneliness he caught on her face made his heart catch.

"I'm staying the night." He kicked off his shoes.

"What?"

"You're clearly shaken up and I don't want you to be

alone."

Her voice hitched when she said, "Being with Mom always makes me emotional."

He dropped down onto her bed and pulled her with him. She rested her head on his shoulder and he held her tight, until her body stopped quivering. When her breathing slowed, he covered them up, and dropped a kiss onto her forehead.

"Try to get some sleep," he said.

"Ryeland," she whispered.

"Yeah."

"Jaelyn texted me."

He cupped her chin, and met her eyes. "It's not what you think."

She looked at him for a long time, then said, "No, then maybe you should leave."

He stiffened. "What are you talking about?"

"From the way Jaelyn explained it, Suzette was all over you and you pushed her away."

His heart pinched, because trust didn't come easy to her, yet she was ever so slowly believing in him. He kissed her, a long, hot kiss that set his heart racing. "I told you before, I only want you."

"She also told me you got into it with Justin."

He fell onto his pillow and pulled her in tighter. "I know you asked me not to say anything, and I hope you're not upset, but you're with me now, Melody, and no one, and I mean no one, is ever going to hurt you again."

Chapter Fifteen

Last night Ryeland had vowed to protect her, but Mel knew the only person who could ever hurt her now was Ryeland Montgomery himself. She was in deep with him, so totally lost in his touch, his taste, the way he cared for her, that she could barely go a minute without thinking of him.

She touched her lips, the kiss he'd given her earlier that morning before he'd left her bed still warming her mouth. But what warmed her the most was that he wanted to be there for her, to hold her and comfort her. Honest to God, he was unlike any other guy she'd ever met.

"Earth to Mel." Fellow counselor Jamie waved her hand in front of Mel's face.

Mel blinked. "What?"

"You look like you're a million miles away."

"Just thinking about the activities planned for tonight," she said, but from the look on Jamie's face, it was obvious she didn't believe her. Mel turned her attention to the little preteens piling into Beaver Lodge, heavy backpacks slung over their shoulders and smiles plastered on their cute little faces. Their parents kissed them goodbye as Mel looked past their shoulders and out the window, noticing the dark clouds moving in to shade the afternoon sun.

Great. The last thing she wanted was for the skies to open up during their overnight adventure. Not only would that put a damper on the late-day bonfire and hot dog roast planned, she had no doubt a few of these girls would be afraid to spend a night in a cabin in the middle of the woods during a thunderstorm.

She clapped her hands to get everyone's attention. "Okay, who's ready for the long hike to Big Bear and dinner over an open fire?"

The girls all started jumping up and down—all except little Sasha, who was tucking her tiny dog into a small pouch on her chest. Shoot. Mel had forgotten that she told her she could take it along. Oh well, there wasn't much she could do about it now. A promise was a promise.

"Let's get a move on then." Mel shouldered her backpack and headed outdoors, Jamie and her group of girls following. Since each bunkhouse housed twenty kids and two camp counselors, Beatrice had paired Mel up with Jamie for the night.

Darkness had settled over them as they pushed their way through the woods and made the trek along the Stone Squaw Trail to the cabins at the top of the mountain. Once they finally reached their destination, they all gathered kindling for a fire. Afterward Mel and Jamie started preparing a bonfire while the girls all ran around excitedly, claiming and making their bunks.

"So you and Ryeland," Jamie began, laying more kindling on the fire. "I thought you said you didn't like him."

Mel shrugged, digging through her backpack for a lighter. "We're friends."

"That's not what I heard."

Squatting, Mel held the lighter to the wood and watched as it caught fire, recalling the couple who'd caught her and Ryeland kissing in the hot springs. No doubt that news had spread quicker than a brush fire. "You can't always believe what you hear."

"Just so you know, Suzette is all over him on the tennis court," Jamie said, adding a few larger pieces of wood to the fire. "I don't like that girl." The concern in Jamie's voice made Mel wonder if she'd had a run-in with Suzette and if she was warning Mel because when faced with a common enemy she'd decided to side with another townie.

Bethany came bouncing over, putting an end to their conversation. "Can we tell ghost stories?" she asked, her blue eyes bright and eager as she clutched a teddy bear to her chest.

"Only if everyone is in agreement," Mel said then put her hands over her ears when the girl shrieked to her friends that they were allowed.

Mel laughed at the girls as they all ran around the camp, but the smile quickly fell from her face when a rumble sounded in the distance.

"Shit," Jamie muttered, poking the fire. "Just what we need."

"We'd better get the food cooked before the storm hits."

Thirty minutes later they all sat around the fire, eating hotdogs, s'mores, and telling ghost stories. While Mel wasn't partial to being scared, especially when she was in the middle of the woods and a storm was brewing overhead, the girls all seemed to enjoy it. The thunder grew closer and Sasha's tiny dog whimpered inside its pouch. They hung outside as long as possible, and when Mel felt the first drop, she stood and hustled the girls into the cabin. Jamie grabbed the supplies and made it inside just as the sky opened and drenched the campsite.

The storm picked up outside, but the girls took it in stride, dry and cozy as they played board games and cards. It wasn't long before the trek through the woods caught up with them and the sounds of yawns filled the cabin.

"Okay, time for bed," Mel announced and grabbed her backpack. She pulled out her cell and tucked it in to her back pocket, hoping to catch a moment alone to send Ryeland a text when the girls were all tucked in.

A tug on her T-shirt had her turning around and she nearly jumped out of her skin when a bolt of lightning shook the walls of the cabin.

"Fluffy needs to go potty," Sasha said. "Will you come with us? There could be a ghost out there." She blinked anxiously up at Mel, and Mel briefly closed her eyes. Dammit, why the hell had she agreed to let Fluffy come in the first place? Now she had to take her outside, in the middle of a downpour, so she could do her nightly business before bed. She certainly couldn't let Sasha do it, or come along. Not only was it dark and stormy, the ghost stories had obviously scared her.

She turned to Jamie who gave her an *it wasn't me who invited the dog along* look when she saw a whimpering Fluffy peeking out from the pouch, obviously in need of a grassy spot to relieve herself.

With a sigh of resolution, Mel reached for her hoodie and pulled it on. "I'll be right back. Fluffy needs to go," Mel muttered under her breath.

Another loud clap of thunder jarred the cabin, causing all the girls to squeal and the lights to dim. Jamie gave a mock shiver. "Better you than me," she said. "I'll just hang here with the girls."

Fluffy whimpered louder as the girls all jumped in their beds, trying to scare each other as they came up with clever ideas on what—or who—was really causing all the noise outside.

Mel grabbed a flashlight and inched opened the door. She stuck her head out and glanced around, hoping like hell she wasn't about to encounter freaky Jason Voorhees. She left the door open slightly, letting a sliver of light spill outside, and was about to put Fluffy on the ground when lighting zigzagged across the sky and the dog bolted from her hands. The little ball of fur disappeared into the night, her yelps growing fainter and fainter as she darted into the woods. Mel waved the flashlight around and peered into the dark but lost sight of her as she ran through the underbrush.

Bloody hell!

Rain poured down her face as she blinked rapidly. She pulled the front of the hood over her face and swiped at her eyes as she glanced around, trying to figure out what to do next.

"Everything okay?" Jamie asked, sticking her head outside.

"The damn dog ran off," she whispered, hopping back up on the porch.

"Fuck no." Jamie stepped out, lowering her voice to match Mel's.

"I have to go find her, but don't tell Sasha. Make something up to buy me some time."

"Like what?"

"I don't know. Tell her Fluffy wanted to go for a walk to find the perfect spot or something."

"Okay, hurry back."

Mel took off into the woods, following the direction Fluffy had gone. "Fluffy," she called out and glanced around, trying not to let the nighttime noises scare the beejesus out of her. She hurried forward, waving her light around and listening for the dog's whimpers. Well off the beaten path, she pushed wet leaves and heavy branches out of her way, but missed the fallen log and stumbled forward. She grasped at a low-hanging branch in an attempt to balance herself but it slipped from her wet hands and she face-planted in the mud.

"Jesus!" she cursed. So this is what she got for being nice and letting Sasha bring her dog along. She wiped her face and cold moved into her bones as the rain fell harder, dripping off the heavy leaves and plastering her hoodie and clothes to her body. She sat still for a moment, trying to catch her breath when she heard the whimpering sound. "Fluffy," she called out softly, and pulled herself to her feet. "Here, girl. It's okay. I'll bring you back to Sasha."

Her light fanned out and she caught a flash of white, but when she made a move to walk she snapped a branch and Fluffy took off again. She ran after her, her light bobbing as she hurried, and the next thing she knew she fell and was sliding down a big, muddy hill. She screamed out for help, but that proved futile, considering she was alone in the woods in the middle of a storm. She slid down the embankment, picking up momentum, and she grasped for something solid to grip on to. Her fingers clawed at the mud with no leverage to be found.

Trees flew by in a whir and when she finally stopped falling she blinked her eyes open to find herself near the lake. Heart pounding like mad against her chest, she glanced around, trying to orient herself. God, she was so lost. She choked back tears and struggled to think. Okay, if she followed the lake it would eventually lead her somewhere, right? Her body began shaking harder, from the cold as well as the stress of losing the dog. Not to mention being alone and lost in the woods.

She pushed to her feet and when she heard a faint bark, she wondered if Fluffy had taken a nosedive down the hill too. "Fluffy," she called out, working hard to keep the panic at bay. The trees thinned and she heard the dog again as she came to a clearing. She was about to call out again when a large, hooded figure dressed in a raincoat stepped in front of her. She gasped, her hands going to her chest as she stumbled backward, every scary story told earlier that night coming back to haunt her.

Before she knew what was happening, a set of strong hands circled her back to balance her.

"Melody, it's me," Ryeland said, pushing his hood off so she could see his face.

"Rye," she choked out breathlessly, nearly sobbing at the sight of him. "You scared me."

"I didn't mean to."

"What are you doing out here?" she asked and that's when she heard Fluffy whimper.

He held the little dog out in his hand. "The same thing you are, I take it?"

"What?" she asked, completely confused and trying to make sense of things. "How did you know she was lost?"

"I was inside studying when I heard barking and came out to see what was going on."

She glanced around, and when lighting lit the sky she caught sight of his family's chalet in the distance. "Oh my God. I got lost but had no idea I'd wandered into the resort housing area."

"Come on, we need to get you inside."

She pushed her hair from her face and shook her head. "I need to get back with Fluffy."

"Not yet you don't," he said, holding both her and the dog close.

Before she could protest, he led her to the boathouse nestled on the lake. They climbed the stairs and he ushered her into the gorgeous upstairs loft overlooking the water, a loft that doubled as a guesthouse.

She stood there dripping wet as he wrapped Fluffy in a blanket and settled her onto the sofa. The little dog curled into a ball and burrowed inside the blanket as Ryeland walked back to Mel.

"Look at you," he said, his smile so adorable as he brushed mud from her cheeks. "We need to get you cleaned up."

"First I need to text Jamie to let her know I found Fluffy." She grabbed her phone from her back pocket, thankful that the counselors had all exchanged numbers a few weeks back, and swiped her finger over the screen. She shot off a text to Jamie, telling her to let Sasha know she'd taken Fluffy to play and everything was fine. After hearing back from Jamie, she powered down her phone, and glanced up to see Ryeland grinning at her.

"What?"

He shook his head. "Do you have any idea how gorgeous you are?"

She wiped her face on her shoulder but only managed to smear the mud. "I'm soaking wet and covered in mud. I'm hardly gorgeous," she countered, but from the hungry way he was looking at her, she couldn't deny that she did feel beautiful, desired by him.

"Come here," he said, his voice deeper than it was only moments before.

He opened his arms and she stepped in them. "But I'm going to get you all dirty," she said.

"I don't care," he murmured and the next thing she knew his lips were closing over hers. He kissed her deeply, his warmth surrounding her as their tongues tangled. His hands wrapped around her waist and he rubbed her back, creating heat with friction. His touch was warm, strong…protective. She sagged against him and a low growl sounded in his throat as their bodies grew needy for one another.

"Melody," he whispered into her mouth, a new, never-before-heard strain in his voice. He shifted his stance and that's when she felt how much he wanted her.

"Yeah?"

He ran his thumb over the wet strings on her mud-coated hoodie. "You need to get out of these clothes."

She inched back and looked into his pewter eyes. The way he looked at her told her how much he ached for her, but it also told her he wanted her out of her clothes not to have sex, but because he cared about her well-being. Except she wanted out of her clothes because *she* needed to get naked—to have sex with him—more than she needed anything in her entire life. In fact, she wanted him so much it scared her.

He took off his raincoat, peeled his shirt off, and gestured toward a closed door as he held it out to her. "You might want to wash up first." He fisted his hair, a look of agony on his face as he took a measured step back. "I can run up to the house and grab you some sweat clothes. They'll be big, but they should work for now."

He made a move to go and Mel touched his shoulder to stop him. She drew a deep breath and let it out slowly when he turned back to her. Their eyes met, every feeling she had for him rising to the surface as his hand tangled with hers.

"Melody?" he asked, his gaze gliding over her face, questioning, assessing.

Instead of answering she lifted her arms.

"Oh, God, Melody," he murmured, understanding moving into his eyes. "Are you sure?"

She gave him a smile that was slow, inviting. "Yes," she whispered. "I'm positive."

His hands went to the hem of her hoodie and his nostrils flared as he gripped it. Her heart raced, and as he peeled the wet cotton over her head, taking her T-shirt with it, she wondered if he could hear the rapid beat against her chest. As he stood back to look at her, her gaze moved over his bare chest, taking pleasure in how toned his body was. She quivered under his inspection, and the next thing she knew he was guiding her to one of the closed doors.

She found herself inside the bathroom, and she stood near the sink as Ryeland reached behind the shower curtain to turn on the spray. Water gushed behind him as he lowered himself to the edge of the tub. With a crook of his finger he gestured her closer. She moved toward him and he widened his legs, pulling her in between them. His mouth moved to her stomach and he buried his face into her flesh, his tongue doing delicious things to her bellybutton.

She gripped his hair, running her fingers through it, and he glanced up at her. The raw need in his eyes excited her all the more. His fingers went to the button on her shorts and lingered there for a moment.

"Tell me you want this, Melody. Tell me you want me. I need to hear it, because I want you so much that once we start this, I'm not sure I'll be able to stop."

"I don't want you to stop," she whispered.

One hand slipped behind her head, and he dragged her mouth to his. Their lips joined and he kissed her with such hunger and intensity it left her shaken. When he pulled back, they both stood there breathless. His hands went back to her shorts. He released the button and the hiss of her zipper cut through the quiet of the room as he pulled it down. Her shorts fell to her ankles as he gripped her panties and slowly tugged them from her hips. He dropped to his knees and unlaced her hiking boots, then tapped her legs. She lifted them one at a time as he took off her boots and removed her shorts and panties.

"I've been dying to taste you again, baby," he murmured into her stomach. "It's all I've been able to think about."

Her toes curled into the bath mat beneath her feet as

his fingers slipped between her thighs, and when he lightly brushed her sex, her trembling hands went to his shoulders for support.

With his one hand between her legs, the other reached around her back and unhooked her bra. It fell away, leaving her complexly bare, completely exposed, completely vulnerable. But she didn't feel afraid. Not with him.

"But first let's get this mud off you," he said, standing up.

As steam filled the room, Ryeland made short work of his clothes. Lacking any sort of modesty, he stood before her, and her breath caught at his beautiful nakedness. He stepped into the shower and pulled her in with him. The hot needle-like spray felt like heaven, but not as good as his soap-lathered hands moving over her body. He touched her gently, taking care to scrub the forest from her skin. God, she loved the way he touched her, wanted her. Her body burned with need as his fingers raced over her eagerly, and unable to help herself, she took the soap from him and lathered him in return. He threw his head back, one hand gripping the metal shower rod as she raced her hands over him, wanting to touch every inch of him. And from the way his body was swelling with need, it was clear he had many inches.

She closed one hand over his hard cock and he growled. "Jesus, Melody." A thrill moved through her and she took pleasure in teasing him, seeing how crazy she could make him with a simple touch.

She gripped him with both hands and stroked lightly. His body shook. Almost violently.

"Fuck," he murmured and moved his hips, pushing into her hands. His soft growls sliced the air and she could feel his veins fill with blood as she squeezed harder.

"Melody," he murmured after a long while and grabbed her hands. He placed them at her sides and leaned into her, his breath warm on her face. He took deep, gulping breaths as they exchanged a long, heated look. "Keep that up and I'll be finished before I start. And there are so many things I need to do to you."

In a move that took her by surprise, he tore open the shower curtain, grabbed a towel off the hook, and wrapped her in it. He grabbed his jeans from the floor and carried her into one of the bedrooms. A second later he was laying her out on the bed. He slid over her, his hot, hard body pressing her into the mattress as his mouth found hers.

She moved beneath him, loving the feel of his hardness meshed against her body. His lips left hers, and he buried his face in her neck as he shifted to the side. His hands slid over her body, touching, reacquainting himself with her curves, as he dipped his head lower to swipe the soft blade of his tongue across her sensitized nipple. She moaned and raked her fingers through his hair as warmth pooled between her thighs.

"You like that, baby?" he asked, his voice practically unrecognizable.

"Yes," she cried out, writhing on the mattress, so needy, so desperate to feel him inside her. His hand pressed between her knees and when his fingers eased her thighs apart, she dug her nails into the bedding.

He slid lower, his breath scorching her skin as he breathed a kiss over her flesh. He drew in the scent of her skin before changing positions. He went up on his knees near the foot of the bed and when he caught her glance, a storm far more volatile and powerful than the one overhead brewed between them. Sexual energy sparked as he widened her legs even more and gave her a look that conveyed his hunger. He dipped his head and the second his mouth moved to the greedy spot between her legs, her chest rose on an intake of breath.

"Oh, God," she whimpered as his tongue seared her clit in the most delicious way. Pleasure raced through her as she moved against his mouth. He continued to bring her higher and higher and the second he inserted a finger and found the hot bundle of nerves inside her, she burst into a million tiny pieces.

"Rye," she cried out, curling her fingers in the sheets as her body let go, giving itself over to the incredible sensations closing in on her. She pinched her eyes shut and concentrated on the pleasure. Ryeland kept licking her, drawing out her orgasm. When her body finally stopped spasming, Rye climbed over her.

She flicked her lids open to find him looking at her, the emotions, the heat backlighting those pewter eyes arousing her all over again. He exhaled a shallow breath and ran his thumb over her kiss-swollen lips.

"I need to be inside you," he said, the urgency in his tone, and longing in his voice doing crazy things to her. She traced her hands over him, unable to get enough, as he grabbed his jeans, pulled out a condom, and quickly sheathed himself.

Overwhelmed by the things he made her feel, she swallowed hard and touched his face. His hand closed over hers, his eyes serious.

"Tell me you want this."

She widened her legs even more as he balanced on one elbow, his crown pressed against her opening. "I want you," she whispered, lifting her hips and inviting him in.

He fisted her hair and jerked his hips forward, driving hard and deep and fueling the need inside her. He began pumping and she moved with him, meeting each powerful thrust.

"You feel so good," he growled as blood pounded through her veins. "So good, baby."

His thick muscles bunched as he shifted his body for deeper thrusts, and as he moved urgently over her, his thumb went to her clit. He circled it, toyed with it, then applied just the right amount of pressure to take her to the precipice again.

"Oh, yes," she murmured, tossing her head from side to side as pleasure exploded through her. He rode her harder, faster, his growls telling her how close he was as her sex fluttered with a second orgasm. "Rye," she called out. "So good." She rode out the waves, working to catch her breath as she gripped him close.

"Jesus," he bit out as her muscles clenched around him. He held her, absorbing her tremor, then between clenched teeth said, "I'm so close."

She pressed her lips to his neck and breathed in his scent, consumed by the things he made her feel. A barrage of emotions raced through her as he drove in once, twice, then buried himself high inside her. She held him tight as he let go, and she whimpered and stilled as he depleted himself completely.

He collapsed on top of her and they remained that way for a long time, each holding on to one another as if their lives depended on it. He eventually slid off her body and discarded the condom. When he fell back onto the bed he pulled her close and a deep sense of belonging settled in her bones.

She took in his profile, beads of sweat plastering his hair to his forehead. Honestly, Ryeland was unlike any man she knew, and being with him like this felt so right. She cuddled into him and put her hand on his chest. He reached for it, and as their fingers linked she closed her eyes, just wanting to hear the sound of his breath.

The storm continued to rage outside, lighting up the sky, but he was in no hurry to move. His arms tightened around her and she gave a soft moan.

"Melody."

"Yeah?"

He shifted to face her, his grin so damn adorable it set her heart racing. "I'm kind of into you."

Butterflies took flight in her stomach and she tried not to giggle like a schoolgirl. "I'm kind of into you too."

His grin widened as he brushed her hair from her face. "I meant to tell you, I registered for the MCATs tonight."

"You did?"

"Yeah. Want to go with me when I take the test?"

"For sure." He went quiet for a moment, like he was a million miles away. She touched his cheek and he looked at her. "What?" she asked. "What are you thinking?"

"What I'm thinking is how you talked about going to Toronto at the end of the summer. If I pass the test, maybe I could apply for schools there next year." He leaned into her, his lips meeting hers. The kiss he gave her was so full of emotion and tenderness it stole the breath from her lungs. "I don't want this thing between us to end come the fall," he whispered.

Mel's heart soared and it took all her effort to refill her lungs as she tried to wrap her brain around what he was saying, how the intimacies they'd just shared had changed everything between them. For the last few weeks she'd simply been living in the moment with Ryeland, too afraid to look ahead, yet he'd been thinking about his future—one with her in it. She resisted the urge to pinch herself, afraid to wake from this amazing dream, because never, ever in her life had things been so perfect, so right. Not only did it frighten her a little, it made her wonder when this bubble would burst and the world would fragment around her, because even though they were great together, and things seemed to be working between them, she couldn't forget she had secrets and he had a family that hated her.

But maybe, just maybe they could overcome the odds and really make this work. She clung to that crumb of hope, needing to hold it close, because after tonight, the alternative was much too painful to consider.

CHAPTER SIXTEEN

Before Ryeland knew it, the summer had breezed by in an idyllic blur as he and Melody continued to lose themselves in each other. They saw each other almost every night, with the exception of the nights she spent with her mom. With Labor Day only a few weeks away, the night mountain air had grown colder, the leaves not too far from changing color. There were still a few weeks left of vacation season, but many families had already started heading home to prepare for the next school year. Ryeland and Melody weren't without their own plans, and Ryeland knew soon enough he'd have to reopen the discussion with his father.

Over the course of the summer he studied while she perfected her chapters, and when she wasn't writing she quizzed him. At times he even helped her plot. He loved her creative mind, her energy, the way she lit up when she talked about her stories. In fact, he loved everything about her and there was no denying how good they were together.

Originally, he hadn't wanted to sneak around with her. She deserved better than that from him. But as their relationship progressed, grew far more serious, they kept things quiet, wanting nothing or no one to come between them—especially his parents. As long as Ryeland continued to practice tennis with Suzette and put on appearances for family functions, his folks had kept quiet about Melody, no doubt hoping he'd simply get her out of his system and leave her behind when he went to law school in the fall.

But today was the day he was scheduled to take his MCATs and if things went according to plan, he'd be moving to Toronto with Mel and changing his path. They'd talked about their future, about having a family together, and had even been looking at apartments online. He knew his folks would go bat-shit crazy if they knew and his father would cut him off, but thanks to Melody, he'd come to learn his freedom, and following his heart was something he needed to do. He hoped someday his father would warm to the idea of Ryeland following his own dreams and they could be friends.

He walked her way when he saw her coming from Wolf Lodge. She hurried toward him. He loved how her face lit up whenever she saw him. He grabbed her backpack and shouldered it, then dropped a kiss onto her mouth.

She kissed him back, so warm and passionate he knew if he didn't break it they'd never make it to Jasper in time to take the test.

"Hey, baby," he said, his heart pounding madly as he inched back. He took a deep breath and let it out slowly, totally blown away by Melody and the things she made him feel. From the first time he gave her a ride, he knew they would be good together, but things were even better than he expected. So much better in fact, it scared him a little.

"You all set?" she asked.

"As ready as I'm going to be, I guess."

She jumped into the passenger seat. "Do you want me to quiz you?"

"No, let's just talk."

He slid behind the wheel and pulled onto the road. Every time he looked at her he found her looking back, a beautiful smile on her face.

"What?" he asked.

"I'm excited for you."

"Don't be too excited. I haven't passed yet."

"You will. I have faith in you."

His heart warmed and he reached for her hand. "So…" he said.

"Sooo…what?" she asked.

"Come on, tell me. Did Marcus like the first three chapters enough to send them off to the publisher?"

Her eyes went wide and she nodded rapidly. "He did!"

"That's great, baby." He pulled her hand to his mouth and kissed it. "They're going to love it."

She made a face that said she wasn't so sure. "I need to get the ending finished. If they ask for more I have to have it ready."

"You can do it. You brought your laptop to write while I'm testing, right?"

"Yeah."

"It's going to be great. I can see it now. I'll work for the next year to support us while you write and get published, then I'll go to medical school and you can support me."

She laughed. "Uh, I'm not sure I'll even be able to support your pinky at first."

He laughed with her. "I don't care. I'd rather be poor and happy with you than rich and without you."

Melody leaned back in her seat, and as she stared at the road ahead, she smiled. Honestly, he'd never seen her so happy or content. They'd come a long way over the summer, growing closer. While they talked and shared everything, there was still a part of her she kept closed off. He wasn't sure what had really happened that night in the hotel he'd heard so many rumors about, or why she was too afraid to tell him, but he hoped that one day she would spill and he could help slay her demons.

They talked quietly about their future and enjoyed the scenery as they drove to Jasper. When he reached the office tower where he'd be testing, he parked and drew a centering breath, realizing he was more nervous than he thought.

Melody leaned into him and planted a soft kiss on his mouth. Then she inched back and licked her lips.

"What was that for?" he asked, his cock thickening.

"Good luck."

"Come here." He grabbed her and pulled her close, his mouth crashing down on hers. "When I'm done today, I'm going to take you back to your place and have my way with you."

She chuckled and said, "On one condition."

"No conditions," he growled. When she angled her head and lifted her chin in defiance, he gave an exaggerated exhale and asked, "Okay, what condition?"

"Well, I'm writing a very complicated sex scene with ropes, and I might need you to help me play it out so I get it right."

"Jesus, Melody." He fisted his hair. "You can't say something like that to me before I'm about to test."

She laughed. "Oops, sorry."

She reached for her backpack from the rear seat but he turned and grabbed it for her. She gestured toward a coffee shop across the street. "I'll be there writing."

"Okay." He gave her another kiss. "I'll be a few hours."

Ryeland watched her cross the street and once she was inside the coffee shop, he made his way to the testing center. He showed his ID and signed in and for the next four hours he, along with twenty other people, sat in front of a computer in their own little cubicles. Exhaustion pulled at him as he finished the third section a moment before he was timed out. He pushed back in his chair and scrubbed a hand over his face. At least everyone else who'd taken it looked as wrung out as he was.

Working to clear his head as he walked outside, daylight long gone, he crossed the road, anxious to see Melody, to take her back to her place and help her out with that scene, but the second he looked at her, and saw the panic on her face, his heart dropped into his stomach.

"Baby, what is it?" he asked.

She held her phone up. "Sattler texted me. My mom. She's in the drunk tank."

He grabbed her and pulled her close. "Oh Jesus."

"I need to go get her."

"Okay," he said and guided her to his vehicle. She remained mostly quiet, nibbling her bottom lip nervously as he drove them back to Deerfield. When he parked outside the police station, Melody jumped from her seat and darted inside.

He finally caught up to her at the front counter, pleading with the officer behind it, but the woman insisted there was nothing she could do. Ryeland grabbed Melody and pulled her away.

"I can't leave her in there, Ryeland," she said.

"I know. I'll call my father. He'll know what to do."

Her lashes fluttered and after a moment of hesitation, she gave a quick nod. "Okay."

Ryeland pulled his phone from his pocket and punched in his dad's number.

"Ryeland," his father said, answering.

"Dad, can you come down to the police station? I need some help."

"Are you in trouble?" his dad asked, his voice hard.

"No. Please just come."

Silence lingered for a second, then his father said, "I'm on my way."

He led Melody outside to wait, and she paced nervously. "I hate the thought of her in there," she said, folding her arms around her chest and hugging herself.

"I know, baby. We'll get her out."

Ten minutes later both his mother and father exited their car. Melody stepped away from Ryeland, moving into the shadows as his mother rushed up the steps toward him. She looked him over, her worried gaze assessing him.

"Ryeland, are you okay? What's going on? What happened?"

He gripped his mother's arms to calm her. "It's okay. I'm okay."

"Then what is all this about?" his father asked, the calmness in his voice belying the anger brewing behind his hard eyes.

Ryeland looked past his mother's shoulders to Melody, who was leaning against the brick wall, her gaze darting nervously between Ryeland and his father. "Melody needs your help. Her mother needs a lawyer to help get her out and I thought you could help."

His mother and father both stiffened, their deadly glances zeroing in on Mel, who started shrinking in on herself.

"Ryeland—" his father began.

"I need you to help her," Ryeland said, his voice low to showcase just how serious he was as he cut his father off. "I need you to do this."

His father glared at him, something dark and worried moving over his face.

"Rita deserves what she gets," his mother Eliza burst out and Ryeland's head came back with a start. What the hell?

"Eliza," his father said harshly. "Go wait in the car."

"You know my mother?" Melody asked, her eyes narrowing as she turned toward Eliza.

"Stay away from this girl, Ryeland," she continued to ramble as she shot a deadly glare Melody's way. "She's trouble. Like her mother."

"Mom," Ryeland bit out harshly and stood between his mother and Melody. He loved his mother but no way in hell was he going to stand there and let her talk about Melody like that.

"Eliza," his father warned again.

Eliza went up on her toes and tried to look over Ryeland's shoulder, her gaze shooting daggers. He shifted his position to prevent her from making eye contact with Melody. She made a huffing sound, then scampered off to the car.

"Ryeland, get in the car and take your mother home."

Ryeland linked his hands together behind his head. "What, no? I'm not going anywhere."

"You will if you want me to help."

He turned to Melody who was staring at him with those haunted eyes of hers. Christ, he hadn't seen her look like she had demons to slay in months now.

"Melody." He grabbed her hands. "I don't want to leave you."

"I need to get her out," she said, her voice tight.

His father stood there glaring at him, his arms folded, his face hard, dangerous.

"Okay," Ryeland finally said, conceding because this was what Melody needed. He turned and made his way to the car. He slid into the front seat, looked at his mother and asked, "How do you know Melody's mother?"

Chapter Seventeen

Mel followed Mr. Montgomery inside the building and stood back as he spoke to the officer behind the counter, the one who'd said she couldn't help. Mel had no idea what he was saying or how he could go about freeing her mother, she was only grateful that he was trying to help. She stayed a few feet back and Mr. Montgomery didn't spare her a glance as he was led through a security door. Mel found a chair and lowered herself into it, wringing her hands as she waited and prayed that he could free her mother. Honestly, she wasn't sure how this would affect Ryeland. His father was pretty harsh with him, and even though Mel had been reluctant to let Ryeland call home, his father was the only chance she had of getting her mom out.

Seconds turned to minutes, and when her mother finally came from the back room, an officer Mel didn't recognize leading her through the security doors to the main counter, Mel jumped to her feet.

"Mel," her mom said, her eyes still glossy, her words harsh as she zeroed in on her, like everything was Mel's fault. "I would rather rot in hell than let that man help me."

Mel flinched at the hard words aimed her way, but not wanting to discuss this here, Mel grabbed her by the waist and led her outside. Her mother straightened slightly as the cool night air washed over them. She looked for Ryeland, but he was long gone.

"Did you want me to leave you in there?" she hissed out.

"Yes." Her mother struggled against her.

Feeling the fight drain out of her, she said, "Mom, come on. Let's get you home."

She practically carried her mom down the sidewalk and when they reached her building, Mel fished the keys from her mother's pocket and dragged her upstairs to her apartment. Her mother threw herself on the sofa and Mel sat down on the coffee table, wanting answers.

"How do you know the Montgomerys?" she asked pointedly.

"You stay away from them," she slurred.

"I'm with their son, so you'd better tell me how you know them."

Her mother jerked up and nearly fell off the sofa, Mel's words having the affect she'd hoped. Honest to God, she was so freaking tired of this, tired of her mother's behavior, her self-pity, all the secrets.

Her mother wagged her finger, but couldn't seem to focus it on Mel. "Mel, you stay away from them. You need to listen to me."

"Tell me how you know them," she demanded.

Her mother fell back on to the sofa, and put her hand over her face, a moment later she began crying. "He…he was my first, Melody. My first love. Seeing him tonight…I never wanted him to see me like that…"

This time Mel nearly fell to the floor. "What?" she asked, shaking her head in disbelief. "What are you talking about?"

"Oh, Arthur was such a beautiful boy, with such a promising future. I was nothing but a poor townie, but he fell for me. We were in love."

Her mother and Arthur were in love?

"Then what happened?"

"Eliza happened."

"Ryeland's mother," she stated.

"Yeah," Rita said, her voice rising. "We were friends, and she was jealous that Arthur was going to take me away and marry me and give me the life I dreamed of." She grabbed Mel's hands. "We were friends and she betrayed me. Arthur betrayed me."

"How did they do that?"

"They slept together." She sobbed harder and Mel ran to the bathroom to grab her some tissues. Rita blew her nose and continued, "Then Eliza got pregnant and the rest is history."

Mel's heart squeezed as understanding dawned. Her gaze moved over her mother's red puffy face. "You never got over him."

She hiccupped, then said quietly, "No."

"What about Dad?"

"He was a rebound. He was never any good. And I'm so sorry, Mel. I'm so sorry. He told me he was taking you for ice cream that night. I had no idea." Mel could feel tears pricking at her eyes, but fought them back, not wanting to think about the events that took place in that hotel room so long ago.

"I want you to go in to rehab, Mom," she said firmly. "You need help."

Her mother nodded slowly and pinched the bridge of her nose. "I know," she whispered.

"I mean it. You need help. Let me take you to rehab in the morning."

"Okay," she said so quietly Mel had to strain to hear. Rita sagged against the pillow and Mel grabbed the blanket at the foot of the sofa. Her mom might be agreeing to it tonight, but tomorrow could very well be a different story. Mel just hoped this run-in with Arthur was enough to show her she'd hit rock bottom and now there was only one way to go—up.

"Mel," her mom said as Mel covered her up.

"Yeah?"

Her mother's frail hands gripped Mel's elbow and she held tight. "Don't let them hurt you the way they hurt me."

"I won't." She swallowed the lump pushing in to her throat. "Why don't you try to get some sleep."

"Will you stay? I don't want to be alone."

"I will."

Mel dropped down onto the floor and laid her head against the cushions. Her mother stroked her hair and soon enough she fell into a drunken sleep. Her frail hand fell from Mel's head. Mel closed her eyes and the next thing she knew dawn was upon them. She stretched out and turned to see her mother blink up at her.

"Mel," she said, her voice thick with emotions. "I'm...I'm sick." The hand reaching out to her trembled. Years of depression and alcohol had deepened the lines around the eyes looking up at her, making her appear so much older than her forty-five years. "I'm so tired of being sick."

"I know." Taking her mother's hand, Mel gave it a comforting squeeze and choked back tears of relief. "I'm going to get you help." She covered her mother back up and pulled her phone from her pocket. Her heart flipped when she saw all the concerned texts from Ryeland. Before she could text back, she made a few phone calls to make arrangements to get her mother placed in rehab at the hospital.

Once done she helped her mother up and packed her a bag. She called for a cab, but when she stepped outside, she found Ryeland leaning against his Jeep waiting for her.

"Rye," she whispered under her breath, her heart squeezing so tight it hurt to breathe. She could hardly believe her was here for her.

He stepped up to her, and tucked a strand of her hair behind her ear. "You okay?" he asked, his eyes narrowing as he assessed her. When she nodded his gaze moved to her mother.

"I'm taking her to the hospital," Mel explained. "I called a cab."

"I'll take you."

"Okay," she said, needing his help, his quiet strength, and steady assuredness to get through this.

Ryeland helped Mel get her mother into the passenger seat. Twenty minutes later, Mel sat in the admissions office of the rehab center, filling out forms while her mother was led off for treatment. Knowing there was nothing more she could do today, she turned and walked in to Ryeland's open arms.

"Let's get you home," he murmured into her hair.

He held her tight as he led her back to his vehicle and drove her home. Once inside her room, he dropped a kiss onto her mouth.

"You okay?"

"I will be," she answered, tears so close to the surface it was all she could do to keep herself together. "I just need some sleep."

Ryeland grabbed the hem of her shirt and lifted it over her head, leaving her in her bra and jeans. He backed her up until her knees hit the bed, then straightened her rumpled sheets. "Climb in," he said.

With exhaustion pulling at her she slid between the sheets and Ryeland peeled off his shirt and moved in beside her. His warmth reached out to her and she snuggled in closer, enjoying the feel of his naked skin next to hers.

As Ryeland ran his hand up and down her arm, she said, "I asked my mother how she knew your mom."

"Yeah, I got the story too. But I'm sure it's different from yours."

"From what my mother told me, she used to date your father back in the day, and then he left her for Eliza, leaving my mom heartbroken. I guess that's why she hates the vacationers now. She married my father as a rebound and has been miserable ever since." She stopped and breathed out a shuddering breath, a chill racing down her spine as her mind went back in time. "Then after he…well, she turned to the bottle."

He cupped her face, everything in his eyes intense, serious. "After he what, Melody?"

She swallowed hard as his gaze moved over her face, and once again she could feel tears threating to spill. God, she did not want to talk about this with Ryeland, especially when she was such an emotional wreck. Sure he said he could never think less of her, but…what if he did?

"Melody," he whispered, his hand so soft on the side of her face, her heart missed a beat. "No one is going to hurt you again. I promise."

As she looked at him, it occurred to her that she believed him, believed in him, and that didn't come easy to her. In that instant, as he held her so tight, so protectively, a barrage of emotions bubbled to the surface. Her heart squeezed as something inside her let go, and this time there was nothing she could do to stop the tears from running down her cheeks as painful memories rose to the surface.

He lightly brushed the tears away, chasing them with soft kisses. "Baby, whatever it is, it's going to be okay."

She nodded as her body sank into his, letting him fill the hollowness inside her with something other than anger and pain. "I was only thirteen," she began on a hiccup. "An innocent kid." She stopped to get her breath, then remained quiet, but Rye's soft hand on her face and the warmth in his eyes gave her the courage to go on. "My father drank for as long as I could remember. And he was mean, always mean, but even worse when he was drunk. One night he got mixed up in the poker games held at the resort each year, and well, he lost everything."

"Everything?"

"Yeah, everything. So he…" Bile rose in her throat and she swallowed at the hurtful things he'd done, to both her, and her mother. She looked away, staring unseeingly at a spot just past his shoulder.

Rye touched her chin, pulling her gaze back to his. The concern in his eyes warmed her heart.

"What did he do, Melody?" he asked, his voice rough with emotions.

Melody looked into Rye's eyes, so full of concern. She reached up, ran her finger along the faint crinkles left from laughter and wondered how he would see her once the whole story was told. If they were going to have any shot at a future together, there could be no secrets between them. It was now or never. She took a cleansing breath, let her hand fall to the mattress, and took the hardest step of her life.

"My father was never an affectionate man. I can't remember him ever going out of his way to spend time with me, so when he came in one evening and said he was taking me out for ice cream, well…" She pulled in another breath, let it shudder out. Rye's arms tightened encouragingly. "Chocolate swirl. He told me I could have any flavor, and I loved chocolate swirl. We drove around a while and then he stopped at the lodge, said he needed to see a guy about something and it would only take a minute. That he was…a special friend and I was to be nice to him."

His forehead dropped to hers, his thumbs gently brushing away the tears that streamed down the sides of her face. "Baby, you don't have to say anything else."

She wrapped her fingers around his wrists, drawing from his strength. "Yes, I do. I have to."

When a drop of moisture fell to her cheek, Melody realized it wasn't only her tears Rye was wiping away. Her heart swelled as she went on.

"He…he used me to pay his debt."

Ryeland stiffened and she could tell it was taking a great effort for him to keep it together. But she knew he would, because right now she needed his strength, and he knew that. He sucked in a couple of deep breaths and held them for a few seconds before he let them out slowly.

"There were a lot of rumors, but I never told anyone what he did to me." A strangled noise sounded in her throat and she shook her head. "How could a man do that to his own daughter? How could he leave me there with that man while he went to his car to wait?"

"I don't know, baby. I don't know," he said, pulling her in tighter, and squeezing her so hard she could barely breathe. "But I'm sorry. I'm so sorry."

Years of pent-up pain and anguish broke free and her tears flowed harder when he ran his hands over her back, holding her in such a tender, possessive way her entire heart opened to him. "No one is ever going to hurt you again. I swear to God. If anyone ever comes near you again, they'll have to go through me first."

She sniffed, her tears soaking his skin as her face pressed against his neck. "I didn't sleep with him, Ryeland. It never came to that," she said, wanting to tell him everything, no matter how ugly the truth was.

He inched back, relief backlighting his eyes. "No?"

"No." She breathed deep, then blurted out, "I killed

him."

He sucked in a breath and let it out slowly. Clearly he hadn't seen that coming.

"How?" he asked, his voice low, his hands practically trembling as they held her.

"He came at me, all drunk and slobbering and grabby. There was a lamp beside me. I reacted and grabbed it. He tripped on the cord and fell and cracked his head wide open."

"Jesus," he said, his thumb rubbing her shoulder as he took a moment to process.

"I was afraid he was going to get back up so I smashed it over his head. Over and over and over again." A hard shiver moved through her and when she shook, violently, he tightened his hold on her. "I can still remember the sound of his bones crushing, see the blood pooling on that awful green carpet."

He hugged her tighter. "It was self defense against a grown man. You're a fighter, baby. I love that about you."

"You do?"

"Yeah, I do."

She looked down, ashamed of herself. "I wanted him dead, Ryeland. It still scares me today how much I wanted him dead." She buried her face in her hands, her stomach clenching when she added, "It scares me how capable I was of doing it."

Ryeland brushed her hair back, put his thumb under her chin, and lifted it until their eyes met. "You were a frightened child. You reacted."

"I murdered a man."

His jaw tightened. "No, you protected yourself from a rapist pedophile, Melody. That's what you did."

"I wanted him dead, Ryeland," she said. "That makes me a bad person."

"No, it doesn't. You're the best person I know."

She sniffed and looked into his eyes. "You don't think any less of me?" she asked, her emotions about that night all over the place. God, she was just a kid then. How was she supposed to deal with what her father had done, what she'd done? Half the time she didn't know whether it was right or wrong, and the counseling she'd received at the time had proved pretty worthless. What she had really needed was her mother, someone she could trust, turn to for comfort, but her mother had turned to the bottle, instead leaving Mel to deal with it herself. Some job she was doing of that.

But Ryeland was here now, giving her the comfort, the support she needed. No one had ever been there for her like him.

"Of course not. You were defending yourself. Christ, if I'd been there I'd have killed the bastard too."

A strange strangled laugh sounded in her throat. "Officer Sattler came. He protected me."

"He still watches out for you, doesn't he?"

"Yeah, and then last summer I slept with his nephew Trevor. I had no trust in men, and Trevor was nice to me. I thought he was one of the good guys, you know, like his uncle. I was wrong." She took a big hiccupping breath. "You were right. I'm a bad judge of character."

Her pulled her head to his chest and ran his hand over her hair. "Oh, baby, I'm sorry."

"There were rumors about what happened in that hotel room," she whispered against his chest. "After I slept with Trevor he bragged about 'bagging' me and told everyone how good I was in the sack." A cold shiver moved through her and she pulled back to see him when she added, "He said that poker player died because I fucked him so good that I gave him a heart attack."

Ryeland rubbed his temple, like he was trying to calm himself down. "What a prick."

"Then I was bullied and harassed by almost

everyone."

The muscles along his jaw rippled and he pressed his fingers over his eyes. "I'm going to get you out of this town, Melody. I promise. I'm going to make things better for you."

She sniffed and pulled his hands from his eyes. When she saw how watery they still were her heart squeezed. "Rye."

He swallowed. "Yeah."

"Thank you."

"You don't have to thank me for anything."

"You helped me with my mom, and well…you're always there for me. No one has ever been there for me before."

"Don't you see?" he said, his voice trembling slightly. "It's because I love you, Melody, and would do anything for you."

"You love me?"

"Hell yeah, I love you."

She sniffed again, more tears falling, but this time they were tears of joy. "I love you too."

"And you're good for me too, baby." He slid his hands over her bare arms and she quivered.

"I need you, Rye." Feeling beaten down after dealing with her mother and sharing her painful memories, she put her palm on his cheek, needing to be touched, caressed, loved by him more than ever. "I need to be with you."

"I need to be with you too."

Ryeland kissed her, his mouth moving slowly over hers as he pressed her back onto her bed. His mouth left hers and he undressed her slowly, his dark gaze never leaving hers. Her heart pounded. God, she had never felt so loved, so close to anyone.

"I love you," she said practically to herself, feeling like a tremendous weight had been lifted off her shoulders.

He made quick work of his clothes, then sheathed himself. With hands that were so gentle, so protective, he touched her all over. Soon he was moving inside her. She closed her eyes, losing herself completely in him, letting go of the past and reveling in the now. She hadn't been prepared for a man like Ryeland, hadn't believed a man like him existed, or how much her life had changed since meeting him.

Her hands moved over his, unable to get enough of him. Her heart swelled as he picked up the pace, his lips closing over hers as her body gave in to the pleasure.

"Melody," he murmured, as he let go, releasing high inside her. "Oh, Jesus, Melody." After they both climaxed, he covered them with the blankets and as she snuggled into him, she was certain nothing or no one could ever come between them.

Chapter Eighteen

Melody sat beside Jaelyn and watched the tennis match under the lights. She'd had no idea just how good Ryeland was and couldn't help but smile every time he was in play.

"You have it bad for him, don't you?" Jaelyn asked.

"Yeah," she said breathlessly, closing her hand over her stomach.

"What's wrong?" Jaelyn asked when she saw her cradling her belly.

"Cramps."

"Oh, crappy. Need a pad?" she teased.

"Hell no." She looked at her friend and lowered her voice. "I'm actually late."

"Oh, shit," Jaelyn said.

"But I have cramps, so that's a good sign, right?" she hurried out. "It must mean I'm going to start soon."

"I think so," Jaelyn said. "I'm sure it's nothing to worry about. I mean you've been using protection right?"

"Yeah. But I mean nothing is one-hundred percent."

"Abstinence is, but where's the fun in that."

Mel nudged her. "You're so bad."

Jaelyn nudged her back, and gestured with her head. "Looks like lover boy and Suzette just won."

The crowd stood and started clapping, and when he was whisked away by his father and Suzette's family, Mel worked to ignore the sinking sensation in her gut. She and Ryeland had plans to move in together, to someday start a family, but with the way his parents treated her, she feared they'd never, ever accept her. For a moment she felt sorry for Ryeland. Weren't his parents doing what they thought was best for him? They were simply doing what parents do, what Mel's had never done. Did Ryeland deserve to lose them, as well as his kid brother and sister, because he fell for the wrong girl?

"Where's he going?" Jaelyn asked.

"After-game party at the country club."

Jaelyn angled her head, her gaze moving over Mel's face. "Are you going?"

"No," she answered, trying to keep her voice steady, like it didn't bother her. Ryeland had invited her, but she knew it would cause nothing but trouble for him.

"Well come on then." Jaelyn glanced at her watch. "We can still make it to the movies."

Nighttime had fallen over the town as they climbed from the stands and caught the shuttle. As they passed the Cave, Jaelyn looked on with longing.

"Still missing, Cole?" Mel asked.

"He texted me earlier and asked if I was coming out tonight."

"And..."

"I don't know, Mel. Maybe I should forgive him. I mean, he seemed sincere enough."

"I don't want to see you get hurt again."

"I know." Jaelyn shrugged and held her hands out to her sides. "But you can't help who you like."

It was true. Mel had certainly learned that over the

summer.

The shuttle stopped and they got off in front of Johnson's pharmacy. As they walked past it and her cramps grew stronger, Mel briefly thought about running in and grabbing a pregnancy test. But surely she was just overreacting. She couldn't be pregnant. Could she?

They made their way to the small movie theater and stood in the outside line under a lamppost waiting for their tickets. The line moved slowly, and when she turned to find Justin and Nikko coming their way, Mel slipped her arm around Jaelyn's and held tightly, hoping they would ignore her.

"Hey, Melody, Jaelyn," Justin said.

No such luck.

Jaelyn turned and glared at him. "Can I help you?" she asked.

Ignoring Jaelyn, Justin turned to Mel. "So I guess lover boy is off with Suzette. I guess that leaves you free for the night." He looked at the line in front of her. "Is this really how you want to spend it when there are so many other…interesting things you can be doing?"

"What do you want?" Mel asked, her voice low, firm like she'd learned in her self-defense classes.

Justin took a step closer, invading her personal space. "Isn't that obvious?"

Unease move through her, every instinct she possessed coming to life. "I think you should leave," she said when she noticed others in the line turning to glare at her.

"I'm not going anywhere."

"Fine, I'll leave."

"How about we all leave together." Justin looked at Nikko who was grinning at them. "I don't mind a foursome. How about you, Nikko? Are you up for a little *four*-play?"

"I'm always up for foreplay," Nikko said.

Mel stepped out of line, pulling Jaelyn with her. Needing to get as far away from those two as possible, she hurried down the sidewalk and turned the corner. Their steps slowed when they were out of sight but when she heard, "What's your fucking problem?" She turned to see Justin and Nikko following.

Justin caught up to her and grabbed her arm. "So what, you'll spread your legs for my buddy, but not me? You think you're too fucking good now or something, Melody?" he asked, drawing her name out slowly.

"Don't talk to her like that," Jaelyn said, shoving him.

He shoved back. "Mind your own fucking business, whore."

Nikko laughed and Justin squeezed Mel's arm harder. "You and me, baby. We're gonna fuck, and fuck hard."

Reacting purely on instinct, Mel kicked Justin right between the legs. It might not have been a move she'd learned in self-defense, but it was an effective move nonetheless. Justin went to the ground clutching himself and cursing, and Nikko grabbed Mel from behind.

She tried to get away but he held her too tight, his fingers biting into her arms hard enough to leave bruises.

"Let her go!" Jaelyn pounded on his back.

Just then Mel's cell phone pinged, but she couldn't go for it, not with Nikko restraining her.

"If that's Ryeland, keep your mouth shut about this, or I'll tell him a few things of my own," Justin said, then nodded to Nikko. He let her go, giving a little shove. "Then you'll be really sorry."

Mel hit the wall and sagged against it, her breath coming in ragged bursts as Justin pushed to his feet.

"Come on, we're wasting our time," Nikko said. "She's not worth it."

"Yeah, maybe you're right," Justin agreed. "I'm liable to get some disease anyway." The two strutted away, disappearing around the corner. Mel leaned forward and braced her hands on her knees. She took deep, gulping breaths. "I need to get out of this town," she whispered, working to fight back the tears as her body trembled.

"Jesus Christ, Mel. What the hell was that all about?" Jaelyn shook her head and added, "You need to tell Ryeland."

Her stomach clenched. Jaelyn was right, but what had Justin meant when he said he'd tell Ryeland a few things of his own? She had no idea what kind of rumors he might spread. While Ryeland might be smart enough not to believe them, she was sure those he was closest to would grasp on to them and use them against her—and him. Plus, summer was almost over, and trouble between friends could mean more trouble between Ryeland and his parents.

"I can't do that," Mel said.

"If you don't I will."

Mel stood and worked to shake off the incident. "Let's just forget it, okay?"

"Mel—"

"Please, Jaelyn."

After a moment, Jaelyn finally conceded and said, "Okay." She hooked her arm in Mel's and guided her down the sidewalk. "You cracked his nuts wide open, my friend. Chipmunks will be following him around for weeks."

God, she loved Jaelyn and her warped sense of humor. Forcing a smile, Mel grabbed her phone from her back pocket and her hand went to her cramped stomach again when she read Ryeland's message.

I snuck away. Meet me at the boathouse. Mom and Dad will be partying for hours and I need to see you.

"Mel?" Jaelyn asked, closing her hand over Mel's. "Are you okay?"

"Ryeland wants to see me."

"From the looks of you, I think you need to see him too. Come on, let's go get the shuttle."

"You go on and get it and head to the Cave. I'll catch the next one. There are a couple things I need to do first."

CHAPTER NINETEEN

Ryeland opened the door to the loft, took one look at Melody, and knew something was wrong.

"What?" he asked and pulled her inside. His glance moved over her face and he braced himself, because everything in his gut told him something bad was going down and she was smack dab in the middle of it. "What's wrong?"

"Rye," she said, her voice wavering slightly. He looked over her body and noticed how shaky she was, how fragile she looked.

"Jesus, Melody. What is it?" He led her to the sofa and sat beside her, twisting his body to face her.

She didn't look at him, instead she stared into her hands. "I…I don't know how to tell you."

"Hey," he said softly, brushing her hair back and angling her chin so she faced him. The fear in her eyes felt like a sucker punch and he knew if anyone had hurt her he'd kill them. "You know you can tell me anything." He talked quietly, working to keep his anger in check so he didn't frighten her.

She opened her mouth then closed it again, her

fingers wringing together. He grabbed her hands and gave a reassuring squeeze. "Melody, what is it?"

She pulled her hand from his and reached into her pocket. She pulled out a white stick and held it out. He looked at it, confused.

"It was positive," she said in a shaky voice. "I don't even really know why I bought it. I never thought…I did it on impulse…the cramps."

He fisted his hair. "What do you mean?"

"There is a pink plus sign and that means…"

He took a moment to sort through what she was saying to him, then his heart slammed against his chest. "You're pregnant," he blurted out. Jesus Christ, she was pregnant. "Holy shit, you're pregnant, aren't you?" He shook his head in disbelief. Honest to God, when she'd come through that door, that was the last thing he'd expected to come out of her mouth.

She nodded, and he watched the way her chest rose and fell erratically, like she could barely catch her breath. Her hands began shaking harder, her glance leaving his and going back to her lap.

"You're not kidding me, right?" When she shook her head now, he asked, "How? When?"

She gulped, her face growing paler by the second. "I didn't mean…I'm sorry."

"Sorry? What are you sorry for? We're going to have a baby. Holy Jesus." He stood, linked his hands behind his head and started pacing. "I'm going to be a father."

"Rye," she said, sounding completely unsure. "I don't know how it happened. We always use protection."

"Melody." He pulled her from the sofa and hugged her so hard he thought he might break her. Then he realized what he was doing and stopped. "Oh, sorry. Sorry. I don't want to hurt the baby." He put his hands on her stomach and rubbed gently, possessiveness racing through him.

Her eyes went wide as she looked at him, like she was trying to figure him out. "You…you want this?"

Emotions pressed against his heart. "Of course I want this. Don't you?"

"Well, yeah but…"

"We talked about this, Melody. I mean, we didn't plan for it until later, but well, we'll just have to adjust. It doesn't change anything. I mean, it changes everything, but it doesn't. You know what I mean?" he asked unable to stop himself from rambling. "Actually, I don't know what I mean," he said, laughing.

I'm going to be a father.

As soon as that thought hit again, so did another one. He'd have to tell his family about his plans sooner rather than later.

But he couldn't think about that right now. Feeling completely protective, he pulled her in gently, holding her soft body next to his, his heart pounding so hard against his chest he thought it might burst free. "How are you feeling? Do you need water, something to eat?"

"I have cramps," she said. "But other than that I'm good."

"Then you need to lay down."

She laughed and whacked his arm. "I do not need to lay down. I'm fine. I just have a few cramps."

"We have to make a doctor appointment." He led her to the bedroom, ignoring her protests. When they reached the bed he pulled her shirt off, then removed her pants, stopping to kiss her belly.

His mouth lingered on her stomach and she closed her hands around his head. "I can't believe we're going to have a baby," he murmured.

"Me neither," she said, a light of excitement in her eyes.

"I want this, Melody. I want you."

"I was worried."

"You shouldn't have been."

"I just…didn't know."

He grinned up at her and winked, wanting to lighten the mood. "If we have a girl I hope she's tough like you."

"And if we have a boy I hope he's adorable like you."

He stood, brushed his thumb over her mouth and whispered, "So you're saying you *do* think I'm adorable."

"Absolutely."

Longing ripped through him. "Want to know what I think?"

"Yes."

"I think, if you're feeling up to it, I'd like to get naked with you and kiss you all over."

She pushed against his erection. "Clearly you're *up* to it."

"Is that a yes?"

"That's a yes, please," she answered, her low, throaty chuckle falling over him.

He finished removing all her clothes then ditched his. After easing her onto the bed, he climbed over her. Her hair tumbled in waves as he kissed her mouth, neck, breasts, belly, and the warm spot between her legs.

He slid back up her body and drew a shaky breath. "I'm so glad you're mine, baby," he murmured into her mouth as perspiration beaded on his forehead. "All mine."

"All yours," she said as he reached for a condom. She stopped him and he gave her a quizzical look.

"We don't need it," she whispered, cupping his cheek.

"Oh, Jesus, you're right."

He widened her legs, positioning his cock at her

entrance. The second he slid into her he nearly went out of his mind. He'd never ridden bareback before and the sensations were unlike anything he'd ever felt.

"Oh baby." He buried his mouth in the soft hollow of her throat as her nails bit into his skin. A tremor moved through him as he sank into her warm, wet heat. "You feel so good."

She moaned and moved against him, her hands racing over him like she couldn't get enough. His body burned everywhere she touched, and he could feel himself reaching the precipice in record time.

"So good, Rye."

Her sex fluttered, a signal he'd long learned meant she was about to come. Her breaths came harder as she palmed his muscles. "That's it, baby," he said, and when he felt her warm heat, and her muscles squeeze his dick, he let go, splashing his seed high inside her.

He growled out loud and stayed inside until he grew flaccid. When he pulled out he shifted beside her and hugged her body to his.

They fell asleep holding one another, everything so right that he was sure nothing could ever come between them. Until Mel's phone rang, the shrill sound piercing their bubble.

CHAPTER TWENTY

Mel grabbed her phone, checked it, and her heart did a little jump when she saw the text from Cole. *Jaelyn's losing her shit. Get here now.*

"I have to go," she said to Ryeland as she pushed the blankets off.

"What's going on?" he asked as he jumped up with her.

"I don't know. Cole said Jaelyn was losing her shit."

"What the hell is that supposed to mean?

"I'm not sure, but I have to go."

"I'm coming with you."

She hesitated a moment. The last time he was at the Cave he got into it with Justin, and the time before he fought with Trevor. "It's okay, I can go."

He squared his shoulders, going all alpha on her. "If you think I'm letting you go alone, then you don't know me at all."

"Okay," she said. "I just…"

"Just what?"

"Nothing. Let's just get Jaelyn and get her home."

They both dressed quickly and hurried to his vehicle.

She clutched her hands together, wondering what the hell was going on as Ryeland sped down the mountain. He parked at the Cave and she sent Cole a text before she jumped out.

"They're down by the water," she said to Ryeland.

They both ran through the sand and when she reached the surf, she found Jaelyn flat on her back, crying. Mel dropped to her knees when she saw her friend's ripped clothes. "Oh God, Jaelyn. Are you hurt?" Just then she heard Cole behind her. She twisted to see him. "What happened?"

"Hey, I didn't do anything." Cole held his hands up. "She got in a fight with Jessica."

"Let's get her up," Ryeland said.

Mel gathered her friend in to her arms. Jaelyn wiped her eyes. "Mel, what are you doing here?"

"Cole texted. He said you needed me."

"Don't you dare believe anything he says," she spit out. "He's a fucking liar. He's still sleeping with Jessica."

Mel looked at Cole and he shook his head. "Jessica said hi to me and it set Jaelyn off. She went after her and they got in a fight."

"Come on." Ryeland helped her hoist her friend up. "I think she's had too much to drink."

Jaelyn angled her head and gave Ryeland a wobbly smile. "Cole's not nice like you." They began leading her up the beach, Cole keeping a few steps behind them, and Jaelyn added, "But your friends suck."

"Come on, Jaelyn," Mel said, not wanting her to bring up his friends. "Let's just concentrate on walking."

"Did you tell him what Justin did?" she asked, her hair flying around her face as her head swung toward Mel.

Mel felt her blood drain to her feet when Ryeland turned her way "What did Justin do?" he asked, his voice hard.

"Oops, wasn't supposed to tell," Jaelyn said and started giggling.

"Melody?" he asked.

Mel shook her head. "It was nothing."

"Nothing?" Jaelyn said, then gave a big hiccup. "It wasn't nothing." She hiccupped again and covered her mouth.

Ryeland glared at Jaelyn. "Tell me," he said through clenched teeth.

Jaelyn held a wobbly finger out. "He said he was gonna fuck her and fuck her hard."

Ryeland went as still as a stealth soldier, and Mel's heart stopped beating.

"Ryeland…" Mel began, her voice trembling.

He stared at her. "You should have told me."

"I didn't want trouble."

"Too late for that." He inched back and when Mel noticed a crowd gathering, watching them, she tried to stop him, to quiet him, but he would have no part of that.

"Ryeland, stop. I'm fine. It's over."

"It's not over. I'm going to kill him," he said and took off, the group watching him turning to go after him to check out the action.

Panic raced through her when he disappeared into the crowd. Jaelyn sank to the ground and Mel was about to go after him when Cameron stepped up to them.

"What's going on?" he asked, worry on his face.

"What's going on is your buddy is about to kill Justin," Cole answered stepping up to them.

"Oh, fuck," Cameron said. He looked through the crowd, then pointedly at Cole as he gestured toward to Mel. "Keep her out of it, okay?"

Cole shrugged. "Sure."

Cameron took off after Ryeland and Mel made a move to go but Cole grabbed her. "Oh no you don't.

You're not getting between them."

"Cole, please. I need to stop this."

She struggled against him and when she heard the crowd chanting *fight, fight, fight*, she punched Cole in the gut. With the hit taking him by surprise, he buckled forward, and she took the opportunity to bolt.

She pushed through the crowd, calling out to Ryeland. When she finally broke through the ring of people circling him, she found him on top of Justin, pummeling his face into the ground.

"Ryeland stop," she screamed and reached for him.

Just then she felt someone grab her by the waist and carry her off. She fought hard to break free, and when she was finally let go, she turned to find Trevor smirking at her.

She started to twist back around, to stop Ryeland, when Trevor pulled her against him. His foul breath fell over her and she knew he'd been drinking.

"Leave me alone, Trevor," she said, and just when she was about to throw a punch, Ryeland came out of nowhere and took Trevor to the ground.

"Ryeland, no!" she yelled, ready to grab him, but then what happened next had her screaming at the top of her lungs. A group of townies swarmed Ryeland, dragging him from Trevor, and she listened to his grunts as fists smashed against his body. She caught a glimpse of something shiny, then a moment later they all ran off. Mel crawled across the sand to find Ryeland flat on his back, bleeding from his side.

"He needs an ambulance," Mel yelled, lifting his shirt and struggling to see the wound through her tears.

"Melody," Ryeland whispered as he struggled to lift his head. "Are you okay?"

"Ryeland," she choked out afraid she was going to lose him. "You're bleeding."

"Yeah, I know," he said, his voice dropping to a faint

whisper.

Sirens sounded in the distance and the next thing she knew Officer Sattler was standing over them, the crowd spreading like wildfire.

"Jesus." Sattler reached for his radio. Everything that happened next seemed to go in slow motion. An ambulance showed up and they took Ryeland off. Sattler gathered her up in his patrol car and drove her to the hospital. A few who'd witnessed the fight came in, and as Sattler questioned them, she sat in the waiting room and watched. Soon Ryeland's parents showed up and were ushered in to see him. Cameron came in and sat across from her. Neither spoke as minutes turned into hours.

Mel had gone to the nurses' station several times looking for information, but because she wasn't family, no one would speak to her or give her answers. Soon night bled into day, and Jaelyn eventually showed up, a stricken look on her face.

"Mel," she said, giving her a big hug. "I'm so sorry. This is all my fault. I was drinking…I didn't mean."

"No one will tell me anything," she said, not wanting to talk about whose fault it was or wasn't.

Jaelyn nodded. "Okay, I'll try to find out something. First let me get you a coffee." Mel sat there clutching her stomach, her eyes heavy, her body exhausted, but there was no way she was leaving. Jaelyn came back with a hot cup of coffee in a paper cup and Mel sipped on it as Jaelyn went in search of answers. Cameron went with her and a short while later they returned.

Cameron came back. "I talked to his mom and she told me that he is out of surgery and is doing okay."

Mel let loose a cry of relief and clutched Jaelyn when she sat down next to her. "Will they let us see him?"

"Take her out of here," a hard voice boomed from behind.

Mel turned around and her stomach tightened when she found Ryeland's father standing there. He glared at her, then looked at Cameron. "She's caused enough trouble as it is."

"Come on," Cameron said, standing up. Mel opened her mouth to protest but Cameron leaned into her and whispered, "Believe me, right now it's about what's best for Ryeland."

Confusion, worry, fear, and every dreadful emotion she'd ever felt rose to the surface. "Okay," she agreed reluctantly and let him lead her outside. The warm morning sun washed over her but did little to thaw the ice inside her. She shaded her eyes and blinked as Cameron led her and Jaelyn to his car.

Cameron dropped them both off at their lodge, and while Jaelyn wanted to stay with her, Mel needed to be alone. With so much to think about, she slipped between her sheets. Even though she was exhausted, she tossed and turned restlessly, dreaming and worrying about Ryeland.

A knock at her door many, many hours later pulled her awake, and she jumped from her bed, hoping it was news about Ryeland. When she saw his father standing there, holding the pregnancy stick she'd forgotten at his chalet, her fight or flight instinct kicked in hard, because she knew nothing, absolutely nothing good could come from this.

CHAPTER TWENTY-ONE

Ryeland blinked against the blaring overhead light as nurses rushed about, poking his arm and hooking him up to machinery. Jesus, it hurt to move, to breathe. He could hear his father's voice in the distance, followed by his mother's. They sounded upset as they whispered—argued—about having his medical files faxed to the hospital.

The nurse called out for his blood type, and Ryeland was certain he heard something about a transfusion. But that's when things became really confusing. It was either the drugs kicking in, or something was seriously off. How could he have such a rare blood type and not be a match with one of his parents. If he was their kid, he had to be a match with at least one of them. Before he could consider it further, the drugs kicked back in and the world around him faded to black.

When Ryeland woke up again, he had no idea what day it was or how long he'd been asleep. He glanced around, looking for Melody, worried about her. "Where's Melody?" he whispered, his throat so dry it hurt to speak.

"Try not to move too much," a nurse said as she adjusted his IV and offered him a few chips of ice on a plastic spoon.

He nibbled on the ice. "How long have I been in here?"

"Close to thirty-six hours," she said.

Thirty-six hours? Christ, he needed to see Melody.

"You're in serious trouble, young man," his father said from the doorway. The nurse stiffened and hurried about her work as his father's large, intimidating frame ate up the small room.

"Hello to you too," Ryeland murmured and turned his attention to Sattler. "What's going on?" Ryeland croaked out.

Sattler rocked on his feet. "Both Justin and Trevor are pressing charges," he said.

Ryeland gave a laugh that made his wound hurt. "I'm the one in bed with a stab wound."

Sattler folded his arms. "I have witnesses that say you started the fight and pulled the knife."

Ryeland tried to get up but the pain in his side stilled him. "That's bullshit and you know it."

"Ryeland," his father warned.

"I even have witnesses saying they overheard you saying you were going to kill him."

His stomach clenched. Oh, Jesus, this was bad. "I might have said that but I didn't mean I was really going to kill him."

When the nurse saw how agitated Ryeland was becoming, she turned to his father and the officer. "I think that's enough for now. He needs his rest."

She ushered them outside to speak and a few minutes later his mom came in. She leaned over him and pushed his hair back. "You really need a hair cut," she said, worry still lingering in the depths of her eyes as she fussed about.

As he looked at her, something niggled at him in the back of his mind. He reached for it and caught it just before it disappeared.

"What's your blood type?" he asked.

Her face paled. "What?"

"What blood type are you?"

"None of that matters now, Ryeland. None of it. You're doing better and that's all that counts."

"How come my blood type doesn't match yours or Dad's?"

"Ryeland, please. That's enough."

His stomach tightened, because in that instant, as he watched her face go white, her bright blue eyes go wide—eyes so different from his—he knew. Jesus Christ, all the pieces of the puzzle known as his father and the way he'd changed after Ryeland's childhood illness suddenly all made sense. He wanted Ryeland working for him, not because he was protective of him, like Melody had thought, but because he was protecting himself—protecting his secrets.

He shook his head, stopping when the room tilted on its axis. "Oh Jesus."

His mother swallowed and tried to pretend nothing was wrong as she fussed with his blanket. But he knew things were wrong, so very, very wrong.

"You should try to get some rest," she said, and he could tell her smile was forced.

"Arthur. He's not my real father, is he?"

"Ryeland," she whispered and darted a nervous glance over her shoulder. "Stop talking like that."

"He's not, is he?"

She turned from him, but not before he caught the worry lines around her eyes. "Ryeland, please don't do this."

"Tell me now, right now," he said, his voice rising.

She dropped down into the chair beside his bed,

panic on her face. "Please, Ryeland."

"Tell me or I'll ask him."

"It was a long time ago." Looking more wary then he'd ever seen her, she sagged in the chair and put her hands on either side of her face. "I made a mistake. That's all."

"A mistake? What was the mistake? Getting pregnant by another man, or trying to pass that kid off as Arthur's?" She went quiet and he added, "That's what you did, didn't you? And Dad figured it out when I got sick with leukemia. I needed blood and mine didn't match with yours or his. There's only one reason for that."

"Ryeland," she whispered, and he could tell by the stricken look on her face it was all true.

He shoved his fingers through his hair. How could he have missed what was right under his nose all along? He thought of his blonde-haired, blue-eyed brother and sister. Both the spitting image of their mom and dad. He scoffed. Now he knew why he was the black sheep—he took after his real father.

"He was going to leave and take Rita with him," she hissed. "I wanted to be the one to leave. I deserved it more than her. So yes, I got pregnant and pretended you were his. But it doesn't change anything. Arthur has raised you like you were one of his own."

Despite the headache and dizziness, Ryeland shook his head, hardly able to believe what he was hearing. Melody's mother wasn't the lying, manipulative whore Eliza had claimed she was when he'd asked about her at the police station. No, *his* mother was. She was the one who'd gotten pregnant by another man and claimed the child was Arthur's so she could get out of Deerfield. No wonder she knew so much about townies and what they'd do to better themselves—because she'd used all the tricks herself.

Holy Jesus Christ.

"Who was my father?" he asked. When she hesitated, he said, "Tell me."

"He was just a ranch hand."

"A ranch hand," he said. "So that's why Arthur hated me in the stable. I guess he thought people would figure out your dirty little secret and it would look bad for him."

"Ryeland, please. Let it go. Don't bring shame upon this family. Your father's work…"

"Let it go. How the hell am I supposed to let it go?"

"Let what go?" his father asked.

Before he could answer, a movement behind his father's shoulders caught Ryeland's attention.

"Melody," he whispered, holding his hand out to her. Oh, God, he needed her so much right now. But when she didn't budge, his heart jumped into his throat because he suddenly had the feeling his day was about to go from bad to worse.

Chapter Twenty-Two

"Ryeland," Mel said, cringing slightly as her gaze moved over his bruised face. "How are you feeling?"

Ryeland's father cleared his throat and Mel stiffened. "Don't you have something to say?" he asked her.

She crossed her arms to keep them from shaking and bit the inside of her cheek, but there was nothing she could do to keep her chest from constricting, making it difficult to talk, to draw in air. She opened her mouth and shut it again, unable to say the words Arthur had put into her mouth. Bile rose into her throat and it was all she could do not to throw up, to run to Ryeland and tell him the truth. But the truth would hurt him—in more ways than one—and that was the last thing she ever wanted to do. She drew a shaky breath and reminded herself that this was what was best for him, and because she loved him with everything inside her, she was going to stand tall and put his well-being above her own. No matter how much it ripped her heart from her chest and destroyed every little bit of her.

She opened her mouth again but when the words wouldn't come, her father blurted out. "I found the pregnancy stick, and the baby isn't yours."

Ryeland tried to sit up on the bed. He struggled and Melody rooted her feet when all she wanted to do was go to him.

"What?" he asked. "No, that's not true." He looked at Melody, and the confusion on his face set fire to her chest.

"It is true," his mother said. She reached into his medical file and pulled out a sheet of paper. "You're sterile, a result of your treatments when you were young."

"Sterile? What are you talking about?"

From the chair beside his bed, his mother patted his hand. "We didn't tell you because we thought you were too young to deal with it."

Melody remained quiet as he pulled his hand away from his mother's, and watched the hurtful exchange from the doorway, unable to move, to speak, to breathe.

"I don't believe you." Ryeland pushed the paper away. "I don't believe any of this."

"Believe it. The indisputable facts are right there in front of you," Arthur stated, his voice as hard as his features.

"She's been sleeping around," her mother added. "I warned you about her, Ryeland. She used the pregnancy to trick you to get a better life for herself." She cast a quick glance Melody's way then turned back to Ryeland. "I bet she even tricked you into using no protection."

"You'd know all about that now wouldn't you?" he bit out and his mother flinched. Then something moved over his face, something that told Mel he was thinking about the last time they had sex—without a condom. Then he blinked away the moment of doubt and said, "And you're wrong about her. The baby is mine."

"I'm not wrong," his mother said, sitting up a little straighter.

"Melody, tell them it's not true," Ryeland said. "Tell them."

Arthur folded his arms. "We know a few people who will attest to it."

"Bullshit," he shot back.

Arthur glared at him. "That's not what Justin says, and it certainly stands to reason why you went after him."

"There is no sense in arguing this with you." He looked at Melody. "Melody, please…"

Mel swallowed hard and in a low voice said, "You passed your law entrance exams, Ryeland. If you were presented with these facts, what would be your conclusion?"

His mouth fell open as he stared at her, the hurt in his eyes cutting into her soul. It took every ounce of strength she had to push the lie through her lips, but if she didn't Ryeland could go to jail, and any future, whether it was in medicine or law, would be ruined.

"Melody, come on." He squeezed his eyes shut. "We spent every night together."

As her heart crumbled into a million broken pieces, she thought about the nights she spent with her mom. "Not every night."

He fisted his hair. "Why are you doing this to me? To us?"

"You wasted your entire summer on her, Ryeland," Arthur said.

"That's not true. Tell me it's not true, Melody. Please tell me it's not true!" he yelled.

"You always said I was the bad judge of character." She stomped down the emotions and met his gaze unflinchingly. "Maybe you're the one who's not so good at reading people."

"Melody, Jesus. No! You're lying. You're fucking lying."

"No, I'm not. Your mother was right. You should have listened to her."

He pulled on his hair and struggled to get up, but his mother stopped him. "You love me. I know you do!" he yelled. She took a small, unstable step backward. "Melody, come on. Please. You're a fighter, you fight for everything and right now I'm the one thing I need you to fight for."

"Goodbye, Ryeland. Go back to school. Don't waste anymore time with me."

CHAPTER TWENTY-THREE

After getting discharged from the hospital, Ryeland went in search of Melody, but she was nowhere to be found. His texts went unanswered and she'd moved from her lodge, no forwarding address. He checked her mother's house and when he found that empty too, he went to the hospital to talk to her. Except her mother hated him with the same ferociousness as his folks hated Melody and wouldn't tell him a thing. Even Jaelyn had said she had no idea where Melody was, but Ryeland didn't believe her.

Two weeks had gone by, two weeks of searching, coming up empty-handed, and going over everything that had happened since he'd met Melody. Over the course of those weeks he had read over his medical file, learning it was true, that his chances of having a child were slim to none. He was going with slim, because deep in his gut he knew the baby was his. He also went looking for answers on his real father and had received the results of his MCAT test. But what good was changing his career track now? That other path included Melody, and if he didn't have her in his life, if she insisted on pushing him out of hers, he might as well go to law school and become a first-class prick like his old man wanted.

He tossed the last of his clothes into his duffle bag and glanced out his bedroom window to see his family drive off. Ryeland had barely spoken to his folks since the hospital, except to ask if his father had been behind all this. He'd insisted he wasn't, naturally, but Ryeland suspected otherwise. Arthur was a man who won at all cost and would do whatever was necessary to gain that win. Except Ryeland wasn't some courtroom case or some protégé son used to help his father build his name and reputation. If anyone caught wind that all was not right in the Montgomery household and that Ryeland wasn't his real son, wouldn't that shit hit the fan?

Ryeland walked down the stairs, his hand feathering the oak rail as he glanced around. So much had changed in the last four months, and while he loved hanging out with Ashley and Evan here, he knew this was the last time he'd ever step foot in this place again. He pushed through the front door and lifted his head to find Jaelyn standing there, holding out the T-shirt he'd given Melody that first day Justin had soaked her.

"Jaelyn," he rushed out, his heart squeezing as he took in the concern in her eyes. "Where is she?"

She looked down and hesitated a moment before saying, "She doesn't want you to know."

His heart raced faster. "Tell me."

She went quiet for a moment, then nodded. "I'm only telling you because I know she needs you."

He crushed his hands in his hair, panic invading his gut. "Is she okay?"

"No. She's not okay at all. That's why I'm here."

He pushed down the stairs past her and opened the door to his Wrangler. "Get in. I need you to take me to her."

"Maybe I should drive," she said.

"Just get in."

After Jaelyn slipped in beside him and gave him directions to some out-of-the-way cabin Sattler owned and was letting Melody use, he took off up the mountain. He took a side road, and when they went over rough terrain Jaelyn grabbed the "oh shit" handle above her door to hang on.

"Slow down or you're going to get us killed. You'll be no good to her dead."

Soon a log cabin came into view and Ryeland slammed on the brakes.

"She's expecting me," Jaelyn said, nervousness lacing her voice. "Should I go in first and give her the head's up?"

"No." Ryeland had his door open before coming to a complete stop. "I need to see her alone." He ran across the wide dirt driveway and pulled open the front door to the cottage.

"That was fast," Melody began. She turned around and her hand went to the back of the sofa when she found Ryeland standing there. "Rye," she whispered.

In two swift strides he crossed the room and gathered her into his arms. He took in the puffiness in her eyes, like she'd been crying for weeks. "Melody," he said emotions choking him as he buried his face in her hair. "Melody, are you okay? I missed you so much."

Her body shook and he held her tighter, absorbing her tremors.

"Rye," she murmured into his chest. "How did you find me?"

He gripped her shoulders and inched back. "Jaelyn. She's outside." His glance moved over her face, accessing her. "How are you feeling? How's the baby?"

She pulled away from him and turned her head, but not before he saw the tears in her eyes. "You shouldn't be here. You need to go."

"I'm not going." Frustration ripped a hole in his gut. "Not until you tell me what's going on. You love me. I love you. I want to know why you lied."

"I didn't lie," she choked out.

"What did my father do?" he asked, struggling to keep his anger in check and wanting her to stop with all the lies. At the mention of his father, she moved to the other side of the sofa. He moved with her, and grabbed her shaky hands. "Tell me what he did."

"I can't do this, Rye. I can't."

"Melody, I love you."

"You're wasting your time here," she said, pulling out of his grasp.

"No, I'm not. I don't get it at all. I know you love me."

"Ryeland, please."

"No. I'm not leaving, Melody. The baby is mine. I know it, and even if it isn't, it doesn't change anything. We love each other. We're going to make a life together. I want you and the baby."

She turned to him, the pain in her eyes so raw and real it cut him deeper than Trevor's blade. "You…you would still want me if the baby wasn't yours?"

"Yes. But it's mine, Melody. I know that."

The sound of her swallowing cut through the air, then she put her hand over her stomach and whispered, "There is no baby. You deserve to know that."

He fell onto the cushiony sofa, air evacuating his lungs. "What? What are you talking about? I know you didn't lie about the baby. I know that much."

"I didn't. I lost the baby."

"Oh, God, I'm so sorry." He buried his face in his hands. "This is my fault. I'm so sorry, baby."

Her voice hitched when she said, "It's not your fault."

He reached for her hand and pulled her onto his lap. He wrapped his arms around her and held tight. "I should have been there for you. I couldn't find you. I couldn't find you anywhere. I searched everywhere. I damn near tore this town apart, but I should have tried harder. I should have forced Jaelyn to tell me."

"Ryeland."

"Yeah." She looked at him, her hair spilling forward. He pushed it off her face and tucked it behind her ears. "I…I…" She stopped speaking and those haunted eyes of hers looked at some distance spot behind his shoulder.

"Why did you push me away? I needed you to fight for me, baby."

"Rye," she said, choking back the tears. "I wanted to. But I couldn't fight him. If I did, he'd ruin your future."

He clenched down hard enough to break his teeth. "What did he do to you? What did he say?" She shook her head and her eyes went wide, like she'd said too much. "Tell me," he commanded in a soft voice. "Tell me, Melody."

"I can't."

"Tell me." He gripped her shoulders. "I deserve that from you too."

Tears ran down her face. "You're right, you do. But then you have to go." He went silent, waiting for her to explain. She sucked in a quick breath, then said, "He came to me and told me he would ruin your life if I didn't back off. He said he wouldn't get the charges dropped and not only would it ruin your future as a lawyer but as a doctor too. He said you'd never get into med school with a criminal record. I couldn't let that happen." She cupped his cheek, her voice bordering on hysteria. "Don't you see, Rye? I couldn't let that happen."

"You should have come to me. You should have told me." He shook his head, anger tearing through him.

"I couldn't…your future."

"That never would have happened. It was just a convenient way to get you out of my life—"

She pressed her fingers to his lips. "Ryeland, stop. He was just doing what parents do. He was doing what my parents never did. He thought I tricked you. How can we fault him for wanting me out of your life?"

"Baby, oh, God, baby, you've got it wrong. He blackmailed you and that's never okay. I know you don't have your own good experiences to draw on but that's never what a good parent should do. From day one he never gave you a chance. He never trusted that I could make good decisions. His every move was about me doing what he wanted, to keep all his secrets."

"Secrets? What do you mean?"

"I have something on him too, something I can use against him so he can never hurt us again."

"You do? What?"

"I'm not his son."

Her eyes widened. "What?"

"When I got sick with leukemia, my father changed. At first I thought it was his way of dealing. But it wasn't. I needed blood and that's when they realized he wasn't a match. My mother tricked him into marrying her. She slept with him, then told him she was pregnant. He married her quickly, to cover the dates. But then later he found out I wasn't his son. I was the son of the resort's ranch hand. But my mom wanted more, wanted out of Deerfield." He scoffed. "I guess that's why Arthur didn't like me hanging out in the horse stables or volunteering. Not only did it remind him too much of my real dad, and my mother's betrayal, he was worried people would figure it out and it would come back on him negatively."

"Why did he stay with her?"

"Appearances. As a lawyer he wanted to come across as unflappable." He held her tighter. "The charges against me have been dropped and he's never going to hurt us again."

The pulse at the base of her neck jumped, and she blinked rapidly. "Ryeland, are you saying…"

"Yes, I'm saying he's out of our life, and he's never going to hurt us again."

"You mean…" she choked out. "We can be—"

"Yes, we can be together."

He cupped her cheeks and planted a warm kiss on her mouth. When he pulled back he caught the flash of emotions in her eyes.

"What?" he asked.

"I know the paper showed you were sterile, but just so you know, I wasn't with anyone but you. Those things your mom said about me, none of them were true."

He briefly closed his eyes, hating the hurt she'd suffered. "I know that, and I know that baby was mine. The report said chances were slim to none, but obviously there is a chance my guys are working." That brought a small smile to her face, and his heart turned over. He cupped her cheeks again.

"I didn't get pregnant on purpose. I was never using you to get out of here. You have to know that."

Ryeland brushed the tears from her eyes. "You're the only person in the world who's never wanted something from me, baby." He dropped a soft kiss onto her mouth. "I'm so sorry I wasn't here for you when you lost the baby."

"I know."

"Melody, I love you so much."

Her tears fell harder. "I love you too."

"I want you in my life. I want to move to Toronto and go to medical school while you follow your dreams of being a writer."

Her glance strayed to her closed laptop. "I want that

too, but I can't write anymore. The words won't come."

He pushed her hair from her face. "You've been through so much."

"We've both been through so much."

He exhaled slowly, and after a long time he said, "I've got an idea. How about we start again."

He caught a ghost of a smile, and his heart swelled because in that instant he knew they were going to be okay. No matter what the world threw at them as long as they had each other they were going to be okay.

"I'd like that," she whispered.

He grinned and, taking them right back to the first time they met, he asked, "What's Mel short for?"

"Melba," she said grinning.

He nudged her with his shoulder, his heart filling with all the love he had for her. "Come on, Melba. We have a lot of work to do."

"We do?"

He stood and lifted her with him. "Yeah, we need to get to work on our happily-ever-after so you'll know how to write one for your book."

She pointed toward the door. "What about Jaelyn, isn't she in the car?"

"Yeah, she is."

"Shouldn't we go tell her—"

He scooped her up and she yelped. "Don't worry, this will only take a minute."

She laughed. "A minute?"

"It's been awhile and I need you so bad," he said, giving her a crooked grin.

"If I'm going to figure out how to write that happily-ever-after, I might need more than a minute from you," she teased, the demons finally gone from her eyes.

"Don't worry, baby. I'm going to give you every minute of every day of every year. Except right now I'm pretty sure I can only give a minute."

She laughed, and the sound warmed his soul. "You're crazy, you know that."

He winked at her. "I think that's already on the list."

"I think you're right," she agreed.

He carried her to the bedroom and laid her on the bed. He stood back to look at her, taking in the flush on her cheeks, the love in her eyes. Jesus, he was the luckiest guy in the world.

"Want to know what I think?" he asked.

"More than anything," she said.

He tore off his shirt, climbed over her, and dropped a soft kiss onto her mouth. "How about I show you instead?"

THANK YOU!

Thank you so much for reading, Wasted Summer. I hope you enjoyed Ryeland and Melody's journey as much as I loved writing it. Please read on, I've included an excerpt from Crashing Down (Book one in the Stone Cliff series) ! I hope you enjoy!

Interested in leaving a review? Please do! Reviews help readers connect with books that work for them. I appreciate all reviews, whether positive or negative.

Happy Reading,
Cathryn

CRASHING DOWN: EXCERPT
By Cathryn Fox

CHAPTER ONE

"You reek of sex."

Noah Ryan grinned at his buddy Jared, a guy he'd gotten to know over the last couple of years while living and working at Stone Cliff Resort in the Canadian Rocky Mountains. Taking his friend's ribbing in stride, Noah scrubbed his hands through his disheveled hair, and sank down onto the driftwood next to him, setting his motorcycle helmet at his feet. He let his glance surf over the crowd gathered around the nightly, beachside bonfire. He zeroed in on a cute blonde with big tits and gave Jared a wry smirk. "Not yet I don't."

Jared reached into the cooler, pulled out a cold brew, and handed it to Noah. "Yeah, well that's a matter of opinion."

"Fuck you." Noah laughed and twisted off the cap, the taste of weed and smoke scratching his dry throat like coarse sandpaper. "How the hell can I reek of sex when I just crawled out of bed, *alone*?"

Jared shrugged. "Well your bed smells like sex, then."

Okay, so that was probably true. His bed likely did smell like sex. Sometimes a hard, mindless fuck chased away the chills that had taken up residency inside him since the accident a little over three years ago. Then again, sometimes it didn't. Sometimes the demons managed to tunnel their way past the wall he'd built despite a warm body lying next to him.

Noah took a long pull from the bottle, and washed the grit from his throat. Too bad the alcohol did little to drown the pain that blackened his soul. Then again, did he really deserve for it to?

He worked to push all dark thoughts aside, and tried to keep things light. He nudged his friend with his elbow. "Ah, come on, Jared. Don't be jealous 'cause I'm getting all the play and you're not."

Jared waved to Ryan and Bobbie, a couple of locals who had just rolled in, before he flicked his beer cap at Noah. "Yeah, well, fuck you. I get all the play I need, or I would be if you weren't always hovering around." Two well-built, dark-haired hotties moved in front of them, smiling flirtatiously at Noah. "Christ, Noah, what the hell is it about you?" He clucked his tongue and added, "You're like nectar to the honey bee, my man."

Laughing, Noah took another swig from the bottle as the cute blonde he'd been eying glanced his way. He caught the mischief in her gaze and pegged her as a local, a rich townie who'd just returned home from university. He knew her type all too well. She'd spend her days lounging on the water with her friends and her nights here at the beach, otherwise known as the Cave, where many of the resort staff and locals alike gathered for a little action. Not that he was judging her. He wasn't. After all, unlike him she was getting an education and going places.

With exhaustion pulling at him, Noah stretched his arms over his head and stifled a yawn. He hadn't planned on hanging out with Jared tonight, but since he couldn't take staring at his ceiling for one more minute, he'd decided if he couldn't sleep, he might as well get laid. The little townie gave him a look that said, *come get some* and his cock twitched, but before he made his move on the blonde, he shifted closer to his friend. He pulled an envelope from his back pocket and slipped it to him, wanting to do this exchange off resort and away from their manager, Donald Brake's, watchful eye.

"Noah..." Jared looked down at the envelope and shook his head. "Shit." He stole a quick glance around before he shoved the bills into his pocket. "But you were saving...you can't afford—"

"And you can't afford not to." He looked pointedly at the swelling beneath Jared's bruised eye. Even though he claimed the injury had happened when he fell off the raft during yesterday's rough, white-water ride down Canyon Run, Noah knew better. Noah pitched his voice low, his words for Jared's ears only. "You keep fucking with these guys and you'll lose more than just your job. You know that, right?"

"Yeah, yeah, I know," Jared said gravely, dark eyes cast downward in worry as he rubbed his temples with his thumbs. "Christ, I had a straight flush. I never thought I could lose." He fisted his short-cropped hair and gave a tug. "I mean come on, what are the fucking odds that the other guy beat me with a royal flush?"

"A trillion to one," Noah said. He didn't need to do the mental math that came so easily to him as he finished off his beer and reached for another, handing one to Jared as well. Even though Jared was as big a fuck up as he was, the guy was a damn hard worker, and in a few short years had climbed his way up from bellboy to concierge. That job was his life, and Noah wasn't about to stand around and see it get taken from him.

It was Jared's job to get to know the guests and see that their needs were being met. What he wasn't supposed to do was socialize with those guests, or get himself invited to the after-hours poker game that the resort's management turned a blind eye to. The high-rolling businessmen, who came to town for the annual weeklong event, weren't the kind of guys who took kindly to getting stiffed. You owed them money, you paid your debt. One way or another.

Noah's glance shot to the blonde. Then again, who was he too lecture about rules, considering he was about to break one himself? Even when off duty, the staff wasn't supposed to do anything to bring negative attention to the resort, which meant that picking up a local for a quick fuck on the rocks was pretty much all kinds of wrong.

"I'll pay you back," Jared said.

The blonde gave Noah a once over and a satisfied grin. "You just keep yourself out of trouble."

Jared followed the direction of Noah's gaze, and when he glimpsed the girl Noah had his sights set on, he shook his head. "You're one to talk. That girl has trouble written all over her."

"Good," Noah said, smirking.

"She's got a boyfriend, Noah," Jared warned. "And he's a big bastard."

"I think you're mistaken." Ignoring Jared's warning, Noah stood and shoved one hand into his pocket, pulling his worn and faded jeans lower on his hips, a not so subtle invitation that brought the blonde's attention right where he wanted it. "I think she's looking for a little play."

Jared gave him a look that suggested he was either crazy, or had a death wish, or possibly both. Maybe he was right.

"Yeah? What makes you say that?" Jared asked.

"She wouldn't be wearing a shirt that showed off her tits if she didn't want me to look."

While Jared cursed under his breath, Noah moved through the throng of people. Seconds before he reached blondie, some douche bag stepped in front of him to block his path. Noah nudged him with his shoulder, shoving him out of the way. With single-minded determination he moved past him, but when the guy said, "Is there a problem here, pal?" it stopped Noah dead in his tracks.

He turned and sized up the steroid-induced mouth breather and shrugged. "Listen dude," Noah began. "As far as I can tell the only problem here is that you're standing between me," he paused to poke his finger in the direction of the girl watching him with big, curious eyes, "and her."

The guy grabbed Noah's arm, his nostrils flaring as he yanked Noah closer. Even at six feet, Noah had to lift his chin to meet the guy's eyes. The ogre gripped him tighter, his sausage fingers digging into Noah's biceps.

Like a wire stretched tight, Noah snapped. "Get the fuck off me." His skin came alive as he jerked his arm free. Christ, he didn't like to be touched. Touching made him feel...well, it made him *feel*.

Old, blood-soaked memories clawed their way to the surface, and visions of his best friend clutching his arm like it was his lifeline swamped him. But Noah hadn't been Jonny's lifeline. Oh no, not at all. Noah was a fuck up, and the sole reason Jonny was dead.

"...Noah."

He heard Jared saying something, pleading with him, but the words were lost in the foggy haze clouding his mind, riding circles around his brain on the pain that came with remembering.

"Maybe you should listen to your boyfriend," the ogre said.

Noah laughed in his face. "Maybe you should suck my dick."

The mouth breather fisted his hands and drew his arm back. Heart racing, Noah stood there, his body braced as he prepared for the pain. Welcomed it.

Deserved it.

Like a hard fuck, sometimes a good punch in the face sent the demons scurrying. For a little while, anyway.

The hit came sure and swift, and Noah's teeth clashed as he flew backwards toward the water. The damp sandy shore padded his fall, but the cold waves crashing over his body snapped his groggy senses back to life faster than a broken condom. He jumped to his feet and spit a mouth full of blood onto the sand as the primate came at him again, his knuckles practically dragging on the ground.

"Stop it, Alex," a shrill voice cried out, and Noah's heart sank as the girl he'd been stalking halted the fight. Jesus, he'd wanted that next blow. Craved it. Noah wiped his mouth with the back of his hand as blondie pounded her fists into Alex's chest.

Fuck if Jared hadn't been right. Blondie did have a boyfriend, and the big bastard's name was Alex.

Alex grabbed the girl's hands, and pinned them to her sides. She squirmed and fought against him, the back of her shirt lifting to show a tramp stamp that Noah was certain her good folks knew nothing about. Damned if she wasn't just the girl he needed tonight.

"Stay out of this, Dara," the ape named Alex warned.

Noah took a threatening step toward Alex. "Take your fucking hands off her."

"Noah," Jared warned again as the crowd gathered around them. The bonfire burned bright, the fiery embers sparking like angry fireflies in the dark night sky, casting a flickering spotlight on the scene playing out before them. "You start this shit again, and Donald won't give you any more chances," he bit out harshly, but Noah was too far gone, too far down the road filled with blood and bad memories to walk away.

"I didn't start it." He swiped his tongue over his swollen lip and jutted his chin toward Alex. "He did. I'm just going to finish it." Noah stood there, sizing up his opponent once again, waiting for him to make another move.

Alex looked at Noah, then at his girlfriend, who continued to struggle against his grip. Suspicion moved into his beady eyes as they locked on hers. "What are you protecting this guy for? Do you know him or something?" he asked, his voice slurring slightly.

"We're all just here to have a good time, Alex."

"A good time?" He jerked his head toward Noah, his lips curling with disgust. "That's the good time you want?" Silence hung heavy for a moment, then sweet tits shrugged, everything in what she didn't say answering Alex's question. "This shit ain't worth it." He shoved Dara away, pushed through the crowd and stormed down the beach.

He watched Alex disappear and then turned his attention to Dara. "You okay?"

Big eyes moved over his swollen lip as her two friends came up behind her. "Are you?" she asked.

Noah scrubbed his hand over his jaw. "Your boyfriend throws one hell of a punch."

She took a sip from the cooler her friend handed her, looking at him over the rim of the bottle. She swallowed and licked her lips before saying, "Maybe he's not my boyfriend anymore."

"Is that right?" Noah asked, inching closer and invading her personal space. Damn she smelled good.

"Well, maybe not tonight, anyway." She nibbled her bottom lip, a seductive move Noah figured she'd perfected in front of a mirror, and then slid her gaze over his body.

"You gotta be fucking kidding me." The sound of Jared's voice from behind him pulled Noah's attention away from those luscious lips.

Noah cast him a quick glance and smirked. "What?"

"Like you even have to ask." Shaking his head, Jared disappeared into the crowd, leaving Noah to do what he did best. Fuck everything up.

With the fight over, the crowd went back to partying, and Dara stepped in and closed the small space that remained between them. She went up on her tiptoes, those nice tits of hers pressing into his chest. Reaching up, she feathered her fingertip over his swollen lip. "Does it hurt?"

"Yeah. It hurts like a son of a bitch. But I guess that's to be expected when I use my face to stop a punch."

She puckered those pouty lips of hers and all Noah could think about was how that sexy mouth would feel around his cock.

"You think I should kiss it better?"

Noah grinned. Christ, she made this so easy. "I think that's a good start."

She handed her cooler back to her friends, and gave the cute brunette a knowing smile before she turned back to Noah. With a tip of her head, she gestured behind her. "Maybe we should...you know...go somewhere private."

She didn't need to ask him twice. Noah grabbed her hand and pulled her away from the crowd. Once they were out of sight, near the rocky cliff at the far end of the beach, he stepped into the water and splashed a palm full into his mouth. He sloshed it around to wash away the blood, and then spat it out.

Not wasting any time, he gripped Dara's hips, his cock swelling inside his jeans as he pushed her up against the rock wall. He dipped his head, his lips so close to hers that he could taste the raspberry cooler on her breath. Goddamn she had a mouth made for sucking. He slipped one hand around the back of her neck, the floral scent of her hair filling his nostrils as his eyes latched on her hot mouth.

"So about that kiss," he murmured.

ACKNOWLEDGEMENTS

A book never comes together alone, and this one is no exception. I would like to give a great big thank you to my street team for all your support. When I asked for beta readers, so many jumped to help and I want to give a HUGE thank you to, Danita Montes, Misty Roule, Cher Kilgore, Jessica Brignoni, Cindy Werner, and Pam Batchelor. I appreciate you all so much!

A special thank you goes out to Jan Meredith, friend, critique partner, talented writer, and sexy nurse. No matter how busy she is, she's always there for me whenever I need her. Thanks Jan, you are a true gem.

To the people behind the scenes who made the book look good: Crocodesigns, for the gorgeous cover, Ironhorse formatting for making the pages perfect, and Tera Cuskaden for the editing…thank you!

Cathryn

OTHER TITLES BY CATHRYN FOX

Hands On with the CEO
Yours to Take
Torn Between Two Brothers
Spring Fling
His Obsession Next Door
Flirty in Whispering Cover
Hold Me Down Hard
Holiday Spirit
Pleasure Control

**To discover even more titles by Cathryn Fox
check out her website at
www.CathrynFox.com**

ABOUT CATHRYN FOX

New York Times and *USA today* Bestselling author, Cathryn is a wife, mom, sister, daughter, and friend. She loves dogs, sunny weather, anything chocolate (she never says no to a brownie) pizza and red wine. She has two teenagers who keep her busy with their never ending activities, and a husband who is convinced he can turn her into a mixed martial arts fan. Cathryn can never find balance in her life, is always trying to find time to go to the gym, can never keep up with emails, Facebook or Twitter and tries to write page-turning books that her readers will love.

Connect with Cathryn:
Newsletter: http://bit.ly/1kpQOzf
Twitter: https://twitter.com/writercatfox
Facebook:
https://www.facebook.com/AuthorCathrynFox?ref=hl
Blog: http://cathrynfox.com/blog/
Goodreads:
https://www.goodreads.com/author/show/91799.Cathryn
_Fox
Pinterest http://www.pinterest.com/catkalen/